Foolish

SAI MECCA

Foolish

Copyright © 2018 by Sai Mecca

Printed in the United States of America
Etherr Publishing, 2018
ISBN 978–1982033170

Cover Image by Lyndsey Stewart
Cover Design and Book Formatting by The Book Khaleesi
www.thebookkhaleesi.com
Editing by Trey West

Dedication

I dedicate this book to my grandfather Elijah Monroe Gray, who gave me the type of childhood that encouraged me to find my magic and dared me to live in it. I love you, and it's my wish and hope that you're resting in eternal peace.

I also dedicate this book to all the black dreamers, all the creatives, shamans, oracles, lightworkers and witches who hide their magic in the shadows. I hear you. I see you. I am you, and I love you. This is for you.

Prologue

August 1932

O dessa knew why she'd returned here. She always knew she would. It didn't make the reality of her situation any better, or the burden she held within her clutches any lighter. She sat up covered in sweat, a sticky wet that only Louisiana heat could produce. Sitting at the edge of her bed, she awaited her visitor. She allowed her body to slide down into the cold, wooden floorboards beneath her and assume a cross legged position. Lighting 7 white candles around her, she prepared a sacred place for her ancestor. With her eyes closed and without uttering an audible word, she welcomed her guest into the room. As many a time as she has done this, the hair on her neck stood still every time.

"You have to do this Dessa, your lineage gotta keep its power," Odessa reasoned with herself. Her mama warned her. Long ago. She warned her about all this "secular, occult mess" that she liked to fool around with. How did Odessa explain that she was called to it? How did she explain the pull she felt to it, like an alcoholic to the bottle? It wasn't something she could stop, because she didn't even know how or where it started.

She was soon to find out.

Odessa cleared her mind, only focusing on the task at hand. She had been gaining strength over the last couple of weeks, and it was taking her a lot less effort to summon and conjure these days. Odessa didn't think she could get any hotter, but the more power she drew to herself she could feel the heat radiating off of her honey complexed skin. Just as her energy reached what seemed like the boiling point, she heard footsteps approaching the door. Odessa opened her eyes as the goosebumps made a guest appearance on her skin with every sloth footed step that dragged.

The door creaked open and what stood before Odessa nearly incapacitated her. Odessa had the chance to experience many visitors, but none like the one who stood before her. Her visitor smiled, and extended a glowing hand, waiting for her to accept. Odessa couldn't move. She wanted to.

"Move Dessa, don't be rude." Odessa thought to herself.

Almost as if her visitor read her mind, she began to chuckle. "It's ok chile, it's a lot. I know. Please, stay seated and I will join you," her visitor replied.

As the door creaked closed behind her, she started to disrobe the glowing golden coat she wore. Underneath she was dressed in an 1800's era fashion, but not just any fashion. Her clothes were neither torn nor tattered and you could tell she came from affluence.

Sitting in front of her visitor, Odessa managed to find words to speak. "Thank you, for coming. I know you don't do this often...or ever. I didn't think you would grace me with your presence quite honestly," Dessa managed to choke out. Her mouth was so dry, and as if she hadn't been sweating bullets before, she was now.

"That's exactly why I'm here. We had to speed up the process, you're stronger than any of us could have ever imagined. You have Dupree blood running through your veins sure, but you have far surpassed anything any of us could have ever imagined child," Odessa's great grandmother stared lovingly at her grandchild.

"So why are you here Granme`? Odessa questioned. She felt like she knew the answer, but under the current circumstances one could never be too sure.

"I'm here chile, because there are things, future things you need to know. This life us chosen Dupree women live is far from an easy one. I sent the ancestors that you've had the pleasure of communicatin' with each for a particular reason, but that's up for you to decipher. What you need to know is through your loins will pass the strongest conjure woman this family will ever know, stronger than me even. You must protect her, and to do this you must be ready. Continue your practicing, immerse yourself in our history and our ways of life. I will be with you, all of us will," Marceline promised her great granddaughter.

She watched her great grandmother's smooth brown skin wrinkle with uncertainty and this concerned Odessa. Watching the matriarch of her family rise and put her jacket back on, so many questions ran through her mind. "Protect her, who is her? What from? Who am I to protect someone?" Odessa questioned herself.

Once again, almost like she was reading her mind,

Marceline turned to her granddaughter.

"Keep your first–born granddaughter close. She will encounter much in her life, but it is she who will prepare us. Don't let her gifts escape her. This task will not be an easy one and you will be tested from every angle," she sternly affirmed.

Marceline was indeed concerned. She knew the obstacles that lie ahead for her family, but the Moreau's could never take them down. Marceline made sure of that, with her life. It was now up to her granddaughter to heed her warning.

Placing a kiss on her granddaughter's head, she turned to make her exit.

"Remember chile," Marceline said, joined by her granddaughter in unison, "I'm just a conjure away," as she disappeared.

CHAPTER 1

Sol

There's not much in life I believe in. I was always the "believe it when I see it" type, ya know? I'm not even sure if I believe the shit imma bout to tell you. One thing I do know...and that is, it happened. This is my story, even if you don't choose to believe it. I'm aight with that. I'm used to getting the strange looks and eye rolls every time I tell this story. Until someone needs me. That's how it goes though right? I'm not looking for a pity party. I've paid my dues, so fuck your judgement. All I'm asking you to do is listen...because I didn't ask for this.

I guess I should tell you a little bit about me, huh? My momma and daddy named me Solelil Marceline Dupree on January 22, 1990. I go by Sol. Momma said I was born still in my amniotic sac... – or with a veil over me like the old folks say. I'm the middle child of the three most dysfunctional siblings to come out of Fayetteville, North Carolina by way of

SAI MECCA

New Orleans, Louisiana. According to Momma that's where our roots are, in New Orleans. My mama thought it was a good idea to move us to Fayetteville versus raising us in the "poverty stricken swamps of New Orleans" but I don't see a difference. There's three of us, like I said. My brother Andre who we call "Dre" is the oldest, I'm the middle child with real life "Middle Child Syndrome," and then comes my baby sister Kyleena.

I was always the wild one of the three. Always getting my assed whooped for something. I liked to live life out loud as opposed to being quiet. Everything about me was loud from my hair color to the color painted on my toes. My mouth was the loudest though. I think what kept me from getting in more trouble is my creativity. My Daddy used to tell me he ain't never seen a child as talented as me. I can make art out of anything, all I need to do is feel it. I can paint it, dance to it, sing it...write it. My brother Dre says it's almost creepy what I can do when I focus.

Aside from the trouble I seemed to always get hemmed up in when I wasn't creating, I was different. Too many nightmares than I care to remember. I could feel when someone was about to die, or when someone was pregnant. I could feel other people's emotions without them having to say shit. That's why it's hard to pull one over on my ass, I'm already knowin'. Let's not even talk about the things I would see at any given time of the day. Now that I look back at it, I really think that's why Momma and me was so close. I was a part of her that she couldn't live out loud. She never really made me feel crazy, but she damn sure wouldn't talk about what I was experiencing out loud. I always had this feeling that she knew more than she let on though.

FOOLISH

I was a mama's girl too. Couldn't tell me shit about my momma. Luna Dupree. I knew she was special. My momma was a quiet woman. Never had too much to say so when she spoke, your ass listened. My momma was the baddest woman that ever walked this planet. She was a light skinned Creole woman, so creole and proud although her and my daddy was married, she kept her last name. "There's something special about women from New Orleans with the last name Dupree," she would always tell me. I never knew what the fuck that meant. She always talked in riddles. She was just strange like that. We also never knew much about her family. I didn't even know my grandparents. She never talked about New Orleans. My daddy though, oh we knew all my daddy family. My daddy, Freddy Monroe was proud of where he came from.

Freddy Monroe stood 6'4 with some of the biggest hands you'd ever see in your life. He knew how to use 'em too. A brown skinned man from Shreveport, Louisiana, my daddy wasn't shy to working hard. As hard as he worked, we rarely ever saw the fruits of his labor. How that saying go? "Jack of all trades, master of none..." or some shit like that. Anyway, my daddy never finished shit. Get rich quick schemes was his shit. Over time, my daddy started going to church "to find what he was missing..." or whatever the hell that meant. All I know is when he started going to church, I guess he found what he was missing and replaced the family with it.

It was like he became a zombie. He wasn't like my daddy anymore. Everything was about saving my momma soul. I didn't know back then what the fuck he was supposed to be saving her from. Whatever is was, drowned their marriage. Not one for divorce, my Momma stuck it out. Faithful Luna. As much as my daddy tried to change her, she stuck to her guns. After a while, they just stopped speaking. It was strange living in the house with your parents who are still very much married, but at the same time very disconnected.

At some point, my family seemed to drift apart. It was like we were family but only when someone asked. I really feel like it started right before my brother Dre went into the Navy. Dre really started distancing himself from the family. He said he was just mentally preparing himself to be away from us for months at a time, but you can't slick a can of oil. I knew better than that. After he left, my sister Kyleena started to change too. A normally outgoing person, she started being real quiet and to herself. She never wanted to talk to or about Dre. It was like Dre took a part of her when he left. I guess he took a part of my Momma and Daddy too because they went from not speaking to each other, to just not speaking period. It was real sudden and strange. For a while, it was as if Dre never existed.

I hated to leave my sister, but I had to get out of there. After I graduated high school, I packed my shit and my best friend Mila and I moved to Brooklyn, NY. I always knew that I wasn't the college type, but that doesn't mean I'm stupid. I didn't know until I got to Brooklyn that I was the strippin' type. I learned a lot about myself in Brooklyn, miles away from my family. I guess that's where you can say I started to spread my wings. I had always been a free spirit, but Brooklyn brought it out of me.

I would call home and talk to my momma and Kyleena, but nothing ever changed. Kyleena was getting closer and closer to graduating high school and to be honest, I was kinda afraid of what would happen to my parents after she left the nest. My sister graduated in the summer of 2015 and ended up going to school to become a social worker back in New Orleans. I guess if she couldn't save our crazy ass family she would make up for it by saving someone else's. With all of us out of the house, my parents grew further and further apart. Momma started going back and forth to New Orleans as much as she could, and daddy became obsessed with the church. He started saying shit like he had to be "reborn" and his sins were "eating him alive."

Life is funny like that though, right? One day everything is all good and the next...well...the next is always unexpected. These six months have made me question who or what I really am. Who or where I came from....and I'm still not entirely sure. I just know its powerful. My story may sound like its straight out of BET'S archives for made for TV movies...but it's mine. And it's real. I really have a damn hard time separating fact from fiction some days.

One thing I need you to remember before we go any further...forget everything you thought you knew about life. Forget everything you thought you knew about death. Just forget everything you thought you knew about anything. All of it. It's bullshit. Before all of this happened, I thought I knew what life was all about. I thought I knew about love, about family....all that good shit. I mean, I knew my life wasn't your cookie cutter life but damn it, I thought I made it out. Life has a way of callin' your bluff. Just listen to my story and decide for yourself, just remember...I don't owe you shit, especially an explanation.

I sat still, legs in a crisscrossed position waiting for the transport back. Flashes of light surrounded me in a golden hue, letting me know it was soon to come. I had never felt this uncomfortable. I had also never been this deep in. Feeling the anxiety rising up in me, I started to attempt to force myself back awake hoping maybe it would speed this shit up. Deep down inside I knew better. I knew these things didn't happen on my time. Lifting my head, my eyes dilated from pure shock. I was not where I was when I initially closed them.

Surrounding me were rows and rows of books, golden glowing books. Shelf upon shelf that stretched on for what seemed like miles. I had never been here before, but my gut told me this was no mistake. Nothing that ever happens during these crazy ass trips is a mistake. Everything is always carefully and strategically placed. Shaken, I got up from my safe position and began to search the shelves, when I felt all the air leave my lungs. Every book I looked at had my name written in the binding. Every book. Visibly shaken and hella disturbed, I reached for the book entitled "The Fool." No sooner as I grabbed the book, my body projected forward into time and space.

I knew what that meant.

Bracing myself for the descend back into my body, I tried to grab hold of what I wanted to remember. Finally back in my bedroom, I stood over my body which was still sleeping peacefully in the position I fell asleep in. I hated this part. Every time I forced myself to rationalize that this wasn't a dream. I matched my limbs one by one until I was comfortable. When I was ready, I forced myself awake.

Lying in what felt like the stickiest pool of sweat, I shot up from my sleep. Grabbing the notebook on my side table just for nights like this, I tried to remember everything that had just taken place. When I'd first started this notebook, these nights and dates were few and far in between. Since my parents died they seemed to get more frequent and more confusing. I kept this notebook so I could remind myself I wasn't crazy. "I mean honestly," I thought. "Who could I tell this crazy shit to? People would have my black ass committed." So, it would continue to be my little secret.

I glanced over at the picture on my desk of my parents. My emotions were still mixed. I knew I should miss them, but that nutty part of me believed they were still here somehow. I still felt them so damn strong, even in their silence. Even though it had been months, it felt like it was just yesterday when shit went left.

~~ * ~~

6 Months Prior...
March 2017

You know that sinking feeling you get when something is wrong, and you know something is wrong...but you can't put your finger on it or rationalize it? Yep. That one. Right before the phone call that would change my life, that feeling had been sitting with me. Made a home out of my body. Nobody should ever have to see the things I've seen in the last six months. Sometimes I'm not entirely sure I'm not crazy.

I stared at my ringing cell phone, not wanting to answer. I had just talked to my little sister Kyleena the night before and was aware of the fighting my parents had been doing. As I glanced at my cell phone and watched my brother's name flash across my screen, I realized I wasn't in the mood to talk to his distant ass either. Selfish? Maybe. I just knew that the reason he was calling me was to talk about my parent's drama and I couldn't began to gather enough fucks. I had shit of my own going on. I finished putting lotion on my smooth brown skin as I watched the stage from the back. I always got anxiety right before I went on stage, but tonight felt different.

As the last dancer finished up and wiped the pole down, I tried to go to my secret place. It's the place I go to when I get on stage that makes my job a little less…everything. I don't even work at one of those hole in the wall spot that bitches with bullet wounds and horrible lace fronts work at. The spot I work at, called Henny's, was an exclusive spot. You had to have guap to come here. This is where all the men (and some bitches) came when they wanted to get their rocks off in private. Literally anything goes here. I'm not into all of the extra shit. I shake my ass on the stage for a couple of minutes, a couple of times a night and take my ass to the house. I'm not judging anybody who does anything extra, that's just not how I get down. I make more money than I need to make here so I can't complain.

I stepped on the stage, kinda in my zone and kinda somewhere else. As PartyNextDoor's "Come and See Me" blared through the speakers I started to twirl my body around the pole. The pole felt stiffer than usual tonight, and the lights hotter. As I made eye contact with my audience, this one chick in particular caught my cat eye. She was a black chick, and truth be told I get a little excited when I see black chicks in here. Not to say they don't get down too, but you rarely see them in Henny's.

All I could see from the stage was the outline of her full lips. They were painted murder red. As I twirled upside down on the pole I could see the blood red stilettos that housed her red painted toes. As I continued my dance, I caught myself in mid–thought. Now, I'm not one to go chase the kitty cat. Don't get it fucked up, I've had many questionable ass nights, but I had never been attracted to a female the way I was attracted to this broad. Brooklyn taught me something new every day.

I could tell she had money because of how modest she dressed. Real ballers don't have to speak too loud. As modest as she was dressed, everything about her still seemed to shine. Everything sparkled. Everything glistened...and I was determined that he was going to pay my rent with her tip. Although I hadn't locked eyes with her yet, I knew I had her wrapped around my finger. I danced through the first song and decided to shift this shit into full gear.

As I snaked around the Main Stage, it felt like she had found me in my secret place. The place where I create. My sexy space, the space where if I were to unleash it into the world it would corrupt the most prude bitch. I never let anybody into that space, yet it feels like she had forced her way anyway. As I prepared for the next dance, I spotted my best friend Mila making her way to the stage to the left of me. Whenever we danced together its like magic happened. I met Mila not too long after we moved to Fayetteville when I was six. Crazy how the universe works. Mila is the spicy Dominican friend that everybody needs in their life was and is still my right hand after all these years. Anytime I had dirty work to do, Mila is always there. I used to love going to her house and listening to the stories her mom and grandma would tell me about Santeria, Brujeria and Las 21 Divisiones.

Little did they know I understood everything they were talking about. By the age of 13, I had experienced most of it...I just didn't have a name to put on it. It was at Mila's house that I really came to understand the crazy shit I was going through. It seemed like around this time my creativity hit an all–time high. I was having crazy visions. One in particular was of this old lady.

They started off as dreams, but she eventually crept her old ass way into my reality. I saw and heard her in everything. I painted her in colors she chose herself. I sang the songs she would hum in my ear. I even picked up a couple dance moves from her. She was everywhere. I felt her energy the most while I was on stage. It was almost as if she took control of my every motor skill. I was no longer myself on stage when she was near. Except tonight. My old lady friend was nowhere to be found, and I had the chance to feel all these emotions for myself.

As Mila twisted and bended her body around, I kept my eyes fixed on what all I could see of my mystery woman. She had yet to make a move, but she had to be crazy not to tip after the show I'd been giving. Feeling Mila's energy amping me up, and low–key pissed off that Mystery Girl still hadn't thrown a single dollar, I started to go harder toward the end of the song. As "Hot Boyz" by Missy came to an end, I snaked my thick brown thighs up the pole. Throwing my body back, head first I let my body expose itself in all the right places. As I tossed my long, freshly twisted locs back and forth while shimming down the pole, I just knew it was a wrap. That tip was mine. As I touched the earth underneath me, I looked up to an empty chair.

Ya'll know I was mad as fuck. There's no fancy words I can say to make you understand it better. I wiped down my pole, collected the rest of my money off the stage and stomped my ass to the dressing room. I had already made up in my mind that I was going home for the night, as early as it was. I put my earbuds on while I counted my cash because, fuck everybody at this point. Honestly, I couldn't be mad because I had already made my quota plus a stack more, but that wasn't the damn point. I felt like I had been toyed with and honestly, I had no idea why I was taking the shit so personally.

I decided to calm down and be thankful for what I did make. As I started to shift my thoughts, Mila's crazy ass ran in the room. "Biiiiiiitccch!! They are showin out tonight! Imma have give an extra special thank you at my alter tonight!!" Mila screamed in her loud ass accent. I chuckled just to appease her because I wasn't in the mood for talking, and Mila is a talker. When I didn't answer her, Mila took a look in my direction and shook her head. "No bitch, you are not about to let one sorry ass ho ruin your night. These niggas are TIPP–ING, do you hear me? Plus you're not leaving me out there by myself." Mila ranted. She could tell by the look in my face I had already made up my mind. This ass was going home.

"Girl, I've made good enough money, plus I work a double tomorrow. I'll be alright. Make you some girl because I already know you're about to take over the Main Stage with your greedy ass." I chuckled as I threw my sweaty bra at her. She stood in front of me poking out her lip, to no avail. "Ugggh, fine. But I don't wanna hear shit next week about you being broke," Mila tried one last attempt. She and I both know it had been MANY moons since I had been broke, so that wasn't even water off my back. I looked at her while I reached in for a hug and watched her jiggle her tan ass back on the Main Stage. I started to get my things together as one of rotating DJ's came into the back calling my name.

I peeped my head from behind the door as I saw Danny's

sexy ass coming my way. I called back to him and in seconds all of his dreadlocked 6'4 chocolate frame was standing in front of me.

What's up, Danny?" I said as a smile stretched across his face.

"I saw you fuckin 'em up out there tonight but Mila told me you out already. You good?" He asked me while I searched for a lie.

"Yea, I'm good Danny. I just have a bunch of shit to do tomorrow and I gotta be up early. You know me, it don't take me long to make my bread like these other chicks." I laughed as I playfully punched him in the arm. "I know you didn't just come back here to ask me was I leaving, what's up?" I asked him now actually curious to why he was back here.

"Oh yea, shit. Some chick dropped this off for you at the DJ booth while you were dancing." Danny said to me as he raised an eyebrow. "You got broads chasin' you around now? Let me find out Sol," Danny joked with a slice of seriousness.

I rolled my eyes at him as he walked back out to the floor.

I sat listening to Jhene Aiko's new album "Trip" to mellow me out. That shit had been my jam for the last week. I ripped open the envelope and laughed mad loud to myself. It was a handwritten card from Mystery Girl. "I know you were expecting a tip, but I could do so much more for you. I wanted to talk to you, but it would fuck shit up. Don't worry though, I'm always around. You'll never have to look too far. Catch me in your dreams, Love yours, S." I sat at my booth trying to decipher what the fuck this woman was talking about when my phone rang. Not looking at the screen, I answered. The voice on the other end was panicking.

"Sol! Sol?! Can you hear me?" The third member of our circle and my second best friend Devon was screaming into the phone. I snapped out of the trance I was in and answered.

"Devon? What's wrong? Yea, I can hear you...calm down. Is everything ok?" I stuttered as I tried to understand what was happening.

"Where the fuck have you been Sol? We've been... well Dre's been calling you and calling you for two days! You need to come the fuck home. Now." Devon screamed at me through the phone. I wasn't used to him talking to me like that, as he was hella soft spoken. I thought back to earlier when my older brother Dre had called me repeatedly all day long. My stomach started to turn as I tried to imagine what was going on. Devon's voice interrupted my thoughts.

"SOL!! Did you hear me? Your parents are dead and you need to bring your ass home. Shit is crazy...." Devon's voiced trailed off as I dropped my phone and tried to comprehend what he was saying to me. Just as I looked up into the mirror, the old woman appeared.

"Time to go home, Pitit Fi," the old lady whispered as I felt my body hit the earth beneath me.

CHAPTER 2

Going Home

D evon.
As much as I had missed my friend, damn near brother because blood couldn't make us any closer, I was nervous about seeing him. Nervous about him seeing me like this. As I stared out the window of the plane that flew my drained body back to RDU in Raleigh, I felt anxiety bubble up in my stomach. It wasn't even anxiety about my parents to be quite honest. It was about facing all the shit I thought I'd left behind in Fayetteville. Shit that Devon so mercilessly brought to my attention during our phone call once I was released from the hospital the night after I'd received the news about my parents.

Devon was the quiet friend in our clique. He was always just kind of there, like a quiet but lethal solider. Back then, we had no idea that Devon was gay, not that it would've mattered one way or another. He hid it very well. He hid a lot of things. That was just Devon's nature. "Mind your fuck ass business", was his motto.

We also didn't know until years of being friends what Devon was going through at home. His mother had some type of mental illness, to this day I have no clue what kind. Devon would never tell us. After years of seeing scars and bruises and being all around concerned about my friend, I asked what the deal was. All he would ever say is, "She'll get what's coming to her one day. They see everything, the world is funny like that." After that, Devon began to change. He became more of a budding rose than a wilting tulip. We tried to protect Devon every way we knew how, and it wasn't until today that I realized he never needed our protection. It's crazy how he would end up protecting me.

I opened my eyes after not even realizing I had fallen asleep. I stretched my tired ass limbs in an attempt to look at least a little bit alive by the time the plane landed. I checked my cellphone and immediately got confused. It was as if time had went back. I stared out the window trying to make sense of the shit, when I heard a familiar voice. I turned my head in disbelief as I took in the fact that Devon was seated beside me. I looked at him as he spoke, mouth moving a mile a damn minute.

"Bitch, why the fuck are you looking at me like you just saw the most beautiful ghost ever?" Devon asked me as he flipped his imaginary ass hair. I continue to stare at him. I'm so confused...I know I'm tired but fuck. I know I got on this plane...without Devon. I looked out of the window just in time to see a clear blue sky change into what seemed like limitless darkness. "Devon, where are we going?" I felt the need to ask, just so I could gauge my level of crazy correctly. Devon looked at me and chuckled, and that shit completely

threw me off. What the fuck was so funny? Most importantly, what the fuck was going on?

"Sometimes, Sol, life takes us places that we aren't sure about. What you can be sure about though bitch, is that everything that happens leads us exactly where the hell we're supposed to be. Humans are so controlling. What I've learned in this life is just sit back, shut your ass up and go for the ride. Life ain't gon' take you nowhere your ass ain't supposed to be. Now, please. You're fuckin up my Zen." Devon placed his sunglasses on his smooth chocolate skin and laid his head back. Irritated that he didn't answer my question, I went to open my mouth as he held his hand up and shook his head. "Girl, hush.", he said to me without even opening his eyes.

As I sat back in my seat, stunned, the flight attendant came over the speaker of the plane. "Thank you so much for choosing Moreau Airlines. We are now at the beginning of our descension back into the earth plane. Please relax your mind and your body as we prepare for landing. If you have any questions or concerns, your higher self is available for service. Once again, thank you for flying Moreau Airlines."

I sat in my seat, not believing what I had just heard. It was my mother's voice. It was clear as day. Luna Dupree had a voice you couldn't mistake for anybody else's. I looked around the cabin and as my eyes made it back to my seat I realized Devon was no longer there. I searched around for someone to help my ass, I spotted a flight attendant coming down the aisle.

"Excuse me, where are we?" I asked the attendant who stopped in front of my chair with her back turned. As she turned around I almost lost it. It was my mother! I knew I wasn't crazy. As I stared at her mouth moving, I didn't hear shit. "What mama? What are you saying?" I said loudly as I started to panic. As I stood up to approach her, the plane shook violently and forced me back into my

seat. My momma bent down, grabbed me by my shoulders and whispered "Odessa, find Odessa... if you find the trunk you can find her. Talk to your higher self..." into my ear as she disappeared into thin air. As I held on to my edges and my seat, I stared out the window fighting back tears hoping it would give me some kind of damn indication of where the fuck I was at.

As I stared out of the window places and times I remembered as I child were flying by. Rim Lake. Places in New Orleans that I knew, but didn't know the name of. The day that Dre left for the Navy. The night Devon called me. The old lady. I shut my eyes as I felt tears creep up and sit on my lash line. I was so close to my mother. She was right there. Her scent. Her soft skin and country drawl. I had her right there and now she was gone. The plane projected forward and all I remember is brightness and an uncontrollable fatigue before slumping over into my chair.

As I my body jerked awake, the lady sitting next to me stared at me like she might need to defend herself. "What?" I asked the lady.

"I thought I needed to call the attendant for you. You fell asleep and started talking and shouting and all this other crazy mess. Are you ok?" the lady asked with concern etched in her smooth but aging brown skin. Her energy was very soothing, damn near familiar. Embarrassed about what had just happened and not wanting to explain it to her of all people, I simply shook my head yes. Realizing that I needed to document this, I went for my carry–on bag to grab my notebook. The lady was still looking at me like she wasn't sure if it was safe or not, so I decided to end the awkward silence.

"Excuse me ma'am I don't mean to keep bothering you, but do you have any idea how far we are from Raleigh?" I asked. Before answering, she looked me up and down.

"We're about an hour away. Are you sure you don't need me to get a flight attendant? I don't know what that mess you were moaning about means, but that shit ain't normal girl," the lady pressed again. I felt my irritation coming to the surface.

"I'm fine, I just haven't had much sleep. That's all," I lied.

I opened up my notebook and began to scribble everything I remembered, even if it didn't make sense. Time was of the essence when it came to these…trips. I had been having trips like these ever since I could remember. I used to think they were just dramatic ass dreams until one day out of nowhere Mila and I got sucked into this conversation about lucid dreaming. I always thought it was weird as fuck that I could control what I do in my dreams and learning about that honestly made it easier to maneuver them. Mila's grandmother also told me about automatic writing which I had also been doing for years without even knowing it. Where did all these gifts come from? I don't fuckin know. As much as my daddy was in to church I doubt he would've known, and momma…everything was a secret with her.

As I put my pen down, I noticed the lady was glancing over my shoulder. Rude ass. I told her ass I was fine. I gave her the dirtiest stare I could muscle up, but she gave not one fuck about my twisted-up face. She looked me up and down, smirked and continued to read her book entitled "Lost Frame." I rolled my eyes and began to look out of the window. I was tryna prepare myself for the fuckery I was sure to walk into, especially if my brother was there already. Kyleena. I couldn't even imagine how she was feeling, and I was sure my fuck ass brother was telling her this was all my fault somehow. He was good for that shit.

My mind rolled back to my recent trip, and what my mother whispered to me. "Odessa," I thought to myself. Who the hell was Odessa and why did momma look so terrified saying her name? What the hell is my higher self and how do I talk to her? Him? Where was I supposed to find this trunk? It's not like I could go ask an auntie or uncle, my mom didn't fuck with her family like that. Hell, I'm not even sure if she had brothers and sisters.

"Going home to see family?" The old lady pulled me out of my thoughts. Her nosiness was beginning to piss me off.

"Something like that," I spat as I looked her up and down, trying to give her a clear indication to mind her damn business. Of course she didn't let up.

"I was like you once." She chuckled as she placed her bookmark in her book. "Young, dumb and mad at the world. Not even realizing what's inside of you." She calmly spoke while she sipped her water.

I wanted to smack that shit out of her hands. Who the fuck was mad and dumb? Before I spoke, I had to calm myself down. My momma would be turnin' over in the coroner's office if I dare disrespected an elder, even if she was judgmental as fuck.

"And just how do you know I'm dumb and mad at the world, lady?" I asked her, waiting for some bullshit answer. You know those hypothetical ass answers all old folks give that sounds like it pertains to you, but it's just some general shit used to get under your skin and make them seem right.

"Actin' like you don't need your family in this world can come back to haunt you," the lady said slowly as she turned to face me. "You don't know what your family did and suffered through to make sure you live a decent life. I remember when I had to put my parents in the ground, I thought all my problems went in there with them too," she stopped to pause and stare out the window. She looked like she went back to wherever the fuck she was from and was having a moment. She turned to face me with a solemn look in her tired eyes, the look that I saw my momma with one too many times.

"Your brother and your sister need you right now. Don't shut them out. You're a Dupree. Act like one. Many people were hurt, killed and sacrificed just to bring your ass into this world...to *protect you. You think you see things and know things for no reason? You a special girl. Find the trunk and you'll find your answers. Dumb ass girl," the lady rolled her eyes and sat back in her seat. I was so shocked you coulda bought me for a penny.*

How the fuck did she know of all of that? As I sat staring at this woman with her eyes closed, my heart damn near stopped. A wind of familiarity took over my body as I recognized this woman's face. She was the old woman who had been coming to me since I was little. The flight attendant came over the intercom to tell us we were arriving in Raleigh. I stood up to gather my carry on, and also gather the nerve to ask this lady some questions before we got off this plane. I grabbed my bag and turned around, prepared to open my mouth but the lady was no longer in her seat. The only thing that was left was her book. I picked up the book and opened it to the page she had bookmarked. It was an empty page. All of the pages were empty. I tucked the book in my bag for safe keeping, not even stopping to contemplate an answer now. At this point I had enough of mufuckas disappearing on my ass. I stopped a flight attendant who was walking down the aisle.

"Excuse me, do you know what happened to the older lady that was sitting here?" I asked the flight attendant. She looked at me with a confused and blank look.

"Ma'am, there's been no one in the seat during this flight," the attendant spoke softly. I looked at her like she had lost her mind.

"Are you sure, I mean...I'm pretty sure there was someone sitting here," I challenged her.

"Ma'am, I can assure you. I do a headcount of people on this plane before we take off and before the landing. There are 52 passengers on this flight. Had someone been sitting in that seat, it would make 53 and I'm never wrong on count," the stuck–up flight attendant stated as she walked off to prepare us for landing.

I sat back in my seat, waiting for the other passengers to unboard. What the hell was going on? It seems like shit has hit the fan and I haven't even made it back to Fayetteville yet. Once the last person walked by me, I got my shit and followed suit. As I entered the terminal, I saw Devon standing there casually on his phone. Dressed in black and gold with enough jewelry on to pawn and feed the homeless for at least the next ten years, Devon paid no attention to the fact that I was walking up to him. I laughed to myself while approaching him. Typical Devon.

I was happy to see him. Out of Mila, Devon and I, Devon was the comforter. He just felt like home anytime he was around. That doesn't mean he won't open hand bust you in your shit. That's his guilty pleasure though. He smiles and hugs just enough to let you know he cares, but don't ever cross him. As he looked up our eyes met, even though he was wearing the darkest shades I had ever seen in my life. I got closer and damn near fell into his arms. We hugged for what felt like forever. I hadn't seen Devon for about a year. We always kept in contact, but it wasn't the same as being in his presence. After our embrace, he took a step back and looked at me.

"Bitch, have you been eating at all? I mean, I know you throwin' that ass in circles every night but shit...we need to get you a plate." Devon yelped as he peered at me over the edge of his shades.

We both busted out laughing, which turned into crying for my crybaby ass. Everything just hit me all at once. I never thought that me coming back to Fayetteville meant I would have to bury my parents. My mom had so much life left in her. She had finally gotten loose from my dad's grip and was starting to live her life. Kyleena would tell me when she would come to visit her in New Orleans that she was just beaming every time she saw her. I couldn't speak for my dad because we rarely spoke to him, but regardless my dad didn't deserve to die either.

Devon stared at me as I let it all out. "C'mon, let's get you a drink before this drive back to Fayetteville. We have a lot to talk about," Devon chirped as he grabbed me by my jacket and pulled me in the direction of a little airport bar. I got my drink, and Devon started to speak.

"Sol, I love you dearly. However, if you ever scare me like that ever again I will beat your ass," Devon squinted at me as he removed his shades.

Trying to down play the fact that I had been ignoring the entire fuck out of everybody in Fayetteville for the last couple of days, I coyly asked, "What are you talking about? How have I been ignoring you?" I lowered my eyes as I sipped through the plastic straw of my now non–existent drink. Damn that was good.

"Bitch don't do it. Sol, everybody and their momma LITERALLY has been calling you for the last week about what happened. Nobody knows what the fuck is going on, and when nobody could get ahold of you everybody thought the worst. Dre, has lost his ever loving fuckin mind. I don't think that boy has slept since he flew home. He swears he's gonna find out who did this shit," Devon stopped speaking as he looked at me as if I knew something I wasn't telling him.

Truth is, I probably knew the least out of every damn

body. Once again here I was, expected to play captain save a ho. And what's with Dre on this vigilante mission all of a sudden, like he really fucked with our family? Guilt maybe? He sure never gave an ounce of a fuck after he got his hefty bonus to join the Navy. The way that nigga acted you would think he was a damn orphan. No phone calls, no Christmas cards, postcards...no nothing. He just dipped out on us. So fuck his sleep and his mission. Devon snapped me out of my feelings.

"Why do I feel like there's something you're not telling me?"

Devon stared at me in a way I never saw him look at me before. It coulda been because I'm tired and now on the verge of tipsy, but I knew better. Something about him was different, he even looked different. Not that kinda different that happens when you haven't seen someone for a while. It was something else.

"Devon," I started to speak and caught myself. I don't think he was ready for what I had been witnessing, so I tried to divert the conversation. "Bitch I haven't seen you in a year and some change, of course there's shit I gotta tell you," I laughed while Devon sat stone faced.

He sensed something. Devon pulled out his wallet and paid the tab along with a tip and got up from his chair. "It's time for you to stop running girl. Let's get home."

CHAPTER 3

2–6

L et me get an All–Star Special, eggs scrambled with cheese, sausage, raisin toast, hashbrowns scattered, smothered, covered and with gravy, a blueberry waffle, and a sweet tea," I stood behind my unsuspecting brother as he placed his order at Waffle House.

We used to always come here with my mom, every Saturday morning. Although I had been back in Fayetteville for a couple of hours at this point, I had yet to make it to the police station to talk to the detectives handling my parents' case. Because my brother is a fuck ass nigga, he had yet to identify their bodies and Kyleena was still on her flight coming into Raleigh from New Orleans. So that left me. I stood behind my brother, trying to suppress all the anger I held inside for him. Devon sat in the red waiting chairs behind me for moral support. My plan was to be nice during this first encounter. I mean, I hadn't seen my brother in almost

6 years. Remembering why I haven't seen him pissed me the fuck off all over again. It's one thing for him to ignore Kyleena and I, but the fact that he treated my mother like shit made me want to grab one of those big ass knives from the grill in front of me and slit his throat.

"So, our parents have been dead for a week and your bitch ass has yet to go identify their bodies? I knew you were a fuck ass person but damn Dre, this is a new low... even for the likes of you." The words slipped outta my mouth before I could catch them, and by the time I put the period at the end I no longer gave a fuck. My brother turned slowly to look at me and I almost dropped my bag when he faced me. This man, looked like a shell of who and what my brother was. His blood shot red eyes, grey skin and skeletal face imprinted itself in my brain. As we stared at each other, a little bit of sympathy crept over me. That was quickly overcome by pride. It was clear all the faking and the "holier than thou" bullshit Dre had been feeding these niggas back home in Fayetteville was such a lie. I'm not going to lie and tell y'all I wasn't happy to have one up on this nigga.

"Sol–" my brother started as I abruptly cut him off.

"Shut the fuck up Dre. I don't wanna hear shit you have to say. I'm on my way down to police station to identify MY parents. The best you can do, is get your food and meet me at the fuckin' house," I snapped as I turned to walk out the door of the restaurant, but not before Dre snapped back to life and hemmed me up in front of a full crowd of people.

He stared at me for a couple of seconds before he snatched me up to go outside. "Devon, get my fuckin food," Dre growled as he dragged me out of the door. Devon continued to busy himself on his phone as we walked outside.

"Listen to me. Even though you're acting like a bitch, I'm not gonna disrespect you like that and treat you like one. You don't know WHAT the fuck I've been going through since momma and daddy were killed. I know that because you never answered your fuckin phone, but I'm all of a sudden the fuck up? Where the fuck have you been Solelil? Feels good pointing your manicured finger huh? Sending Momma and Daddy money don't mean a damn thing, not when I had to sit there and–" Dre paused before he continued. "Nah. You damn right you're gonna go down there and identify them. You're the angel, right?" Dre screamed at me with tears in his eyes. I had never seen him look nor act like this. "Now, I'm going to the house. I'm going to eat my food, and wait for Ky. I'll see you at the fuckin house." Dre said with his back turned to me as he walked back in the Waffle House.

I stood outside for a few minutes trying to collect my thoughts. What was really going on? I know Dre and I had our issues but seeing him this way caught me totally off guard. What was the real reason he hadn't been downtown to identify momma and daddy? Ky said he'd been acting strange, but shit. I knocked on the window to let Devon know I was ready. Before walking out, Devon stopped and mean mugged the shit out of my brother. I had to laugh to myself. That's Devon, always ready.

As we drove through Fayetteville, my emotions were mixed as hell. It's like everywhere I looked there was a memory of Momma and Daddy lurkin' around the corner. The jump house they used to take us to on the weekends. Douglas Bird High School, where all three of us graduated from, and where momma spent a lot of time volunteering. The closer we got to downtown, the more surreal it became to me that my parents are actually dead. I would have to look at them knowing they weren't coming back. As we parked, I sat in the car for a minute just thinking quietly to myself. Or so I thought.

"Who the fuck would kill MY parents?" I yelled to nobody in particular. "I mean shit, they weren't perfect but damn man...MY parents? Luna and Freddy? Everybody here fuckin loved them! What if Dre had—" Devon cut me off. He took his glasses off and looked at me for a couple of seconds.

"I was wondering when it was gonna hit you bitch. You can't keep holding shit in and pretending like it doesn't bother you. I know that's your specialty. Stone Cold Sol. Hell, they not even my parents and a bitch is crushed like a cup of Sonic's ice, you hear me? Now, I don't know what the fuck was about to come out of your mouth, but swallow that shit before you get back to that house. That's some ground you might not wanna go stomping in just yet," Devon looked at me with his thick eyebrow raised. He was right, though. I always tried to be the one that shit didn't get to. I had to be a rock. Hard...but these were my parents, and as much I hated Dre in this moment, he is my brother.

Devon popped open his middle console and handed me some tissue. "So ummm...do you have any concealer, you know...some light foundation, lip gloss or glaze, a highlight...SOMETHING in your bag because...no ma'am. You will not walk up in there looking like what you done been through," I side–eyed the shit out of him but I couldn't help but crack a smile.

"My makeup bag is in the trunk, could you grab it for me?" I asked as I flipped open the mirror above me and looked at my puffy face. Devon sat and looked at me, puzzled.

"Oh…you thought you were bringing all that powder and shit in my car? Ha! Bitch, you know better." Devon laughed as he opened my door from his side of the car. I had been meaning to ask him where he got this fancy ass, expensive ass black on black Mercedes G63. Questions needed answers, but I had bigger fish to fry.

I opened my eyes trying to get them to adjust to all these bright ass lights that were around me. Trying to remember where I was, I looked around for some clues. The last thing I remembered, I was sitting in Devon's car about to come into the police station and speak with the detectives that were handling my parents' homicide case. Fuck. My parents. As I looked around the room, I noticed all of the surgical tools lying on a table beside me. Was I in a fuckin hospital? I don't have time to be sitting up at Cape Fear. As I looked down, I noticed that the clothes I had on were replaced with some thin ass hospital gown, with my ass exposed. I walked over to the window to be met with pitch blackness on the other side of the curtains. No buildings. No stars. Just…an existence of some sort. One that told my ass I wasn't going anywhere.

I made my way toward the door and walked down a bright, sterile ass hallway. Everybody was moving so fast, like they had some important shit to do. I made it to the desk where a lady sat with her back turned to me, clicking away on a computer. She was the only one who seemed to be moving in real time, so I decided she'd be my best hope.

"Excuse me, can you tell me where I am?" I asked the lady as she turned around to face me. This couldn't be real. It was the same lady from the plane. The old lady who had been around most of my life. She smiled warmly at me as she stood up and came from around the desk space.

FOOLISH

"Solelil, you're finally up. How do you feel love?" The lady asked me while cupping my face in her hands.

I jerked back not knowing how to respond. I felt fine, but I also felt like something wasn't right.

The old lady snapped her fingers and pulled me back into reality, or whatever this is. "Pitit fi, do you hear me? Are you ready to go?" The old lady still wore a warm smile as she tried to get my attention.

Hell no I wasn't ready to go. Go where? We're literally in the middle of no-fucking-where. I held my head trying to make sense of all of this shit. Before I could respond, I felt my body project. When I opened my eyes again, I was standing alongside the old lady in front of two huge windows. I squinted my eyes to see inside of the room and almost screamed. Lying on two cold slabs of metal were my parents. I felt the tears well up in my eyes as the old lady started talking.

"We've been waiting for someone to come and identify these two. I dare not imagine that as big your family is nobody was coming. I knew it would be you, Sol. Are those your parents, Freddy and Luna?"

I stared at my parent's lifeless bodies trying to tell my brain to speak, but nothing came out but a nod.

"I need to hear you verbally say it Solelil. Are these your parents? Freddy Monroe Sr. and Luna Dupree?" The old lady asked again.

"Yes," I stuttered quietly.

As I stared at my parents, all the emotions I had been holding back came to the surface. Who in the fuck killed my parents? Was it random? Even as I asked myself that question I knew for some reason it wasn't. Why was Dre, of all people, the first to pop up in my head as having something to do with it? My momma always told me to go with my first mind. I had a ton of questions for this lady. Hell, she's been following me around most of my life, she had to know the answers to something. As I turned around to ask my questions, I was met with two black, shiny ass bodybuilder lookin' ass niggas. They weren't there before. One of them stood in the back of a wheel chair, while the other held restraints. The kind that you saw when you did some fucked up shit in jail and they had to pin your ass down. I started to silently panic as one of them moved closer to me.

"Solelil, the therapist will see you now," the one with the wheelchair moved closer.

"I'm fine, I can walk if you just tell me where to go," I tried to bargain. I knew somehow, I wasn't getting out of this, and they were smart enough to sense my plan. I promise you, had they let me walk myself I would have found the closest exit outta this bitch.

"Sorry Madame, we've been strictly instructed to deliver you there, personally." They spoke in unison.

Deliver me? Nope. I'd heard enough. Without a second thought I took off running, ass out and everything. I looked back to see them gaining on me with some freakish ass quickness. Who the fuck runs that fast? Just as I turned the corner and saw a big ass red "EXIT" sign, I was met with a stinging sensation that traveled up my spine, as I hit the floor.

As I woke up and tried to focus my eyes, I saw the old lady seated in front of me. Y'all know my first instinct was to dip. I went to move my arm just to notice that one of those black, shiny ass dudes had damn near locked me to the chair. Before I could form another thought, the old lady started to speak.

"I'm surprised you haven't realized who I am, Solelil. I mean, I've followed you your entire life. It is interesting though, to see how people treat others who they think they'll never have to encounter *again," The old lady pulled off her glasses.*

I wasn't in the mood for riddles. At all.

"Confused pitit fi? You don't remember our plane trip? I do believe you have my book, 'Lost Frame' by the way. No worries, you should give that to Devon," she spoke softly as she got up from her seat. "Unchain her," she commanded the beings in the back of the room. I say beings because there is no way in any universe that those niggas are human.

Just as she ordered, both stepped forward and undid the chains that tied around my body. These extra ass niggas. My whole body though? Arm and leg restraints would have been just fine.

"Now, I hate that we had to have this conversation under these circumstances. I would have very much liked to personally meet my namesake under other conditions," she spoke as she walked around me.

Namesake? I don't even know who this lady is, but I'm named after her? I started getting irritated. I need answers.

"I am Marceline Dupree, and you pitit fi are my great great–granddaughter. I know you don't know much about me, or anybody else on this side of the family thanks to your mother, but we really don't have the time to get into all of that at this precise moment. You'll learn as we go along." she hissed as she shuffled papers on her desk.

I sat completely still trying to comprehend where this conversation was going. I swear fo' skittles I was losing my damn mind.

"You are not crazy, chile. Before you were born, your existence and your gifts were chosen for you. You may come to see it as a burden, but I promise you in due time you'll come to like it. The things you've seen, dreamed or experienced are by no mistake, even your seemingly surface level knowledge of the occult. You haven't

remembered everything yet. You were given all these things at birth." Marceline circled my chair as my breathing became shallow.

This lady had to be on some murder one type shit, none of this was making sense. Was she like the "Godmother" of the family? What if she was the one that killed my parents?

"I promise you, it will all make sense in time," she exasperated as she sat on the edge of her desk in front of me. "Right now, I need you to tap in. Pay attention. Dig. Take nothing with a grain of salt, but everything seriously. TRUST NO ONE. I know this is a lot, and I will be there to help you, but this family's survival depends on you. Do some meditating and connect to your higher self, she will help guide you," she cautioned.

"My higher self? How will I meet my higher self? I don't know how to do this shit!" I screamed frantically. How in the hell is it possible that I'm more confused now than when this conversation started?

Marceline looked at me with a smug smile on her face. She walked over and snapped her fingers as a card appeared in her hands. "Oh, but you've met her already…at that job of yours, hmm?" she assured as she handed me the card. It was the card from Mystery Girl.

"What the fuck?" was all I could get out before the floor opened underneath me and swallowed me into its darkness.

I gasped as cold water hit my face, ice cubes and all. Above me stood Devon and a member of Fayetteville's Finest. To the left of me, I saw the underbelly of Devon's car which meant my ass was on the ground.

"So…we just fall out of our friend's vehicles? That's what the young folks are doing now?" Devon sarcastically asked me as he helped me up off the ground.

"Your friend here was pretty concerned about you ma'am. Everything okay?" the cop asked out of what seemed like sincere concern.

I wanted to tell him no, but how do you tell someone that you just spoke to one of your great, great ass grandmothers who has, by the way, been dead for CENTURIES, you're supposed to save your family because you're the "chosen one" but first you have to go identify your parents? Exactly.

I mustered out "I'm fine," while I dusted myself off and set on the edge of the sidewalk.

"Seriously Solelil, are you okay? You've been acting like those weird bitches we used to talk about. All shaky and shit. You know you can trust me with the tea, what's up? Devon quizzed me. I wanted so badly to tell my friend what was going on with me, but the timing didn't feel right. I felt like I had to tackle this shit in order, and next on the menu was identifying my parents.

"I promise, once I get this out of the way, I will tell you everything...but I'm not crazy Devon," I gave him a warning beforehand.

He looked at me and laughed. "Ho, you not no more crazier than any of us walking around here. Some of us just hide it well bitch," Devon laughed as we got up and faced the police station. "You ready?" Devon asked as he grabbed grab my hand.

Without saying a word, I walked toward the police station. Before I could complete a full step, I heard a familiar voice in the back of me.

"I'd notice that ass anywhere," a small voice squeaked as it moved closer. I was about to turn around and unleash the demon I've been holding inside until I saw my baby sister's face.

"Ky?!" I screamed as my sister and I ran to each other. I couldn't believe how grown she looked. When I left, Kyleena was the epitome of an old woman trapped in a teenager's body. All this skin she was showing caught me off guard. "Girl, where are your clothes? You're not in NOLA no more, its chilly as hell out here," I caught myself easily sliding into overprotective sister mode.

"Girl who you tellin, I need to find a hoodie or something out this ho, imma fuck around and be sick," Kyleena admitted in the most southern drawl I have ever heard slip out of her mouth. I couldn't believe I was staring at what once was my baby sister, all grown up and a woman of her own.

"So what the hell are you doing here? Your brother said he was going home to wait on you," I asked lighting a cigarette.

Kyleena looked at me and shook her head. "Old habits die hard huh? Anyway, I know what YOUR brother said, but there was no way I was letting you come do this by yourself. That would be some fuck shit, and Dre knows his ass should be here too. Somebody gotta be levelheaded in this family, shit." Kyleena objected as she rolled her big almond eyes.

Kyleena took her shades off and looked at Devon like she was seeing him for the first time. "Devon? I know that's not you looking like you're straight out of Forbes ho! What are you doing here?" Kyleena squealed as they embraced one another.

"You know I had to come support this one," Devon said as he eyed me up and down. "Plus, you know Momma and Daddy was like my momma and daddy too, I wouldn't let y'all go through this alone. Hell, I'll be damned if they haunt me for the rest of my life," Devon laughed.

Kyleena's face got really serious. "Speaking of haunting, we really, really need to fucking talk," Kyleena murmured as she looked at me with wide eyes accompanied with some serious bags underneath. "I know I used to give you shit and call you crazy when we were kids, but everybody lowkey knew you were special Sol. I didn't know how special though until I started experiencing shit myself," Kyleena whispered.

Devon looked back and forth between us. "See! I knew it! I knew this was on some other shit! Bitch my knowin' be knowin! I gotta call Mila! Yea we ALL are gonna talk tonight ho," Devon screamed as he jumped around.

That shocked me. I thought I was the only one in my family who was cursed with this shit. As much hell as I caught from Ky and Dre back in the day, you would think they attended church with Daddy. I'm not gonna lie, it brought me some comfort.

"Yea, we can definitely talk tonight, but right now can we please get this out of the way?" I pleaded as I pointed to the police station.

"That's what I'm here for," Ky whispered as she grabbed my hand.

As we walked into the police station, I thought my stomach was going to fall outta my ass. Kyleena was surprisingly calm with a stone face. I wonder how she felt inside. I hadn't talked to her at all since all of this happened. I looked at my sister and felt so proud. My mom would be so proud of both of us, handling business unlike our pussy ass brother. I'm not even gonna lie, sometimes I felt like Dre was a weird fit in our family. I mean he was nothing like any of us, not my mom, not daddy and he damn sure wasn't like Kyleena and I. I remember feeling so lonely when it was just him and I, before Kyleena came along. I felt like…I was supposed to have a brother, it just wasn't supposed to be Andre.

We walked up to the desk and asked to speak with Detective Moreau. The lady at the front desk took a wild guess and asked, "You must be the Dupree girls, she's being waiting on you all for quite a while," the lady smiled. "I'll walk you to her office." The secretary turned on her heels and started to lead the way.

As we entered her office, I was shocked to meet her. For whatever reason, I thought she was going to be some older woman beaten down by life. Instead, she was beautiful and young, still full of life. Detective Moreau sat at her desk staring at some files in a file folder, concern etched across her face. As we came into the room, she closed the folder and forced a smile. I didn't like the way I was starting to feel. I already felt as though something was off. Why would we be asked to come to the police station before going to identify bodies? I watch a lot of Crime TV and that's not the procedure.

"You must be Kyleena and Solelil, thank you ladies for agreeing to meet with me. Especially under these circumstances. Let me first start off by saying I'm tremendously sorry for your loss. I know this is a difficult time for you and your remaining family. Your parents were a strong staple in our community, and we're going to do everything we can to make sure their killer be brought to the light," Detective Moreau stated without making much eye contact. Thank God Kyleena started speakin' because I had nothing to say. I didn't even want to be here, and she was dragging this shit out.

"Thank you so much for your condolences. I'm sorry my brother Andre couldn't be here, he's taking it really hard," Kyleena lied as I held back the urge to roll my eyes into eternity.

Almost as if she read my mind, Kyleena asked the question that had been bothering me since we got here. "So, I understand this isn't normal procedure for identifying a body. Has there been some developments in the case or something that we need to know about?" Kyleena asked as she gently grabbed my hand a little tighter.

Detective Moreau shifted a little in her chair and looked like she was really tryna choose her words wisely. "So, there's certain things that happen during a crime scene investigation to make sure everything is secured not only on the crime scene, but after the bodies come to the Coroner's Office. I have been working cases for many years and I have never had to explain what I'm about to explain to you all, and I hate that I'm the one who has to deliver this to you without answers," Detective Moreau hung her head before she continued. "I regret to inform you that we don't currently know the whereabouts of your parent's bodies…"

CHAPTER 4

M.I.A.

As we sat in silence, so many thoughts ran through my head. How the entire fuck do you lose two whole bodies? Something wasn't sitting right with me. I felt my phone vibrate in my lap. As I looked down, Mila's name flashed across my screen. I ignored the call. I wasn't in the right frame of mind to deal with anybody right now.

Kyleena squinted her eyes and squeezed my hand before she spoke. "So, you mean to tell me that someone...lost my parents' corpses? Like...how is that even a possibility?" Kyleena shouted, expecting an answer. Detective Moreau who was still avoiding eye contact stood up behind her desk.

"Ladies, I wish I had an answer for you. We have been working trying to find the answers to how this could've happened or who could've done it. Like I stated, this isn't something that has ever happened before, but believe me. The

Fayetteville Police Department is working around the clock to find out. Any leads that we have we assure you, you will be contacted," she asserted, as if that was supposed to make that shit feel any better.

Not wanting to hear shit else, I got up and walked out. This shit was getting heavier and heavier by the minute and between great great grand–who the fuck ever and this shit, I was well on my way to being locked away in a hug me jacket. As I walked up to where Devon was sitting, I felt dreaded anticipation in having to repeat what I just heard. Luckily, I heard Ky's heels clicking fast, trying to catch up with me. As she shouted my name, I couldn't make my body stop moving. I felt like if I stopped, everything would be that much more real. As I walked past Devon, I grabbed his car keys out of his hand. Running toward the car, I felt like I was about to implode.

Why was all of this happening right now? Great, Great Grand who– the– fuck– ever talkin about I'm chosen. Does this shit come with a side of therapy? A manual? Something?! I felt safe as I hopped into Devon's truck and closed the door. I watched Devon and Ky stand outside of the truck talking, Devon's face stretched in horror as Ky filled him in on what's going on. Devon and my sister hugged it out, and Devon walked around to the driver's side of the truck. Knocking twice on the window for me to unlock it, he hopped in.

"Sol, I'm not gonna sit here and pretend that I know what to say to you right now, but I'm here," Devon reassured me. "Don't be mad at me, but Mila is flying in tonight and I think we all need to sit down and talk," Devon's voice quivered as he waited for my reaction.

All I could muster was a death stare. I swear if looks could kill. I knew what that meant. If Mila was coming, this is way bigger than what I originally thought. Mila is the person that we call when some OTHER shit is going down. I started to think maybe that's why I've been having so many dreams, and visions. Speaking of dreams and visions, I remembered the book my great great grandmother asked me to give to Devon. I decided to wait until we were all together collectively to give it to him. Nobody needed any more surprises now.

"Sooooo... where do you wanna go?" Devon asked, trying to let me direct the moves.

I had been avoiding my parents' house all day and couldn't really avoid it any longer. Yea, I could get a hotel room but I wouldn't feel right. After a long thought out pause, I told Devon to take me home.

As we pulled up, I noticed there were a couple of cars in the driveway. I didn't really pay any mind to it, you know how it is in black families when someone passes. Their family house is the hot spot to mourn. My parents knew a lot of people so it wasn't surprising. Hell, I'm honestly glad people were there because who knows what the fuck Dre's crazy ass has been in here doing. As I walked up on the front porch of my childhood home, I felt a sense of foreboding urgency wash over my ass. I just felt like some stale ass, unwelcoming energy smacked me in the face. I looked behind me to see Devon digging around in the car. As bad as I wanted to walk in, I waited for Devon to come on the porch.

"You ok? I mean I can take you somewhere else if you wanna go, a bitch is always down for somebody's Hilton, I'm just sayin'," Devon offered as he read the worry on my face.

Feeling a little more confident now that he was backing me, I turned the knob on the heavy oak door to my parents' house and walked in. In the living room sat Samuel and Luciana, who are Mila's parents, Marisol who is Mila's grandmother and my brother. Fuck. Something definitely was not right. I turned and looked at Devon and his look confirmed what I was feeling.

Luciana, who is like a second mother to me jumped out of her seat and greeted me at the door. Without saying a word, I knew she could tell I knew something was going on.

"Come mija, sit," she urged, pushing me toward the family room.

After getting hugs from everyone not including my asshole of a brother, I had to acknowledge the elephant in the room. "Sooo, what are you guys doing here? I thought Mila's flight wasn't landing until in the morning," I tried to act totally oblivious to what I was feeling. Luciana looked at me with this look I'd never seen in her eyes before.

She stared at me long and hard before she started speaking. "How did um...how did everything go down at the police station," she quizzed me.

I had this sinking feeling she was diverting the issue. Well, that and I just wasn't ready to talk about the police station. I had to eventually tell my brother, and that shock value was gon' be high enough.

"Um, everything went smooth, I guess," I replied trying to really hide the fact that it was some utter bullshit. As I looked straight in front of me, Dre was stone cold zoned out and not here. I didn't notice I was staring at him as I was until I looked up and realized Mila and Devon were standing in front of me. MILA! Before I could form words outta my mouth my punk ass started sobbing. I don't know where it came from, but it felt so good to be released into the arms of someone you know cares. Mila pulled me up from my seat and walked me outside, where Ky was standing against the hood of her rental car.

We all just stood for a couple of minutes, taking everything in. It had been such a long time since we had all been together. It made me realize how much I missed my friends and family. We had all been through so much together, collectively, and being here with them in this moment felt right. For a few minutes, everything in the world didn't seem so bad.

Ky busted me out of my thought with her growling ass stomach. We all looked at each other and cracked the fuck up laughing.

"So, I'm guessing we're going to get food before Ky hungry ass makes us a snack," Mila joked, laughing hysterically at her own wise crack. Just like back in the day we all piled into one car, cranked the music up, sparked a spliff and vibed the whole way there. We all knew there was much to be said, so we decided to save our breath until we got there.

We pulled up at one of my favorite spots in Fayetteville, The Orleanian. They have some of the best Cajun, down home cooking I've ever tasted, outside of my momma. We all sat around the table waiting for someone to talk.

Mila started. "So, we all know why I'm here. Somethin' in the Morir Soñando ain't clean. Spill," Mila demanded.

I tried to concentrate on my catfish and let someone else talk, but in the midst of chewing I looked up and everyone was staring at me. "Why the hell yall gawkin', I haven't eaten today. Damn," I replied, knowing exactly what they were waiting for.

"Bitch I hung my thongs up, took as long as needed off of work at Henny's...talk," Mila screeched.

I put my fork down, trying to figure out where to start. I started with the craziest shit. "My parent's bodies are missing," I blurted out as Mila looked at me confused.

"What do you mean they're missing? Missing as in somebody misplaced them, or missing as in...I don't even fuckin know. How the fuck did they misplace two whole human bodies Solelil?" Mila screamed.

I looked at Mila like she had the answer to her own question. Hell, I would love to know the answer too.

"The detective was very vague," Ky followed up. "I don't feel like she was telling us everything. I feel like you Mila, something foul happened. I just don't know right now what it is," Ky mentioned as she stared off into space.

Devon nudged me under the table. That meant he was waiting for me to tell them about my dreams. I cleared my throat as I reached in my bag and pulled out the book with the blank pages, "Lost Frame". As I handed Devon the book, his eyes damn near popped out of his head.

"Solelil Marceline Dupree, where did you find this? Who have you been talking to?" Devon asked me, visibly shaken.

I wasn't prepared for him to react like that, so I was at a loss for words. "It came from a dream I had while on the flight here from New York," I started. "Marceline left it in the seat when she disappeared," I continued. Everybody's eyes were glued to me. "On the way here, I had like two dreams. The first one, I saw my mother. She kept telling me to find Odessa and use my higher self. You were in my dream too D. You were so real, I swear you were sitting there. Its like I was talking to you one minute and the next you were gone. That's when I saw momma. I'm still tryna figure that out," I chuckled and paused before continuing my crazy ass dreams. Everybody looked to be in deep thought and I really wanted to know if they were thinking about putting me in straight jacket. "The next dream I met my great great grandmother, Marceline. She gave me this book to give to you Devon. That's all she said, was give it to Devon," I answered.

Everybody took a minute to digest what I had just spilled. Mila, filled with questions broke the silence. "So you've been having these dreams since we were little, right?" she half asked, half told me. Trying to figure out how she knew that, I just nodded. Almost like she read my mind she replied. "You don't remember your first journal? You left it over my house. I'm nosey. I read it. At that moment I realized we were meant to be friends," Mila smiled as she kicked me under the table. "That's why you finding Devon's journal makes so much sense," she continued.

Devon closed his eyes as he held on to the book for dear life. "This was my journal growing up. I named it "Lost Frame" because I felt like it was a part of my life I couldn't tell anybody about, the missing link. It was my book of spells. I lost it right before you started at our school," Devon looked at me teary eyed. "Bitch you're not the only one with visions. We all have them. Tell them about the one at the police station," Devon urged.

I closed my eyes to try and recapture the dream since I didn't write it down like the other ones. "I woke up in some type of hospital. Marceline was there. She basically told me

I'm supposed to save our family. That I have gifts, and I needed to find Odessa" I told them as it all came back to me. "She said that I needed to use my higher self, and when I told her I didn't know how, she gave me the card that Mystery Girl gave me that night at the strip club," I reminded Mila. When I opened my eyes Kyleena's face was pale.

"Sol, you haven't made a connection yet?" Ky looked at me. "My middle name Sol. My middle name is Odessa," she spoke softly.

I sat up in my chair and stared at my sister. Was she a link to something?

"Let's all take this back a minute before we get ahead of ourselves," Mila reasoned. "Before we go putting Kyleena somewhere she's not supposed to be, let's rest on this. You guys have a crazy couple of when the fuck ever's ahead of you," Mila proposed.

She was right. Why would my baby sister be a clue to my Captain Save a Family duties? Something was tying all of us together, and as tired as I was I wanted to do some digging. Something told me I was going to be dreaming out the ass tonight.

As we got take-out trays for our food, Mila's phone rang. Looking at her phone and rolling her eyes, she switched it to silent.

"Alright hot stuff, let me find out you back in Fayetteville looking for some country meat," I laughed as I teased her.

"Girl that would be moving backward, and we don't do that. Not when I have a deli selection waiting for me back in NYC," Mila laughed as I slapped her a high five. "But nah, my parents man. My mom has been blowing my phone up since we sat down. Like I know I'm back in town and she wants this family togetherness but damn, a person can only eat so much Salami. Shit," Mila scrunched her face up.

As I laughed, I felt a little jealous. Not only were her parents still together and happy, they were alive. I would've given anything to walk in my Momma's house and smell her gumbo cooking. Now it just feels, empty. Very much a shell of what that house used to be. I decided I couldn't stay there. I wasn't ready.

We all got up and hopped in the car, but before we could get in, Devon's phone rang. Before he answered he looked up at us. "Ca–Mi–La, girl why is mama Luci calling me? Call her, it's gotta be deeper than some salami and plantains bitch," Devon joked as he ignored the call.

As we left, Mila called her mom back. "Mami, I'm sorry I don't get good signal out here! Ok I understand but calm do–" Mila started speaking Spanish, so I missed that part of the conversation. "Ok. Ok! We're on the way," Mila screamed as she ended the call. "I gotta get you and Ky to the house Sol, this is some fuck shit..." Mila murmured as she sped down Yadkin Rd.

As we pulled up to our blocked off driveway, the flames stood taller than the trees in the yard. Before Mila put her car in park, I hopped out of the car and ran in the direction of what was left of my parents' home. Pushing past the officer on the scene, Luciana ran toward me to stop me going any further. I was in shock. I know bad things come in threes, but this? Now this? I couldn't process this shit. I saw Luciana's lips moving but I'll be damned if I could tell you what she was saying. 27 years of memories in that house, gone.

"Sol, Sol baby do you hear me? Sol, I need you to go talk to the police," Luciana whispered as she walked me over to the officer.

I felt Kyleena walk up beside me and lock her arm into mine. As if shit couldn't get any worse, he started explaining his theory on what happened.

"Ma'am do you know of anyone who maybe had it out for your parents? I know you've had a horrible week, but really would like to help you get to the bottom of this as fast as possible and we need your help," The officer fed me lines I'm sure he's said about a thousand times to a thousand different suffering ass people.

I turned around to see Mila motioning for me to come to her. Totally forgetting the conversation that was at hand, I walked over to her.

"Sol, Ky..." Mila whispered. "Please tell me you know where Andre is," she looked at me with hopeful eyes. The look we gave back confirmed what she already knew.

CHAPTER 5

Rose Colored Glasses

I heard them. I heard their voices loud and clear. Some things you just know. As I opened my eyes, I realized that I was laying on the porch of my parent's house. Right away I knew I was in another world, because in my world, that house no longer existed. I squinted my eyes to block the sun's rays, and in the distance, I heard the laughs. Those laughs that weren't tainted by the fucked up world of reality. As I sat up and forced my body to move in the direction of the voices, a sadness hit me. Sadness because I realized how far we had come as a family to where those laughs didn't exist anymore, at least not right now. Off in the distance I saw a little girl. Brown skin, slanted eyes and nappy hair pulled into that ponytail that you only wore when you went outside to play. I watched her run around the yard, in and out between my mother's rose garden. Black girl joy.

I got up with every intention to chase her, until I heard my mother's voice. A voice that I had to catch in the wind because I knew she didn't exist here anymore. With hesitation, I pushed open the flimsy door that lead into my parents' house. It's crazy that every part of this house held some type of memory. I remember the day my parents argued about that door.

Momma had been on daddy's back about finishing it. He never finished shit, and my momma was tired of repeating herself. "Dammit Freddy, I worked all my life to have nice things, this nice house. Between you and these kids this door is hanging on for dear life. You always bumpin' your gums about how handy you are but you handy everywhere else but here. Maybe if I pray hard enough I'll get me my damn door," Luna stood with her hands on her hips, ready for battle. A battle that Freddy already knew he'd lost.

"Aw Luna stop your mess. I'ma get to it. Hell, if you want it so bad then you build it. You build everything else around here according to you. If you can handle it, what the hell am I here for?" Freddy shouted back across the kitchen towards Luna.

I stood invisible in the door way of the kitchen, listening to my parents argue. Maybe this is where it started. They did a good job of hiding things from us kids. I never knew this conversation even happened. He looked defeated and tired. They both did.

Before I knew it, Momma chucked a bowl across the room, hitting Daddy square in the face. "So this is how you want to play Luna? Three kids and 20 years together and this is how you treat me? One of these womens would be lucky to have ol' Freddy, but here I am tryna stick it out with you. Doing all of this unholy mess in our house, burning candles and shit. What's wrong with you Luna? This mess is driving you crazy woman. It's bad enough I have to put up with your family bullshit. You said that boy would get better but he just as crazy as shit. You think a spell is gonna fix his ass? What if she comes from him? I swear every day you turn more and more into Od—"... My momma stopped him dead in his tracks *with her eyes.*

"Freddy, now I take a lot of shit from you. I put up with your Jesus and your bible. I let you walk around this house like you run the place. One thing I won't accept is you comparing me to my momma. You might wanna watch your mouth Freddy Monroe," my momma warned him.

Even though I knew I wasn't visible, I felt like I shouldn't be here. I never knew things were this bad between them, and even seeing it didn't make me a believer. Over the last couple of days my whole life has been one big question mark, and the one thing I thought I was sure of just came tumbling down right along with it.

Just as the conversation was getting heated, three of most beautiful kids ran up on porch and into the house. Damn we looked so innocent.

"Mamaaaaaa! Sol was playing in your rose bushes! I told her to stop but she don't listen to nobody," Andre's snitchin' ass alerted my mom. I saw her face light up the way it always did when it came to us kids. It's crazy how she was able to hide what was really going on. We really had no clue.

"Now Sol, what have I told your hard headed behind about Mama's rose bushes, huh girl? Head just like a rock. Andre, Ky, go get washed up for dinner while I deal with your sister," Momma ordered them out of the room. I was almost scared for little Sol until momma softened her face as they ran their bad asses down the hallway.

"Baby, I know you like nature, you just like your mama," my smiled as she stroked my sweaty ass face. "Andre and Ky don't understand you yet, but momma knows. I also don't want you getting hurt, you hear? Stay away from those roses until I pick them Solelil." Momma swooned as she smiled like only she could.

"But momma they just so pretty, you always say beauty is pain.

FOOLISH

I didn't even cut myself momma. Andre just a big ole cry baby scaredy cat," I watched myself pout.

Momma laughed as she sliced lemons for her lemonade. "Sol, you heard what I said. Don't mama always make sure you get the roses? Now go on and get cleaned up. We're doing a crawfish boil tonight and Mila and her parents should be here any minute. Go on now," my momma pushed me toward the hall bathroom.

I watched as Luciana, Samuel, Camila and her older sister Julissa pulled into the yard, and it put a smile on my face. I remember this day, it was Mila's 8th birthday. Mila hopped out of the car and before she could get to the porch I was running toward her. As she showed me her new doll, we ran out in the yard to play. My mom and Mila's parents sat on the back patio and talked.

"Luna where's Freddy?" Samuel asked.

I could already see he was tired of the woman talk that had ensued.

"He might be in his shed Sam, you can go on back," my momma pointed out. As soon as he left, that's when the real gossip started. "Girl I don't know what I'm going to do with Freddy. Every day he's on my case more and more. I try to get him to understand this is who I am, hell he knew this before he married me. He keeps bringing up Andre and I'm scared to death he's gonna slip up and say something in front of the kids Luci. Then what am I supposed to do then?" my mom asked, concerned etched across her smooth brown skin.

"I don't want to be the friend that says I told you so, but I told you not to do this Luna. How did you really think this was going to turn out? Hell, I'm surprised nobody else has caught on," Luci hissed with a raised eyebrow.

My momma looked lost in her thoughts. What were they talking about? Suddenly all the feelings I had about Andre came back to the surface. In this very moment I knew his bitch ass had something to do with my parents murder, and couldn't nobody tell me any different. I tried to listen to more of their conversation, get some more clues, but I shoulda known the universe wasn't gonna give me too much to go on. As I sat and watched my mom and her best friend talk, their mouths were moving but I couldn't make out what they were saying. I was trying hard to read their lips when I realized that the world around me was turning black. I knew what that meant. I braced myself as I felt my body project into another timeline.

I opened my eyes to total darkness. It smelled like straight shit and wilderness wherever the fuck I was. I was getting so tired of this shit. It was one thing when I was jumpin' every now and then, but it seems like since my parents died they've been more and more frequent. I never visited 2 timelines at once. I was doing a hell of a lot of traveling across timelines for somebody who didn't want this damn gift to begin with.

As my eyes focused, I noticed I was in the middle of my momma's huge garden. I turned around and behind me far off, and I do mean far off in the distance I could see the back of my parents' house. As I walked toward the backyard, because you know niggas don't do darkness of any kind, I heard voices nearby. I stopped so I wouldn't be noticed, forgetting nobody could see or hear my ass anyway. As soon as I quieted my breathing, I recognized the voice immediately. It was Andre.

"Luna, they're on my back more than usual. You have got to either talk to them, or give me back. If I could give myself back I would, because I don't want to be caught in this drama. In all my decades of living, I've never seen somebody try the Moreau's the way you do. You always talkin' about it's for the best of the family, woman you gon' mess around and not have one. Sol is getting stronger and stronger, you don't need me anymore," Andre half *yelled, half whispered.*

I tried to make sense of what the fuck Andre was talking about. Give him back? Where the hell did we get this nigga from? I knew he couldn't be my brother, but that's not even the most important part. Why did my strength depend on him? They continued talking in hushed tones.

"I already told you Andre, I'll give you back when I'm good and damn ready. The Moreau's don't shake shit around here. I'm Luna fuckin Dupree. They didn't consult me when they took Freddy Jr. Now did they? We will do this shit on my time and my time only. I just want to see my son, to know that he's ok. I'm not asking for a lot. When they show me my child, they can have you back. Until then, we're on my time," my momma fumed.

I felt like all the breath was leaving my body. It was one thing for Andre not to be my brother, but who in the eternal fuck was Freddy Jr.? Why wasn't he ever talked about and more importantly who the fuck has him? The more I thought about it, the madder I got. It's not like I could pick up the phone and ask her this shit. My last resort would be to ask Andre, but from this conversation it seems like he's playin both sides. I made a mental note that he's not to be trusted.

"Shit!!" I cussed out loud to myself.

As soon as the word left my lips, Andre and momma turned around, as though they could hear me. I knew I was trippin, they couldn't have heard me. I took a step backward and stepped on a random branch. When it crackled under my foot, my momma called out and my heart stopped.

"WHO'S THERE?! EAVESDROPPING GIVES ME A GOOD REASON TO LET THIS SHOTGUN OFF!" my momma threatened. All the New Orleans in her blood came up and out of her mouth when she was mad.

I didn't know whether to walk to her or call out, seeing as though she was holdin. When the fuck did Luna Dupree start shootin' niggas? I swear every day I find out more and more about this woman. Maybe she's where my "beat your ass, ask questions later" mentality comes from. Why and how could she hear me though? This had never happened before, I was always unseen and unheard. I thought it would be smarter to just call out to her, give her a warning of sorts.

"Momma, don't shoot. It's me. It's Solelil," I squeaked.

"I don't believe you, show your damn self," momma demanded. Slowly walking toward her and Andre, I was tryna figure out how I was going to explain that the only daughter she knew, 8 year old me, was now 27 years old and not have her shoot my ass. She didn't know this Sol yet, and I damn sure didn't wanna get shot. Can you feel bullet wounds in the Ether? I wasn't tryna find out tonight. I stepped out of momma's garden and into my parents' back yard. When I stood in front of them, their eyes almost popped out of their heads.

"You can't be Sol, my Sol is still a little girl, she's still a baby...they told me this could happen but..." my momma looked me up and down with tears in her eyes.

I wish I had a word for the confusion I was experiencing. As momma stood and looked at me, it dawned on me how much I had missed her and the rambling started. "Momma, it's me. It's Solelil. I'm 27 now and I live in New York momma..." That's all I managed to choke out before I burst into tears that rocked my entire frame.

Momma walked up to me slowly and reached out for me, but not before Andre stopped her. "Luna, remember what Odessa said. We're not supposed to blur timelines like this. It's dangerous," Andre's cock blocking ass tried to persuade momma.

Momma looked him up and down before proceeding. "My rules, remember? You don't like them you know what you can do. I would assume you wouldn't like that very much, now would you?" Momma asked Andre as his eyes lowered and stared at the ground and out of our business. Momma looked at me and wiped her tears.

"So this is what Solelil looks like grown huh? I guess I did a pretty good job. I knew you would grow into those lips of yours" Momma chuckled. A concerned look washed over her face. "How much of the conversation did you hear? She questioned me. My eyes darted to Andre.

"Enough to know this bitch isn't my brother," I spat.

Andre looked at me with equal hate in his eyes. I know he knew what I was referring to. Maybe my Higher Self told me, I don't know...but his ass knew.

My momma looked between the both of us confused. She had no idea what a piece of shit her "son" had turned into as an adult. Feeling the tension between us, she made a suggestion. "Why don't we all sit down and talk? Clearly there's some things you should know about—" she offered before Andre cut her off.

"Luna, that is NOT a good idea. We're already doing way too much just standing here with her. Did you listen to anything Odessa said? What if she alters something on her plane?" Andre begged my momma. Momma wasn't tryna hear it.

"Look here, if I have to tell you ONE more time that we are doing things MY way, Jaqueline Moreau or Odessa Dupree will be the least of your worries. Solelil isn't stupid. Are you baby?" my momma looked to me for reassurance.

With a smirk on my face, I replied, "No momma, you didn't raise no fool. A stripper maybe, but no fools," I held back my laughter as Momma's jaw dropped. Before I knew she was laughing so hard it shook her whole body.

"Well I guess I couldn't expect less when you got your ass from *my side of the family, come on here and let's go talk," momma grabbed for me as she wiped her tears away from laughing so hard.*

As we walked toward what my momma referred to as "The House Roses Built," which was a greenhouse momma had daddy build when she became obsessed with roses around my 3rd birthday, a thought hit me. Odessa! I can ask momma who Odessa is! Maybe that will put me one step closer to figuring out who the hell killed my parents. As we walked into the greenhouse and sat down, Andre kept staring at me with this disgust in his eyes, jealousy even. I was waiting for him to pop off because growing up I could never beat his ass. He was always bigger than me, but oh bitch. I wanted him to try me on this night.

"So," Momma started "How exactly did you find us baby?" she quizzed me.

I assumed she was asking the questions first. Typical Luna. I thought about my answer before I replied. I didn't know how much I should say and how much I should hold back. Honestly, how the hell do you tell somebody their gonna die in like 19 years? Don't nobody wanna know that morbid shit, but I needed answers if I was ever gonna find out who killed them. Shit, Marceline's cryptic ass sure wasn't any help.

"I uh, I travel. Dimension travel. I can never tell when it happens. I have noticed though it happens more often when I'm stressed about something," I murmured as I made an entry way into the conversation. If I knew anything about my momma is was that she couldn't stand to see her kids stressing, about anything. Just as expected, she picked up the conversation.

"Stressed? What are you stressed about Solelil Marceline? You're even more beautiful than I could ever imagine. You have a nice paying...job. You sound like you doin good girl. What I always hoped you would do," she smiled. "Andre said that around this age

you would start to time jump. He said it's dangerous for me to see you from the future because I could "influence" thoughts in you that will make you alter the timeline," Momma rolled her eyes as she looked at Andre. It was really killing me having to break this to her. Nobody wants to know when or how they die, but I needed answers. Andre looked at me like he wanted to shoot me in the forehead with Momma's shot gun that sat propped up on her side. He had been quiet since the last time Momma warned him, but you could tell he was busting at the damn seams.

"Solelil," Andre started, making damn sure not to make eye contact with my momma. "I don't know if you should be telling her this," he looked at me like he knew exactly what I planned on asking. "This could change everything, especially getting your twin back," he stated as he looked at momma.

I cleared my ears to make sure I heard him correctly. "My twin? I don't have a twin, right momma?" I chuckled as I waited for Momma to respond. I kept waiting and Momma said nothing with her mouth, but her eyes said it all. It just hadn't made it to her lips yet. Andre continued talking.

"You wanna know how I know all of this right? I was your brother's sacrifice. I see Luna hasn't told you about her side of the family, huh?" Andre asked as he raised an eyebrow. "See, Sol. I dimension and timeline jump too. I hardly age. You didn't notice that growing up? Andre chuckled. "Of course you didn't. I forgot you were blind to my magic. Nice little spell that was put on you when you turned about three years old. You do indeed have a twin. His name is Freddy Jr. I am a Moreau, one of the few remaining members of my bloodline. Your brother was taken," he spat "as a payment of sorts. A payment that your family owed to my family. I suggest you talk to your great great grandmother," Andre snickered.

SAI MECCA

My momma got up and without warning back handed the shit out of Andre, so hard that it sent him flying across the greenhouse. "If you're gonna tell the story, tell it right boy. The Dupree's don't owe your family shit, Marceline made sure of that. Your family has always been jealous of the power that runs through the veins of the Dupree women. Your sorry ass Momma don't hold a candle to what my Sol can do, now watch your damn mouth boy," Momma shrieked as she stood directly over Andre.

I had no idea what in the entire fuck was going on, but it lit a fire in me to see my momma like this. All my life she had been quiet, not much to say. Not quick to anger. It seems like the momma I knew was a whole different person. I always wondered where I got my fiery attitude from and now I knew.

Andre got up and rubbed his cheek, and within milliseconds he was yet again standing in front of me. "Your brother," Andre flinched as he watched Luna, "Your brother was taken because of the blood that runs through his veins. Dupree magic was only ever known to exist in the women of the blood line. Since you two came out as twins, I guess you can say you rubbed off on him," Andre rolled his eyes as sat back down. I looked over at my momma as she held her chest.

"Momma, is this true? Where is he? Can I see him?" I panicked and spoke at the same time. My momma took a deep breath before she spoke.

"Your brother is dead Solelil. Jaqueline Moreau, who just so happens to be Andre's jealous ass momma killed him and took him into the Ether with her. That is why I had your great great grandmother bring me Andre. All of the Dupree women hold their magic and their strength in a certain part of their bodies. For my momma it was her mind. She could conjure with little to no tools. For me, it's in my hands. Hence the roses. Remember when you were

younger and yall would get hurt and I would rub that rose ointment on you? Chile, that was a cover up. All I needed to do was touch yall and you'd be good as new. You brother carried his magic through his speaking. His words. Kyleena through her eyes. She can see things before they happen, but you? Girl you got them all, and some," Momma chuckled. "You hold gifts from ancestors thousands of years old. Every gift that was given to us Dupree women lies inside of you," Momma smiled.

"That's why she took my baby. The two of yall were gonna do some damage. It was destined that you wipe out the Moreau family for all the evil they've done, it was written. The Moreau's run everything. Those old white men that everybody thinks run the entire world? Cover up. They are all distant family members of the Moreau's. They run the media, the money, the resources. Everything. You and your brother were destined to bring light to all of that, so she took him. You can't do it by yourself, and as long as she has Freddy Jr, she holds leverage over this family," my momma finished as she began to fiddle with her roses again.

"I know I'll never be able to see my baby boy grow up. No matter what these fairy tale ass stories and shit say, once your lessons have been learned, you don't come back to this plane in another meat suit. This was Freddy Jr's last reincarnation. I just wanted to see him. So, until I do Andre stays here. With me. If I have to suffer, so does she. Mother to Mother," my mom screamed as she kicked the shit out of Andre's chair.

I had gotten answers I didn't come for. Now it made sense why Momma and Daddy were having so many issues behind the scenes. It wasn't Daddy's church that got between him. He missed his son, and I got the feeling that maybe he resented Momma and blamed her for it. That means that I had grown up with a complete stranger as a brother. It all made sense now. The hate I felt for him was now justified in my eyes. It also shed light on why I always felt like a part of me was missing and why I always felt lonely. Andre's bitch ass voice interrupted my train of thought.

"Sol, understand that everything, every fuckin thing that you have come in to contact with has been strategically placed there. From Mila to Devon and everything and everybody in between. They're all guides. I've hopped timelines and I know you've met Marceline. Marceline is only gonna tell you so much. I know you hate me, well future me anyway...but I can help you," Andre pleaded with his eyes.

I looked over at my Momma who sat in the corner picking petals off rose stems that had dried out. "Momma, can I trust him? I mean, it seems to me like he's playing for both sides. How do I know he's not tryna trap me. It sounds like some bitch ass Andre shit," I grilled him as I spoke. Momma put her plants down and walked in between Andre and me.

"Nothing screams untrustworthy more than anybody walking around with the last name Moreau, but he has been a great help Solelil. Let him help you. He can hop any timeline, any time he chooses and that can become a great asset to you. You can come back and talk to me whenever you can," Momma looked at me with tears in her eyes. As bad as I wanted to ask her a billion questions, I couldn't let her know that she would eventually die without ever seeing Freddy Jr. again. I would save that for later. I was however gonna ask her about Odessa.

"Momma, who is Odessa? I keep hearing her name thrown around," I asked innocently.

Momma took a deep breath and reached into her bra and pulled out a key. "Odessa is your grandmother chile. I can't tell you much more than that right now. There is a trunk in the attic with things that have been held just for you, for centuries. These things will *guide you to her," Momma told me as she wiped her eyes. "Now baby, you better get going. We weren't supposed to talk this long but I enjoyed your company," momma wept as she pulled me into a hug.*

I hugged my mother as tight as I possibly could. Who knew if this was the last time I would ever see her or not.

As I pulled away, I felt Andre grab my arm. The lights in the greenhouse started to fade to black. I watched as my mother got further and further away from me. When I woke up, I was in the back of an ambulance with my friends staring at me.

"Bitch, how many times can one person pass out in a day? I mean shit, I know I'm dramatic but you're really milking this shit," Devon hollered as soon as I opened my eyes. I looked back at what remained of parents' house when a thought hit the front of my mind. I started to rip out the IV's in my arms and told my friends to come on.

"Ma'am we don't think it's safe for you to leave yet. Your vitals were really low for a minute there and–"

I took off running before the EMT could finish her sentence. Once in the car, I collected my thoughts. Kyleena turned and looked at me and for once I knew what that meant.

"Where is he?' Kyleena asked me, knowing that I knew.

"Tonight, when all of the commotion dies down, meet me in my momma's green house."

CHAPTER 6

Beef in the Ether

The cold, frozen ground crunched underneath my Nike Boots as I walked across the yard to my mother's greenhouse, "The House That Roses Built." I finally felt like I was gettin' somewhere with some damn answers, no matter how crazy they sounded. I was beginning to realize that crazy is a social construct, and in my life the crazier it seemed the more true to life it was. I got to the door of the greenhouse, hesitant to go in.

The last time I saw my Momma alive, it was in this greenhouse. I remember she had looked so sad about me leaving. I hadn't been coming home often, and anytime I did she never wanted me to leave. I guess it felt good to her to have someone around who understood her. As usual, I did my best to reassure her that I'd be fine, and I'd be back to visit soon. I remember watching her tear–filled eyes as I pulled away in an Uber. I never once thought that would be the last time I would see my mother in the flesh.

I pulled open the flimsy door and stepped inside. Momma was always one for creating some type of ambiance, so her choice of light in the greenhouse was always pillar candles. I reached for my lighter while I lit up the room with the flashlight on my phone.

"Sol please, the lights hurt," a soft and tired voice spoke up behind me. I lit the candle closest to the door and turned around. "How did you know to find me here Sol? Has it happened yet? Have you talked to Momma?" Andre's voice shook with every ho ass word he spoke.

I lit my blunt as I moved from candle to candle. I would be a damn liar to say that I wasn't still disgusted with him, and the fact that I now knew he wasn't my brother didn't make it any better.

Walking around lighting candles, I decided to entertain his conversation until squad arrived. "As a matter of fact, I did. I ran up on Momma AND you. I know you come here to do your dirty work, whatever the fuck that may be. So why wouldn't you be here now? Wanna toke?" I taunted him.

Hell he clearly needed it. Now that the room was lit up, I could see his face more clearly. He looked a hot, stank ass mess. His grey eyes looked dull and his skin pale as fuck like he had been drained of every liquid in his body. Fuckin' disgusting. Something in me knew that Andre had something to do with all of this, and tonight I was determined to at least catch a clue.

I stared at Dre, trying to find some type of sympathy for him but I couldn't. He didn't really lose anything behind any of this. I glared at him.

"So, what do you know Andre? Did you hide their bodies

to buy time? Burn the house down to destroy evidence? I hope you don't think that you're getting any insurance money from that shit, it all goes to me and Ky."

Andre looked at me with an emptiness I hadn't seen from him before. He seemed like he didn't care if I felt sorry for him or not. He was tired of something. What, I just hadn't figured out yet.

"If you met Luna and I here, then I already know what you're mad about. Its understandable. I'm not doing this shit Sol, you know me better than that," Andre growled. I shook my head in disbelief as I took another pull of the perfectly rolled blunt and laughed.

Mila damn sure knew how to roll up.

"Nigga, I've lived the last 27 years thinking you were my brother and you knew all along you weren't, so no. I don't know shit about you, Andre." I walked toward him, prepared to kick him in the face if his ass gave me the wrong answers.

"So, you must know who is behind this shit then, huh? Don't tell me you don't know Andre. I would hate to have to beat the fuck outta you in Momma's sacred place."

Andre pulled himself up off the cold damp earth and walked towards me. All of a sudden his eyes were burning a amber brown, filled with anger.

"There's not gonna be too much more of your ass threatening me. I could kill you right here and now, and not serve a day in jail. You went to Brooklyn and that shit got you thinkin' you hard. Don't you dare forget who I am."

With every word that came out his mouth, my skin got hotter and hotter. Yea, I had went to Brooklyn but it didn't make me think I'm hard. If Brooklyn did anything it made me realize my personal power. Speaking of personal power, that's not something I fully had control over in terms of anger yet. Before I knew it, I took my foot with all my force and kicked Dre in his stomach. I watched as he doubled over and looked up at me. There was no way he was gonna disrespect me or my intelligence in Momma's space, especially knowing what I know. As he rushed toward me, I quickly moved to the side as he fell face first into one of Momma's potting plants, cutting his face on a thorn. He turned around and looked at me as I smirked my ass off. Bitch.

My proud ass must have been a little too proud because the next thing I know, Dre's hand was around my throat.

"Uh huh. Its gonna take a lot more than you to beat my ass Solelil. I'm not one of these fuck niggas out here that you ho around like I'm your bitch," he whispered as I felt his hot, stank ass breath on the side of my face.

I felt him feeling around for something, but not wanting to let me go. He had the right idea, because had he...it woulda been poppin' in this greenhouse. I was starting to lose oxygen and was tired as hell of trying to free myself from his grip. As the world was blackening out around me, I heard a voice.

"Can you hear me Love? If you can hear me, follow the sound of my voice. Look up," a deep, southern voice sounded like it was being blasted through a speaker system.

As I looked up, I tried to focus my vision. The voice continued. "That's right. Just like that. I want to you repeat what I say Sol. Tell him 12 not dead, and him and his bitch ass Momma need to study their Book of Shadows better. I'm chillin right now, but time is ticking. I'm coming for his ass."

Confused but still trying not to pass completely the fuck out, I had no choice but answer the voice back in my head.

"What? Who are you? When did I start hearing voices?"

It felt as though it took forever for me to get an answer. Convinced I was dying, and this is just one of those things that happen when you're about to die, the only thing I could do was pray that Squad was on the way. Leave it to niggas to be late, every time.

Just as I was about to close my eyes, I heard the voice again.

"Sol, lift your fuckin head up. I can't tell you who I am right now, you're not ready for that. Just know I'm always here. I've always been here. Remember my words. TELL THAT NIGGA WHAT I SAID!"

I'm not gon' lie, that shit shook me awake. Gasping for air, I managed to choke out what I had been told to say. "12 ain't dead nigga." I felt Dre's grip loosen.

"What the fuck did you just say?" Dre shouted as he let my body go and I dropped to the ground.

For whatever reason, saying that shit made me feel bossed up like a mufucka. I don't know who the fuck this was, but they sounded like no games were being played and they were on my side. So yea, I felt like the shit. I gathered up all the strength I had so he could hear me clearly.

"I said, 12 AIN'T DEAD MUFUCKA." I watched as Dre's eyeballs grew to the size of Mangoes. The voice in my head laughed the loudest laugh I had heard in my life.

"Yea. That nigga ain't so tough now. There's a gun behind the flower pot to your left. I put it there for you. Grab it and put it behind your back," the voice demanded. Scared to be like "hell the fuck no", I fumbled around behind the flower pot.

I had been to the gun range plenty with my Daddy, but never did I ever in my life think I'd have to use one. Trying to remember what gun I shot with my daddy, I continued to fidget around until I felt the cold steel. A .357. The same gun I had shot over and over again in our backyard.

"Who the fuck you been talking to? Huh? What the fuck do you know Sol?" Andre inched toward me slowly.

I held the Glock behind my back as I forced myself to sit up. "Oh so you ain't saying shit now huh? One thing your family was always good about was keeping secrets," he chuckled.

Noticing that my face lacked fear of his ho ass, his smile disappeared. "Well the next time you talk to that nigga 12, tell him I said that shit not possible. I did what I had to do and watched that nigga die. He don't scare no damn body," Andre half chuckled.

The voice in my head chuckled back. I swear I was starting to feel like AOL Instant Messenger. I had no idea what the two of them were talking about, but it was clear there was some beef here at some point. I wasn't tryna get my black ass caught up in the middle of it. Bullets don't have names, in the ether or this bitch ass plane. As I waited for a response like all of us waited for a diss record response from Mase, I heard the voice again.

"Tell him he talks a good game. Funny his brothers said the same thing, see where that got their asses. Bitch." As Dre inched closer, I gripped the handle tighter behind my back.

"Take one more step and you'll regret it Andre," I threatened.

Andre laughed in my face. Y'all know that did nothing more than piss me off. "By the way," I smirked. "You don't have to be scared...evidently your brothers weren't scared either," I laughed as I saw the rage building. I heard footsteps coming toward the greenhouse. Squad.

I saw Kyleena peeping through the hole her and I had made when we were little and wanted to spy on Momma. I let her know I saw her and shook my head for her not to come in yet.

"You know, I promised your Momma I would keep my hands off of you, but you make it really fuckin' hard bitch. I shoulda killed you like I killed your pussy ass brother" Andre growled as he walked toward me.

This nigga was really testing me. My daddy always told me you should never underestimate your opponent. Andre seems to forget that I grew up with him. I knew all his strengths. All his weaknesses. That could be dangerous in the hands of the wrong person, like myself. I smirked harder.

"And I promised my Momma I would give you a chance. I didn't say that I wouldn't kill you if I had to. I suggest you stay where the fuck you are Andre, three deaths in one week is just too much for anyone to bear, right?" I asked as I prepared myself.

"Sol, I really don't wanna play games with you. I'm here to help you but you're just like your damn mother. Don't wanna listen for shit!" Andre's voiced echoed through the green house. That was the last straw. I pulled myself off the ground, and in one motion felt the chrome handle of the gun crack Andre in the jaw. I stood over him, enraged.

"You talk a little bit too much about my Momma nigga. She's not the one you should be concerned with. You right though. I am like my Momma. Unpredictable. What you should know though, is I'm just like my Daddy, and I don't give a fuck," I stood over Andre and cocked the gun back. Andre smirked as I stood over him. "You and I both know you not shootin' shit. Where did you get that from?" Andre laughed. I felt the rage stirring around in my veins and I never felt like this before. It was almost like someone had taken over my body and I wasn't in control for shit. Seriously, when the hell did my ass start pistol whippin' people?!

Everything that had happened up to this point was sitting in the front of my brain. All I know is somebody is gonna have to pay for this shit. Why not him?

"You said it best nigga, we're a family full of secrets," I taunted as I wrapped my finger around the trigger and let it loose.

I wish I'd killed him.

I heard Kyleena scream as I held the gun tight and squeezed the trigger over and over again. Don't get it fucked up, a killer I am not...but his ass was gon' bleed today. I watched as Andre's body fell to the ground as he grasped his shoulder in agony. Remember when I said that his ass must have forgotten that I knew everything about him? When we were bad ass teenagers, Andre damn near shattered his clavicle in an accident when he was about 16.

The doctor told his dumb ass that he needed to not only let the shit heal, but he needed physical therapy. Of course, his dumb ass did neither. The last appointment he went to, the doctor told him that his shoulder would never heal properly at this point without surgery, and because he didn't allow it to heal, any minor trauma to any area of his shoulder would have him fucked up for the rest of his life.

As I stood over him as he screamed like a little bitch, I wanted to do more. I wanted to empty the rest of the rounds into his fuckin' chest, but I still had use for him. He just needed to know I'm done fuckin' around with him. I heard

Squad burst in a few seconds before, and I turned around to face them. Kyleena stood behind me with her hand on her chest, being dramatic as fuck, as per usual. Everybody looked shocked yet grateful that Andre was still breathing.

Kyleena ran to his side to see if there was anything she could do. "Fuck Solelil...what the fuck is wrong you?! You blew his fuckin' shoulder open, how the fuck are we supposed to explain this? Our parents were just murdered and then you shoot our brother in the fuckin shoulder? How the fuck do you not expect them to think you had something to do with it?! I know y'all are beefin' but damn!"

Kyleena shouted from a clearly overly emotional place. And for the record, I didn't "blow his shoulder open," that nigga would be alright. I hadn't spilled the tea that the bitch made nigga wiggling around on the ground wasn't our brother. To be completely honest, it kinda pissed me off to see her still vouching for him and coming to his defense. The kettle on this tea was screeching however and it was time to pour.

I looked in his direction and smiled.

"Would you like me to tell her or do you want to do the honors, brother?" Right after the words left my mouth I decided I wouldn't let him get the satisfaction. Ky, Mila and Devon looked at me confused as fuck. I hopped up on an unoccupied table and cleared my throat.

"So, in an interesting chain of events, I found out that Andre here isn't our brother. He's not related to us. At all," I spat as I watch Ky's eyes get big, and anger took the place of sadness.

"Sol I know you're mad but chill bruh. He's hurting just like we are," Kyleena little honest ass tried to make sense of what I had said.

"Kyleena," Andre moaned through his pain as he rolled around on the ground. "She's telling the truth. You have a brother, but it's not me. I should've told you a long time ago, and I didn't mean for the shit to drag on this long. I hope you can–" Kyleena cut him off.

"You bitch ass, ho ass nigga. No wonder Sol thought your ass is behind all of this. How the fuck do you hide something like this Andre?!" Ky screamed as she bent down and smacked the shit out of him.

Mila grabbed Ky before she could do anymore damage. She carried her outside kicking and screaming so she could get her shit together. Devon walked over to me, and it wasn't until he took the gun out of my hands that I realized I was even still holding it. I felt numb, and I didn't like feeling like this. Feeling like I wasn't in control of my body. Devon crouched down in front of Andre and scratched his head with the tip of the Glock before he spoke.

"So, what do you think we should do about this shit Dre? Clearly we're not taking you to the hospital. Do you wanna talk or do I have to use this too?" Devon asked him, eyes locked in place waiting for Andre to choose his fate.

Andre's eyes darted back and forth between Devon and I, and to be real I was losing patience. Had been lost it. I just wanted to find out who killed Momma, and didn't feel like I should have to jump through hoops to do so.

Andre answered in between the shallow breaths he was taking. "Sol already knows. She can tell you. I don't know much more than her. I'm just here to help," Andre looked up at Devon as if to beg of him to believe him.

Devon glanced over at me. I knew if I told Devon to blow

his head off he would have, but that would've been too easy. Well, that and he was accessible to both sides. I kinda needed him and I hated that shit.

I walked over and stood over him. I wasn't in the mood for games. "Where is he?" I mustered the strength to form my lips to speak. Andre looked up at me with fear in his eyes.

He was hiding something, and whatever it was I knew that Momma didn't know, which pissed me off even more. "Can you sit me up please? Sit me up and I'll tell you anything you need to know," Andre pleaded.

I told Devon to go get Kyleena and Mila. They needed to hear this too.

I sat him up in a chair that was in the corner and lit a blunt that Mila passed in my direction, waiting for him to start talking. He looked around at each of us, and as his eyes met Kyleena's you could see it hurt him to some extent. Of all of the available fucks in the world, I couldn't catch one. He cleared his throat as he started to speak.

"Your brother Freddy Jr. was special. Y'all were special. Your mother did everything she could to keep her pregnancy under wraps and hidden from my family, but everybody knew about the twins. It was already written. Some people nicknamed y'all Ibeyi, I personally thought that was kind of a reach.," I looked at him with as much evil as I could muster until he got my point.

"That gun still has bullets my nigga. I suggest you keep it cute," I warned him. He looked as if he wanted to say some shit, but instead attempted to continue with his story until Ky interrupted him.

"What the hell is Ibeyi?" Mila of course being the history buff she is gladly answered her question.

FOOLISH

"OOOOHH let me tell you girl, Ibeyi is lit. They were Orisha twins, they call them the "Divine Twins" in Yoruba. In Yoruba culture twins are sacred as hell. They are said to be the offspring of Chango and Oshun. I know you know who they are," Mila stopped for a minute to make sure Ky was following.

"Yea, somebody went through a phase where they were obsessed with learning everything about Orishas" Ky chuckled as she looked in my direction.

She wasn't lying though. I did go through a time period where I wanted to know everything about every spiritual practice, and when I got to the Orishas and African Traditional Religon, I got stuck because it was just so intriguing to me. I rolled my eyes because I swore I told her all about Ibeyi. Must have been one of the times she was ignoring my ass.

Mila continued. "So, when Oshun had them, she was called a witch by the people in her village because at that point, only animals had twins. They told her to get her ass out the village, so she threw the twins out and told people she wasn't their Momma. After that, she damn near went crazy. Lost everything. Eventually, according to who tells the story, Oya or Yemaya took them in. They are said to bring fortune and happiness to anyone who is around them."

Ky nodded her head. "Ohhhh, so they were like, the lit twins huh?"

Andre cleared his throat. "Yea. Mila is right. Can I finish?"

"It wasn't supposed to be like this. Nobody thought that your magic would have any type of effect on him. When Luna had you two, it was like he knew exactly what he was born for. I didn't kill him right away. I kidnapped him and took him to my mom in New Orleans in another dimension. The plan was to kill him so you two could never link back up, because like your Momma told you that would be dangerous to my family. Eventually, as you got stronger, my momma realized that because yall are twins the energy is transferable. Even if we killed him, you would just get his energy so there was no point. So, she kept him and hid him in another timeline. Luna, thinking that he was dead had your grandmother Odessa dimension jump and steal me in retaliation for taking him. Luna and Freddy Sr. decided to raise me as their own until she gave Freddy Jr. back, and Odessa hexed me to never be able to age past the age of 21. I made up a lie that I was going to the Airforce so you and Kyleena wouldn't notice. I really left to find your brother and kill him."

We all sat in silence, not sure of what to say or what questions to ask. It seemed like there were so many secrets wrapped up in this situation, and just like that this situation had become bigger than my parents, and bigger than my abilities. Knowing that I had a brother out there somewhere, a twin at that, made me wanna find out what the fuck was going on that much more. I looked over at Andre, unsure of how to feel. He literally just sat here and said that he was gone for 6 years, with the intent to kill my brother. I wanted to strangle him and watch the air leave his bitch made ass body.

"So what the fuck was the point of your deranged ass Momma keeping my brother if she wasn't gonna kill him? Why not give him back so she can get your average bitch ass back?" I questioned.

I watched Andre's jaw flex before he answered. "Our

family has a beef that goes back generations. Your great, great grandmother Marceline was close with my Momma at one point. They were thick as thieves, they conjured together, hexed together...everything. At some point during their friendship, they attempted to do a spell that would give the both of them stronger ablilites. Something went all the way left though. My momma got greedy and tried to alter to the spell to where she would have more power, and it backfired. It gave the Duprees' the power. When Marceline became pregnant with her first child, they realized that with every girl child born into your family your ancestral magic and abilities got stronger. Our bloodline wasn't capable of magic like that, so my momma was jealous.

"By the time Odessa was born, my momma was already plottin'. She didn't want the magic in your bloodline to increase anymore, and she already knew what was written. She knew that if it did, our bloodline would cease to exist because the strength of your gifts would drain ours. Momma was gifted with immortality, but it came with a clause. The only way that my momma could keep her immortality if eldest child born into the sixth generation of your family was a boy. If a girl was born instead, she would harness the gifts of not only her bloodline, but ours also and my momma will die by the hands of her.

"You Sol, are the oldest girl in the sixth generation. Not only is Momma pissed off that you are the oldest twin, but you shared some of your power with Freddy. So, she cursed you two. His magic is limited unless he's around you and you can't carry out my family take down without him. Not only did she hide him, she hid your grandmother too."

I was...flabbergasted. So many questions ran through my

mind, but I had the answer to why my mother never spoke of my grandmother. Maybe it was easier for her to act like she didn't exist than to admit that my grandmother was basically hidden from the family because of her offspring. He still didn't answer my question about killing my brother though. He wasn't just about to skip over that shit.

"So when you left to go the Airforce, you really went to kill my brother? How did that work out for you?" I smirked.

Andre was now up and pacing the greenhouse while holding his shoulder. "I found him. He knew who I was and wasted no time trying to off my ass first. I tried my hardest to beat him senseless without using magic, but he was too much even on his own. So I stopped his heart with a spell and never mentioned it to anybody but my Momma. After that, we never saw or heard from him again, he literally disappeared. A couple of months later, my brothers turned up dead in New Orleans in this current timeline, victims of a stick up in a drug deal gone wrong. I didn't think anything fishy until tonight," Andre said as he turned and looked at me along with everybody else.

While I was trying to understand why everybody's eyes were glued to me, the obvious hit me like a ton of bricks.

12. Freddy Jr is 12, and he was the voice I heard earlier.

That's why Andre got so shook. My eyes teared up as I realized I had heard my twin. That softness quickly turned right back to anger as I remembered what this fuck nigga standing in front of me had tried to do.

"So what you're telling me is that you tried to kill my brother and it didn't work so in retaliation he killed YOUR brothers. You really thought he was dead this whole time?" I screamed at Andre.

FOOLISH

He looked at me with remorse, I guess he finally felt something in that icy ass heart of his. How did he live all these years knowing all of this and didn't warn us?

"I couldn't warn you Sol. If I had said anything your Momma promised to do me in. She didn't want you or Ky getting caught up in anything until yall developed your gifts. I couldn't have my Momma losing another son. Its bad enough already that she was cursed to out live all of her kids. I couldn't do that to her," he responded as if I had said it out loud. "That's another one of my gifts. I can hear thoughts of people I'm near," he answered.

At that moment, I realized what Momma had said about our gifts, and it totally escaped my mind that Ky had them too. Momma said that Ky could see things before they happened. Made me wonder if she knew something she wasn't telling me, but I wasn't gonna freak her out anymore and put her on the spot. That was a conversation that we needed to have alone.

Devon, who hadn't said much of anything chimed in. "So what does she need to do to find her brother? It's clear he's alive and you gotta know she's gonna look for him."

Andre's eyes darted back and forth between the three of us. "He has to be timeline jumping if my Momma doesn't know where he is. What timeline that's in I don't know, but I'm pretty sure your grandmother might and who knows what timeline she's in. If you can find her, you have a good chance of finding your brother. Just like your momma said, there were things put up for you to guide you, but with the house being burnt down, I don't know if that's even an option anymore."

Ky spoke up. "So you really didn't burn the house down?

I mean you are a great suspect. You could be trying to hide some shit."

Once again, I could see the hurt in his eyes. He and Ky were close, so I knew every word she said sliced at him. "No Ky, I have a good idea who may have done it, but it wasn't me, and right now the less you know about the house being burned down and your parent's bodies missing is best. You could be walking into a trap and not even knowing it. Right now, your main goal should be finding your grandmother so you can find 12 and complete your bloodline circle. You'll all be stronger that way," he muttered.

"The best thing you could do right now is retrace your steps" he continued. "There were things placed in each dimension, including this one that are supposed to guide you. I told you, nothing in your life is by mistake. From the places you've gone, to the people you've met and the jobs you've worked at. You have to look at your life with a microscope right now and make connections," he urged.

"So, we should start at the house? Wouldn't that be dangerous right now?" I questioned.

Andre got up and started walking toward the door. "Let the noise here die down. You don't know who is watching. Take some time to get your thoughts together. I'll be in contact whether that be on this plane or another. Be careful," Andre warned as he walked out.

We all stood there, trying to process the conversation that had just happened. I didn't know what direction to go in, but I was glad Squad was here to help me.

Kyleena walked over and pulled me into a hug. "I know you have the weight of the world on your shoulders right now. We need some type of closure. I say we plan a memorial service for Momma and Daddy. Too many people knew them and they might start asking too many questions if we put off a service too much longer." She was right.

"Why don't we get two rooms and decide what we're going to do tomorrow. Tonight was a lot to take in, and we all need some sleep," Mila offered. I didn't realize I hadn't slept until she mentioned it.

"That actually sounds like a good idea, but I wanna stay back for a while and sit here and collect my thoughts," I mentioned.

"We drove two cars," Devon said as he threw me his keys. "We'll get the rooms and I'll text you where we're at and the room numbers. Bitch, this is first time I'm letting somebody whip Alejandro. Don't make me regret it. No eating, drinking or breathing too hard," Devon joked.

I couldn't help but crack the fuck up. "Alejandro nigga? Really?" I laughed. Devon looked at me and rolled his eyes. "Look, long story, I'll have to tell you about my Latin dealings later. Don't judge and don't fuck up my shit Sol," he reiterated as he bounced to Mila's rental.

Mila came over and embraced me. "Be careful, ok? You know we have y'all's back. Whatever you need. Text me when you're on your way."

I watched the three of them get into the car and pull off. I sat there for a minute and took in my surroundings. I looked at my mom's roses and wondered to myself how they were still alive without being taken care of. Typical Momma. I pulled my hood up and made my way towards the smoldering pile of what was left of my childhood home. I hated lying to them, but niggas are nosey. I couldn't trust Andre's word worth a shit, so his warning to stay out of the house fell on deaf ears.

I walked across the lawn and stood in front of the house. Something was in there and I was gonna find out what. Holding on to my black tourmaline necklace, I made my way inside of the only place that could hold answers.

CHAPTER 7

Ibeyi

The hair on my arms stood up as I walked up to what remained of the house I spent 15 years of my life in. It seemed like all the memories were scribbled into the walls, incapable of destruction that the fire bought. It still smelled like fire, and I took the top of my shirt to cover my nose and my mouth. I stood in what used to be the front entrance hallway and looked into the skeleton of the house.

Looking up, I could see all the way up into what used to be the attic. Tears welled up in my eyes when I thought about all of the work that my parents put into this house. It was another one of those things where we kids had no idea the struggles that my parents went through to provide us with the lifestyle we lived. Don't get me wrong, it wasn't extra grand, we still went without. My parents were just the type of parents that believed that children should be allowed to be children and not worry about the things that were supposed to be taken care of by the adults, so we never knew.

I watched my steps as I walked through the house, careful not to step in any possible still smoldering embers. I looked up the steps to see if there was a way that I could get to my bedroom without hurting myself. I carefully climbed what was left of the steps and had to damn near jump from the middle of the stairs to the top because of a massive hole left by the fire. Holding on the railing on the left side of the wall, I made my way into my room.

When I opened the door, my heart sank to my ass. Nothing was left in my room but ashes basically. I took pride in the fact that my room was one of the rooms in the house that never changed, no matter how old I got. It was like a permanent reminder of happier times every time I came home. With that being the case, all the memories stored in my room were gone.

After standing in my doorway for a few minutes and taking it all in, I had to find what I was coming for and it clearly didn't lie in the destruction that sat in my room. I tried to think like my Momma's cryptic ass would and imagine where she would hide something she knew she had to hold on to. At the same time, that wasn't any help because Luna was famous from hiding things from herself. I chuckled at the thought of all the damn times she would try hiding stuff from us just for us to end up helping her look for it.

I didn't realize I had gotten lost in my thoughts until I realized I was standing in front of what used to be the attic door. Y'all should already know what I was thinking. There's not much I'm afraid of, but I am black. I don't do attics. I turned around to walk away when I stopped. Something was pulling me toward this attic. As much as I didn't want to go in there, part of me knew that this would probably be somewhere Momma would hide some shit. After going back and forth in my mind about it, I decided to at least check it out for a couple of seconds.

I walked into the room, which had the least damage. Thank God the fire didn't start up here with all the paper and shit my parents had stored up here. I looked around at what seemed like a million boxes, not knowing where to start or even what the hell I was looking for.

"Fuck," I muttered out loud to myself as I opened and closed boxes. I used the light on my phone to read what was printed on each box, and I noticed something. For the first three years of my life there were no boxes with any pictures or anything. I found that odd since I had seen baby pictures of myself but there were so few. Momma always told me that I would never cooperate for pictures as a baby, so she gave up trying to make me take them.

The boxes that I did see started in 1993 and went forward. I made a mental note of that as I started going through the rest of the boxes. I found a box that Momma had evidently started right after she had Kyleena. I had to be about three years old at the time. I smiled as I looked through all of the pictures of Kyleena and I playing in random places my parents took us. The park. The backyard. Momma's rose garden. One thing that stuck out is that Andre stuck out like a sore thumb in any picture he was in. I don't know how I didn't notice these things once I got older. I guess that dumb ass spell worked. I remember being in high school and people not knowing that Andre was my brother. We literally looked nothing a like, but the genes between Ky and I were so strong.

Lost in my thoughts and still flipping through pictures, a

picture caught my eye. I almost glanced over it because I thought it was one of the baby pictures they had of me and I had seen enough pictures of baby Sol rockin' a baby high top fade with no edges and a watermelon head to last me the rest of this life and the next. I dug the picture out and tried to make out my Mommas scribble at the bottom of the polaroid. The black marker had faded, but if you squinted hard enough you could make it out. "Junior, March 1991."

I froze as I realized what I was looking at. It wasn't me in the picture at all, it was my twin brother. I checked the dates on the box that I was looking at. The box I was going through was labeled "Summer 1994", so I could only assume that Momma didn't mean for this picture to be in there. Staring at my brother was literally like staring at myself. We were indeed twins. Same eyes. Same face. Same watermelon head courtesy of our father Freddy Sr. I didn't realize I was crying until I felt the wetness drop on my hand.

I stared at the picture trying to take it all in. In a matter of hours, I went from just knowing about my brother, to hearing his voice, to seeing the only picture that may exist of him. My mind started wondering to what he would have looked like now. Or what he does look like now, where he is, and how can I find him. I tried to imagine what my life would have been like with a twin. I laughed as I pictured Momma tryna handle a male version of me. Right as I felt myself about to literally start sobbing, I heard what I thought was a voice. I looked around. For what, I don't know because I just know my black ass came up here by my damn self. This is why I told y'all I don't do attics. I stood still to see if I could hear it again.

"Don't be scared, it's just me Sol. It's 12," the voice repeated itself.

FOOLISH

Do I really have to tell y'all what I did next? If you guessed scream you've been paying attention. In the midst of me screaming, the plan was to run however I couldn't move my feet fast enough. Damn heavy ass Nike Boots. As I turned to the door to take a step, my exit was blocked by a figure standing in what would've been the doorway.

As I started backing up, the figure moved closer. As I moved backward, I could partially see thanks to the moonlight, features of this...person or thing. As it moved closer into the light I swear my soul left my body. Standing in front of me was the male version of myself equipped with medium length dreads and a shirtless top half filled with tattoos, one of which was glowing. In complete and utter shock, I felt myself getting lightheaded. I'm not the one to ever have a loss for words, but I couldn't force my mouth to form words. 12. Standing in front of me. He reached out his hand and because I'm scary as fuck, my whole body jumped backward. The next thing I knew my body was hitting what was left of the floor.

I gotta be more careful, nobody should be that scary and clumsy.

As I opened my eyes, I tried to make my vision focus. Before I had the chance to, the most lit scent caught my bell pepper shaped nose. Momma's gumbo. I knew at that point I had jumped timelines. As I sat up, I realized I was sitting on the floor of a dining room. I looked around the room and noticed my daddy looking younger and completely buff and in shape, and Momma who looked just like a chocolate version of Kyleena. I watched as my parents sat at the table among people I didn't recognize.

They were so into each other. If you didn't know any better, you would think they were in the room alone. I watched as my Daddy whispered into Momma's ear while she giggled like a damn school girl. I stood up and walked over slowly, not sure if they could see me or not. I waved my hand in front of Daddy and Momma, but they didn't budge. That kinda sucked. I was hoping we had a repeat of the other night and I could talk to them. I stood staring at my parents, looking so young and in love.

Out of nowhere I heard what sounded like a baby crying, and that's when it clicked in my mind. I must have traveled back to when she had us. I'm starting at this point to realize that I only really travel when there's a piece of the puzzle I gotta connect. I gotta learn to leave my emotions out of it to see what needs to be seen. Like clockwork, my parents hopped up and walk into the other room, with me following closely behind. I watched as they walked over to two bassinets and each gently picked up a baby. I walked over to where they were standing to get a glimpse. Jr. and I were two of the cutest babies I had ever seen, minus that head. Damn we had some big heads.

We both took after Daddy, but Jr. had Mommas complexion. In all honesty outside of that, you wouldn't think Momma had anything to do with our creation. We were definitely Daddy's kids. I looked up at my parents who were beaming with joy. They walked back into the dining room and the room lit up with "ooohhhs" and "aww let me see!" from the house guests. I guess we were kinda popular. At the head of the table, a fairly older lady sat, unenthused. Momma walked over to her and tried to hand Jr. off to her but was met with the meanest look I'd ever seen in my life.

"Momma, you don't wanna hold your first grandson? C'mon, don't act like that. Not today Momma," I watched as my Momma begged.

I started to tear up as I realized who I was looking at. Odessa. I had never even seen a picture of my grandma, but I knew it was her.

FOOLISH

They don't be lying when they say those Dupree genes are strong. My grandma got up and walked into the kitchen, and Momma passed Jr. off to my godmother and followed. Being nosey, my black ass followed behind them. As I stood in the doorway of the kitchen, the two women immediately began to argue.

"One thing us Dupree women are known for is our feisty mouths and attitudes," I chuckled to myself.

"Momma, do you have to act like that in front of company? You don't have to let all of New Orleans how you feel," Momma snapped.

"Girl don't you tell me how to do shit. I keep tellin' y'all hard headed asses stop letting everybody near those babies. Everybody that smile in your face don't mean you no damn good Luna," Odessa warned.

Momma rolled her eyes. "Momma, we hear you, but we all friends here. Who out there ain't happy for us Momma? Huh? If the twins were in danger, don't you think I would know it?" Momma asked with tears in her eyes. Odessa stared at her daughter and I could tell she was conflicted about something.

"I done told you Luna. I got to protect Solelil. She's special. Now I gotta protect two of em. Who knows what happened when they was in your womb. We gotta be careful, that's all. I don't dislike my grandchildren Luna, you know me better than that. I just got this feeling, you need to watch that Jackie," Odessa confessed as tears welled up in her eyes. Momma walked over and gave her a hug.

"Momma Jackie wouldn't hurt a fly, where are you getting this from? Hell, she's your friend," Momma looked concerned.

"As sure as my name is Odessa Dupree, that woman is jealous of us Luna. I see the way she look at them babies, especially Junior. It's like she knows something we don't. I'm telling you what I know and you know I've never been wrong with these hunches girl. Keep your eye on that one. Hell, she done stole a husband from half of

Lafayette Parish, what makes you think she won't steal your babies?" Odessa questioned as she stirred the pot of gumbo on the stove.

I felt my body getting lighter and that meant it was time to go. I watched as my Momma and Grandma continued their conversation, but I couldn't hear. When I woke up, I was lying beside my phone which still had the flashlight on. I felt like I had found enough for one night and decided it was time to go.

I sat up and dusted myself off and tucked the picture of 12 inside of my hoodie pocket.

"12," I chuckled out loud to myself. "Who the fuck names themselves 12?"

"Don't you think you should practice not passing out before you talk shit," I heard a deep voice chuckle from behind me. Determined not to jump outta my skin, I turned around to face my brother.

He wasn't glowing this time, which helped me calm the fuck down. He looked like a regular ass human being. We stared at each other for what seemed like a million years. Instantly I felt like I had been unconsciously searching for him my whole life. I had a shared a womb with this now grown man, and here we were standing in front of each other after being apart for so long.

"Damn, you're even more beautiful in person love," 12 damn near whispered with tears in his eyes.

"That means you must think pretty highly of yourself too," I laughed as he joined in.

I had so many questions for him. "How did you find me?" He was now tossing around boxes as if he were looking for something.

"What makes you think I ever lost you to begin with? We're twins. I always knew where you were. Even at Henny's," I felt my cheeks get hot as he turned around and looked at me with a stern look.

He continued. "I just couldn't talk to you. If I did, Jackie woulda been able to find me. Couldn't risk that happening, so I kinda watched you grow up from afar," he smiled at me as he continued to toss boxes around. He paused for a second and walked over to me.

"Ah, here it is," he whispered as he dusted a trunk off. "Leave it to you to fall and hit your head on exactly what I was looking for girl," he laughed. I felt my face and realized that hot place I thought was me blushing actually turned out to be a cut.

"Don't worry, I'ma walk you out. We'll take care of that with Momma's roses. You gots to be more careful," he laughed. "Matter of fact, lemme see somethin'. Come here," he instructed.

I walked over to him and he wrapped his arms around me. Kinda took my breath away to be so close to the other half of myself. This nigga was ripped too, talk about protection. Guess that's what happens when you thuggin' across timelines. He took the trunk and slid it between his legs.

"Now, wrap your arms around me and no matter what, don't let go. Your ass is still fully mortal, and I'll be damned if you fall and it be my fault. You might wanna close your eyes too, I know you're scared of heights," he laughed.

As I wrapped my arms around my brother, I had never felt so safe and peaceful in my life. I closed my eyes and buried my face into his shoulder as I felt our bodies lift. The cold air seemed to hit my face hard and I wanted to know what was going on but I knew my ass would freak the fuck out, so I waited. After a few seconds, I felt my feet touch the ground again.

"Alright, you can look now. Scary ass," he teased while walking to Devon's truck. I hit the unlock button to pop the trunk open and stood back as he slid the trunk into the back.

"That's the trunk that Momma was talking about. Under no circumstances does Andre bitch ass see what's in that trunk. Kyleena or your little friends either, not until we go through it together. Until then, this is for your eyes only. If you get confused about anything in here, you're thinking too hard about it. There's a book inside of there with instructions. Read it," he warned.

Realizing it was late and I should be getting back, I started to get sad. It seemed like our time together was so short. "When can I see you again?" I asked, choking back tears.

12 shook his head. "Girl I told you I never went anywhere. I was always there. You just weren't listening hard enough. Whenever you need me, just think of me...and stop being so jumpy when I talk to you. You should be used to my voice by now," he replied as he lit a blunt. I busted out laughing.

"So they have blunts in the Ether?" I joked. He cracked up laughing.

"Man, I be all over the place. Hell, you act like a nigga dead and shit. I enjoy ganja like the next gifted mufucka," he joked. "Oh shit, come on. Let me fix your damn head. Clumsy ass," he remembered as he guided me back into Momma's greenhouse.

I sat in the chair while he plucked a couple of rose petals off of one of Momma's roses and pressed them against my head. I sat there trying to understand why he was pressing some damn rose petals against my head. "Momma enchanted her rose petals with her healing touch. This shit is better than going to the hospital," Jr. smirked.

"We're gonna find out what happened Sol, don't worry. You're not by yourself anymore. You got a whole team around you, and I can tell they some loyal mufuckas. You don't find niggas like them every day. I can tell they gon' ride with you, and you already know I'm locked and loaded. You gotta listen to your higher self baby girl," he mentioned as I rolled my eyes.

"You know, I wish one of y'all would tell me what the fuck that means. Momma said it, Marceline said it and now you. I'm new to a lot of this shit you know," I spat.

12 chuckled. "Read the book girl. You'll figure it out," he grinned as we walked back to the truck. It was kinda bittersweet. I had so many more questions I wanted to ask him, I felt like I had barely said anything.

"Don't worry. We have all the time in the world to catch up. Shit is about to get real, so you'll be seeing and hearing from me a lot more often," he responded as if he'd read my mind.

"Let me guess, you can read minds too?" I asked rolling my eyes. He laughed while digging in his pocket.

"Nope, just yours. You're my twin dummy," he laughed. He grabbed my hand and placed a stone wrapped in copper in the form of a ring on my finger. "Keep this with you at all times. It's black tourmaline, it'll protect you. I'll be in contact," he whispered as he hugged me tight. I got in the truck and started it as he kissed me on the forehead and shut the door. I shot a quick text to Mila to let her know I was finished. She gave me the address to a hotel on Skibo Road.

As I pulled off, I looked back in the rearview mirror to get one last glance at him, but he was already gone.

CHAPTER 8

Hide & Seek

I sat in the parking lot of the Marriott, getting myself together before I went in. I knew as soon as I stepped foot in the door there would be a lot I would have to tell Kyleena, and I didn't know how she would handle it. She seemed like she was on edge, but Ky can be just like me. We're good at hiding how we really feel. Speaking of how people felt, I was still on an emotional high. Even though things had been crazy with the loss of my parents both literally and figuratively, meeting my brother and knowing that he was alive brought some much needed comfort. I just hate that all this fuck shit had to happen in order to meet him.

I felt myself getting kinda angry again. Who was this Jackie person, and why the hell was she so jealous of some shit that she had a hand in creating? Nobody told her to be greedy. Why was Andre trying to help, what was his motive? I couldn't imagine going against my mother to help our arch nemesis. Maybe he felt guilty, who knows with him. I sat in Devon's truck trying to put pieces together, but that just ended up in a headache. I decided that I needed a good nights sleep, and a shower felt like a lit idea. I hopped out of Devon's truck, making sure I chirped the alarm and made my way to the room number Mila gave me.

I knocked on the door and waited for Kyleena to answer. The first couple of times I knocked, she didn't answer but I could hear voices behind the door. Getting aggravated, I started to knock again when the door opened, and Devon stood in the door way looking startled.

"Hey Sol, why didn't you text us you were on your way?" he asked tryna avoid eye contact.

I pushed past him and walked into the room. My spidey senses were tingling. As I entered the room, I walked into a cloud of incense and Ky and Mila sitting on the floor across from each other. Neither of them noticed me standing above them. I cleared my throat to get their attention. Kyleena glanced up and when she saw me standing there, nudged Mila.

"Damn it Ky, if you wanna tap in you have to be still, nudging me is not helping," Mila muttered before she looked up. When she did notice me standing there, her cheeks turned flush.

"Hey Sol, you got here fast as hell," Mila stuttered.

Sensing something was up that they weren't telling me, I mentally prepared my questions as well as exhaled as to not come off too hostile. I knew what Mila is capable of, she grew up practicing what we were just breaking into. I know how powerful she is despite the fact she always tries to downplay it.

FOOLISH

"Mila, what are yall doing? Tapping in? Tapping into what?" I questioned my best friend. I really didn't wanna come off suspicious, and I hate that I felt like this. These days I was finding it hard to trust anybody and it shouldn't have been that way but I have to protect my sister. Kyleena avoided making eye contact with me as I stared a hole in her face.

"Kyleena Marie," I called her name louder. Mila and Devon stood on the sidelines, not sure whether to say something or stay out of it. Ky finally looked up at me with anger in her eyes.

"You're not the only person in this family with gifts, just so we're clear," she called herself telling me. I knew this already, but she wasn't aware that I did. I realized at that moment that so much had been going on in the last few weeks that I hadn't talked to her at all about anything I've been experiencing. It was now or never. I looked over at my friends apologetically.

"Can ya'll give me and Ky some time? I need to talk to her about some stuff." I asked of them.

"Sure, we'll be in the next room over if you need us" Mila reassured me. Mila walked to the door, but Devon was still standing there with his eyebrow raised.

"Um, Miss Ma'am, my keys?" he reminded me. I laughed and handed his keys to him and watched them walk out of the room. It was game time. I had no idea where to even start this conversation with Ky. I didn't know how she was gonna react and to be truthfully honest, I'm not in the headspace for other people's mental breakdowns.

"Ky, I know we've been through a lot over the past couple of weeks. I get it. I get that you wanna find answers on your own but I wanna talk to you first," I lead into the conversation. Ky came and sat on the edge of the bed and crossed her legs.

"I'm listening," she mumbled. My hands were sweaty, and my heart felt like it was gonna bust through my double D's. How do I tell her this shit without seeming bat shit crazy?

I cleared my throat and proceeded to talk. "I know you have gifts. Every woman in our family on Momma's side does. Momma talked to me about it." Ky looked at me like she was curious as to what I meant by that. "You know I timeline jump, that's one of my gifts. My last three jumps have been...crazy. In one of them I found Momma and Andre talking and I'm guessing in the timeline that I jumped to, we were still little because Momma lost her shit when she saw me grown. Like, pulled a gun on me lost her shit," I chuckled.

Ky's eyes got big as hell. "Wait. Luna Dupree, the woman who wouldn't even let Daddy have a gun in the house pulled a gun on you? What the fuck did you do Sol, damn!"

"I didn't do shit!" I cackled. "Up until then, when I timeline jump nobody could see me or hear me. It's like I'm just there to observe or some shit. When I rolled up on Momma and Andre, Momma heard me somehow. I don't know, I'm still tryna figure that one out," I stammered. I stopped talking for a second to let all of what I told her sink in, even though I hadn't told her much at all. This was gonna be a long night.

"So what did Momma say to you that was so special?", Ky questioned. I ran down the whole thing to her, reiterating what she already knew because of Andre. I told her that Momma told me about each one of our gifts, and told her she had the gift of sight. When I told her that, she didn't look too shocked, so of course imma ask questions. Before I could get the chance to, she started spilling.

"So, remember when I told you I wanted to talk to you at the police station? I swear I used to think you were making shit up when we were little. Right before I left for college, I started seeing things. At first, they were just dreams. It kinda creeped me out because I would dream about shit and it would happen, exactly how I dreamed it. When I got to college, it started happening while I was awake, you know like Raven from That's So Raven? Except I didn't look all dumb in the face like her," She giggled a little, but her smile turned to this eerie expression. She looked at me like she was going to regret what she was about to say. I braced myself because I couldn't take any more bad news.

"Sol, I saw Momma and Daddy's death months before it happened. I don't know how they were killed, I don't know who did it and I don't know where the bodies are, but I saw it. I saw them laying there, in the house. Dead," she whimpered as she teared up.

"I didn't know how to tell you without you freakin' out, because I know you woulda believed me. I wasn't worrying about that. About two weeks before they died Momma had flown down here to handle some business. She didn't say what business, but whatever it was aggravated the shit outta her because when she came to my house she was in a bad mood. I tried to talk to her about it, but she just kept telling me I wouldn't understand but I would see what she was talking about soon. I knew when she said that she didn't mean in the physical." She wiped her tears on the edge of her shirt.

I felt bad for my sister. I felt bad because I know how it feels to deal with something like that and feel like you have nobody to talk to. Even though Momma and me didn't really talk about it much, I at least knew that she understood and knew what I was going through. I wonder why she wasn't the same way with Ky.

Ky's voice broke my thoughts. "So what did you do at the Greenhouse? Honestly, that shit looked mad creepy with the house half way burnt down in the background. You couldn't pay me to stay there by myself." I prepared myself to tell her the only part I hadn't mentioned, and I was still debating on how much to tell her. Twin said not to let anybody see inside the trunk that he found, but he didn't say I couldn't say shit. I had to tell somebody, I was tired of all these damn secrets.

"So I um...I went into the house tonight," I muttered. Ky looked at me in shock.

"Sol, why the fuck would go in the house. Like they JUST put the fire out, you coulda got hurt! Sometimes I swear I don't know who's older, me or you. Why didn't you ask me to stay back with you, I wasn't gon' say shit," she exploded. If she was acting like that about me going in a damn house, she was really about to be .38 hot.

"First of all, chill the fuck out. I had to do some sneaking around. I don't know about you but I want some damn answers. Besides, I wasn't by myself." I threw in.

Ky rolled her eyes so hard I didn't think they were gon' open again. "Bitch if you say God was with you imma smack fire outta you. Don't play with me Solelil."

I don't know why it was so nerve wracking to tell her this. Maybe because part of me felt like maybe she shoulda been there. "No dumb ass." I retorted. "Our brother was there." I blurted out.

If looks could kill Ky woulda been a cold–blooded murderer. "So you mean to tell me that you let Andre, the nigga we can't trust...the nigga who is still under suspicion of killing our parents...you let HIM go with you but not me? What the fuck is his gift besides reading minds Sol? How was that gonna help you, was he gonna tell you how the walls felt when they were being burnt the fuck up? You get on my damn nerves!"

I let her rant as long as she needed to. I didn't even say anything when she finished. I just looked. When she realized what that meant and put two and two together, her whole rant changed.

"Stop playin! You saw your twin?!" she squealed and ran around the room. " Ok, so you know I have a million fuckin questions but go ahead and spill."

Trying to control my laughter, I waited for her to calm down before I started talking. "So, he looks like Daddy, just like I do. He's light skinned like Momma. Clearly, we're fraternal. He is like the male version of me when it comes to his humor, he's gonna fit in perfectly with us. Momma said that his gift was his words, but we didn't really get to talk about that too much because I ended up passing the fuck out and timeline jumping, which I'll tell you about tomorrow when Devon and Mila are around so I don't have to tell it twice."

Kyleena sat on the edge of her seat with tears on her waterline. "Remember I used to say all the time I know we were supposed to have a brother but it couldn't be Andre when he would piss me off?" I laughed. We used to be so mean to each other.

"Who the hell knew that shit was true? He gave me a trunk. Momma had told me about the trunk already, but I didn't know where to find it. I honestly thought it had burnt up in the house. According to Momma, there's things in this trunk that have been passed down from generations ago specifically for me. I can't let nobody see it, not even twin." I confided in my sister.

Ky sat looking curious. "So, what exactly is supposed to be in this trunk that's supposed to be passed down to you?"

I shrugged. "I don't know. Momma said there's things in there that are supposed to lead me to grandma evidently. I guess she has all the answers."

"NOBODY HAS THE ANSWERS SWAY!" my sister blurted out and killed the tense moment. We both laughed so hard, harder than we had in days. Leave it to my goofball sister.

"So, what are we gonna do about a service for Momma and Daddy. Like I said, you know they had hella friends and associates and they're already in my Facebook inbox asking questions about a service," Ky groaned. To be honest, I hadn't even thought about it, especially seeing as though there were no bodies at the moment. I knew we couldn't leave it open ended like that though.

"I say we set up a memorial service at the funeral home and leave it at that. Before they even have a chance to ask about a burial we'll just let everybody know that the family wants to do the burial privately." I blurted out off the top of my head.

Ky nodded in agreement "Yea that's cool and all, and I'm down...but what do we do when the bodies turn up? We can't have a whole 'nother funeral for them. People are gonna really start asking questions then."

Honestly, all of this hadn't even crossed my mind. I knew in the back of my head that none of this would seem real until we found their bodies. I really didn't care what other people thought. Hell, up until this point people had always figured me crazy. I guess Ky didn't want our crazy broadcasted through all of Fayetteville.

I walked into the bathroom to wash my face. "We'll cross that bridge when we get it to it."

~~ * ~~

The smell of off brand coffee woke me up out of my sleep.

I rubbed my eyes, trying to adjust to my surroundings and remember where I was. I turned over to see my sister sitting up in her bed, holding a paper cup of said off brand coffee and staring off into space. Not wanting to bother her, I grabbed my phone and began my morning ritual of scrolling through social media. At least I tried to. As I unlocked my phone, I realized I had about a dozen texts from various family members and friends of my parents about funeral arrangements.

Fuck.

Realizing that today was the day that we needed to actually go to the funeral home and speak with them about my parent's service sent a chill up my spine. I would have to be around Andre. I wish that twin could be here instead of him but again, gotta save face.

"He's already downstairs waiting in the lobby." Kyleena's lips moved but she continued to stare out into space.

Not even turning my full body around, I sighed mad loud. "You know, you and twin really gotta stop doing that mind reading shit. People's thoughts are supposed to be private."

Ky chuckled, not even a full chuckle. "Don't have to read your mind. Your body language says enough. Plus, your mind is the last mind I would wanna read. Bitch, you crazy." We giggled together.

I gave up trying to respond to all of the text messages individually and decided just to make a post on Facebook. After I let my whole news feed know that I would have details later on today, I got up and headed to my suitcase to find something to wear. Realizing I hadn't packed anything for a memorial service, I made a mental note to grab something while we were out. I grabbed all of my stuff and headed to the shower while Kylenna watched her monthly tarot reading by our favorite reader on YouTube, Amber from The Quietest Revolution.

As I showered, I began to think about everything that had been happening. If anybody woulda told me a year ago that I would be planning a funeral for my parents I woulda laughed. When they say cherish your parents while they're here, that's no joke. I couldn't begin to imagine life without them. My Daddy would never have the chance to walk me down the aisle. My Momma would never have the chance to spoil her future grandkids, something she always talked about. They would never get to physically be here to see how me, Ky and Junior turned out. I felt my emotions bubbling up inside of me, so I decided to end my shower. I couldn't be out here all puffy eyed.

I wrapped my towel around me and wiped the steam off of the mirror so I could wash my face. I splashed water on my face and looked up into the mirror to apply my black soap, and there was a face that wasn't mine staring back at me. Of course, my first reaction was to scream, in which I did. Twin covered my mouth with his hand while laughing uncontrollably. Once I realized it was him, I tried my best to cave his chest in with my fist.

Kyleena came to the bathroom door trying to jiggle the locked door open. "Um are you ok in there?!"

Giving the evil eye to my brother who was still crackin' the fuck up, I let her know I was ok.

"I'm fine Ky, I'm sorry! The water just got too hot, you know I have temperature sensitive skin!"

"You gotta chill out with the skittish shit girl." He continued to laugh.

"Well excuse the fuck outta me for not thinking you would pop up in a bathroom of all places! Did you not think that through?" I held my chest to protect my heart which was bound to pop the fuck out. "What's so important that you couldn't wait until I was out of the damn bathroom?"

"I came to warn you about Andre. You need to keep an eye on him. I've been tryna track his movements because I know you think he's playing both sides. The thing is, I'm able to follow him most of the time, but there's some places that he goes where I lose him." 12 sat on the edge of the shower, rolling up a blunt.

"So where is it that you think he goes when you lose him?" I asked while rubbing the black soap into my face.

"The only thing I can think of is that he's meeting up with his Momma, and nothing good could come out of that as you already know. I really feel like that nigga is hiding something, but I can't put my finger on it." He replied.

I knew it. I knew this nigga was playing both sides and I couldn't trust him. I tried really hard because Momma said that he could help, but I don't think Momma completely got the full scoop on Andre. I know if she knew she woulda never suggested his help, which means it's open season on his ass.

Reading my mind, 12 chuckled and shook his head. "Hold on before you go all Kill Bill on his ass sis, he fighting on a whole different level. This isn't something you can do by yourself, but I can't do it from behind the scenes."

I laughed as I rinsed my face off. "Nigga what you know about Kill Bill in these streets? Who knew you watched TV!"

He pushed my head under the faucet as he laughed. "I told you I be outchea! But for real though, did you tell Ky about me? Imma have to show face and I don't wanna scare the shit out of her. Hell, if she acts scary like you I have to come at her gently."

"I told her about you. She knows. She was kinda pissed that I went into the house without her until I told her you were there. Ky is not like me. She gets a kick outta this shit." I laughed.

"Bet. Ya'll go take care of Momma and Daddy's memorial service. I'll wait here for you. Whatever you do, don't let Andre know I'm here. That would fuck everything up, I have reason to believe he's a snitch ass nigga." He shook his head.

"I mean, I have reason to believe that he's a lot of things, but why do you feel like he's a snitch?" I started to get concerned.

12 lit the blunt and took a huge pull. "I told you, I can't track this nigga. If I can't track him that means he's going somewhere that he knows he can't be traced. That's grounds for hiding something. If you can bounce all over the universe and I can see you, and then all of a sudden you drop off the grid...that screams sneaky to me. Especially seeing as though

nobody knows where his Momma is at."

I started to understand what he was saying, and it did sound mad sneaky. "So Kyleena knows about you, like in depth. My friends don't though. They just know you exist, kinda. What should I tell them because I know they're gonna come back to our room after we handle the memorial service arrangements."

"The question is can you trust them? You don't have to keep me a secret, but everybody don't need to know about me just yet. If you think you can trust them, go for it."

"I can trust them. They're like us," I replied as I put my foundation on.

"So, who's this Mila girl you be with? She single? What's her type?" my twin had a look on his face that grossed me out.

"Could you not? I'm sure she doesn't want any of your ghost dick bruh." Disgusting.

12 almost fell in the tub laughing. "Nigga I'm very much alive, nothing ghostly about me. Why don't you let her tell me no and stop cock blocking...twin."

This kid. "Nigga I have to get ready. Ky is in the room. You might wanna go introduce yourself."

"Nah, I'll wait until yall get back. I'm hungry as shit anyway, I'm about to go grab something to eat. I'll be here when you get back."

I turned around to tell him I was leaving a room key for him, but he was already gone. I have one magical ass, crazy ass family man.

As we waited downstairs in the lobby for Mila and Devon, I watched the traffic on busy ass Skibo Road speed past. My thoughts were doing the same thing, racing. How you do you prepare yourself to say goodbye to your parents? To top it off, its not like I could see them one more time. I hated the idea of lying to everyone, but this shit was too far out to make public.

I looked over at Andre, standing off to the side by himself. Asshole. Since 12 told me what he told me, it made him even more like a snake. I hated that I had to grin and bear it just to get these plans underway. Part of me wished he would just gracefully bow out and be the prodigal son that never returned.

"There's the bitch I know, yaass for this boho hood outfit you're serving!" I knew that could only be Devon extra ass. I turned around to see him and Mila walking in our direction.

"Yaaaaas for this highlight and bold lip! You look alive finally." Mila joked while she hugged me.

I peeked over my shades and rolled my eyes. "Girl you know I can't walk around here lookin' tore up. You will end up a meme with the quickness around here."

Andre finally joined the four of us.

We all stood in the middle of the lobby, I decided to go ahead and direct the game plan for today. "Ok, so aside from the obvious which is going down to the funeral home, there's other things that have to be done too. We need to get the flowers done, the obituaries, and we need to find somewhere that can blow up pictures of them. I say we split up and meet later for lunch."

Ky nodded in agreement. "Sounds good to me. Which one do you wanna tackle?

I thought about what would make me less weepy and as crazy as it sounds, looking at pictures of them wouldn't help my fragile ass mental state right now. Undertakers it was.

FOOLISH

"I'll go handle the funeral directors. Fuckin around with you they be done talked you into a trillion–dollar service with drive thru options included." I poked fun at Ky.

She rolled her eyes and stuck her tongue out. "That's fine, you go talk to the creepy dead people pushers and we'll deal with the living and breathing folks."

I decided to ride with Mila since I hadn't spent that much alone time with her. I also didn't want to be in a car with Andre, I'd rather let Ky have her fun torturing him. It was a perfect time to fill her in. Half way down the road, it dawned on me that I hadn't taken the trunk out of the back of Devon's truck. I started to panic and dug through my purse for my phone.

"I already took it out. It's in your hotel room. You're welcome." 12's voice echoed through my head.

"Gee, thanks. Can you not randomly put yourself on speaker phone in my head? You loud af for no reason." I responded back to him silently.

"Well turn your ethereal hearing aids down, twin. By the way, tell Mila I said what's REALLY good! Aha!" His laugh vibrated my whole body. I couldn't help it and laughed out loud. Mila turned and looked at me like I completely lost my mind. I guess its time for me to spill the beans.

"Bitch, are you ok? Did you sleep at all last night? You actin' real sleep deprived." Mila asked while glancing out the corner of her eye.

"Ok, so I got some shit to tell you, but don't think I'm crazy Mila. Seriously." I begged.

Mila let out the loudest cackle ever. "Did you forget who raised me? Girl, there's nothing that surprises me anymore. Try living with Luciana all your life and then talk about crazy!"

I laughed at the truest statement she'd ever made. "So, remember last night back at the greenhouse when Andre said that we have a brother that he was supposed to have killed? He's not dead. At all. He's actually back at the hotel room waiting on us to get back."

Mila kept driving like she didn't hear what I said. "Um, hello? Did you hear me? My supposedly dead brother is waiting in my room."

She smirked. "I heard you. How's it felt having him around? You feel complete? I know it has to feel better than having Andre's psychopathic ass as a brother."

That smirk threw me off, but I would address that later. "It feels...strange, but I'm hella happy about it though. He's just like me and Ky, like the missing puzzle piece. He's funny as hell and his sense of humor reminds me of Daddy."

Mila laughed. "Girl if he's anything like your daddy you need Depends because I swear Mr. Freddy was the funniest nigga alive."

That was true. Back before shit took a weird turn for the worst, my Daddy would crack jokes at the drop of a dime. You couldn't stay mad at him. I hate that he had turned into a different person in his last days.

"Yea he was. Back to my brother though. So you know Mommy said we all had gifts, right? Well evidently, me and him can talk to each other telepathically. Its some weird ass shit. That's why I laughed earlier. He wanted me to tell you wassup." I cracked up laughing.

Mila's cheeks turned red as she laughed with me. "So, are you like the only person that can see him?"

"No but he can make himself scarce when he wants to. He

can jump timelines like me too. I wanted to tell you about him before we got back to the hotel room, so you wouldn't be shocked." I checked out her expressions, and the more we talked about him I definitely had some questions about her responses.

We pulled up at the funeral home and I immediately had an eerie feeling. Mila stood outside of the car waiting for me to get out. When she noticed I hadn't budged, she walked around to my side of the car and opened the door.

"Don't feel right, huh?" Mila questioned. Unable to really put into words how I was feeling, I nodded my head in agreement.

Mila bit down on her bottom lip, a sure sign she wasn't feelin' it either. "I figured. I feel it too. Let's just go in and talk to them and see what they talkin' about. If we get in there and it still doesn't feel right, we can dip. You know I don't play with bad vibes."

I got out of the car and Mila locked her arm into mine. I'm kinda glad she did because I felt faint as shit. As we entered the funeral home, it smelled like death and sadness. Don't ask me how I know what that smells like, but if it had a smell that would've been it. Funeral parlors always creeped me out. I didn't understand how somebody would actually choose to work with dead people. I chuckled to myself at the irony of that thought.

We walked up to the receptionist window where a tall brown skinned lady sat smiling ready to greet us. She kinda reminded me of the lady from "Get Out."

"Hi, what can I do for you?" She asked, perky as hell. I thought the reason that we were here would be obvious...people don't just hang around funeral homes for no reason, but whatever. I tried to find my voice to answer her, but I just couldn't fix my mouth to say the words.

Mila squeezed my hand, letting me know she got it. "My best friend recently lost her parents and we were wanting to check out any options that you have for memorial services." I don't know where Mila gets this white girl professional voice from, but ok sis.

"Ok, not a problem! So, have the bodies already been shipped here or would we need to arrange to have them sent from the coroner's office?" The lady's eyes seemed to stare a hole through me. I didn't like that shit.

"So, that's the thing, we kinda wanted to know if the bodies were actually needed because we don't have access to them at the moment." Mila stammered. The lady looked confused.

"What happened to the bodies? I mean, it's perfectly normal to have a service without them. I just want to be clear before I present you with some options." The lady frowned her face up. I don't know why but that pissed me off.

I couldn't hold my annoyance in anymore. "Look Ma'am, we don't have the bodies right now. I will be doing a funeral just for the family when the bodies are found and released to us. I don't understand where the confusion is coming from. People have memorial services all the time for people whose remains haven't been found. WHAT'S THE PROBLEM?"

The lady's face didn't change whatsoever. Mila looked at me like I had lost my mind, and in the moment, I didn't care. I didn't feel like explaining anything I didn't feel like I should have to.

"Don't tell her nothing else. She looks familiar and I don't trust her energy. Just walk out." 12's voice boomed through my head.

Trying to ignore him, I turned to Mila. "Look, can you deal with her please? I need a minute." I didn't have shit left to say anyway. As I walked out, I dug through my bag for my Newports. As I puffed away, I tried to let the tension melt off of me. Why did the lady piss me off so much? She was honestly just doing her job.

"She pissed you off because you're sensing what I did, something ain't right with her. She knows something." 12's voice boomed in my head again. I swear having a brother that can talk to you through thought can be the most aggravating thing ever in life.

"Stop tryna ignore me too nigga. I heard that." I rolled my eyes as his voice echoed through my thoughts. As I put my cigarette out, Mila walked out of the funeral home.

"Yo, what was that all about? You know I got ya back, but she was just doing her job. What's really good?" Mila stood in front of me waiting for an explanation. I felt myself getting faint. I wanted to answer her, but just like earlier my lips couldn't form the words. I looked around as the scenery in front of the funeral home seemed to morph and change in front of my eyes. I closed my eyes to make sure I wasn't trippin, and when I opened them what was in front of me was totally different.

I looked to the left of me, and instead of Mila being there it was my brother. I looked around trying to place where we were. We were still in front of the funeral home, but something was different. I couldn't put my finger on it. I had never really timeline jumped back to exactly where I was. My brother cupped his hands against the window of the funeral home to look inside. Out of nowhere, he grabbed my hand and whispered "Run!"

You don't have to tell my black ass twice.

I took off running behind him until we were behind the building, hiding behind one of the trashcans. I didn't want whatever or whoever the fuck we were running from to hear us, so I shot a thought to 12.

"Why the fuck are we hiding, and where are we?" I thought waiting for him to respond.

He looked at me with his finger over his mouth. "Be quiet. They can hear our thoughts. Don't say shit until I tell you to. You still got that ring I gave you?"

I showed him my hand where the chunky ring sat on my right ring finger. "Bet. Put your hand on your forehead and don't move it."He instructed.

We watched as the woman I had just talked to came out of the back door and dialed a number on her phone. As she waited for it to ring, she looked around the vicinity. I knew she was looking for us. Someone answered on the other line.

'Yea, where are you? The oldest bitch came in just now to try and make some plans. She got real pissy with me when I asked about the bodies. You sure their kids don't know where the bodies are? She came up in here like she knew what she was talking about." You can tell she was pissed off at whoever she was talking to.

I looked at my brother and went to ask a question when he shook his head no. Who the fuck was this lady and why was she so concerned with my parent's bodies? I knew something was off about her, hence my immediate attitude.

"You keep fuckin up and you're gonna get us all caught up. We shouldn't even be having these problems, they shoulda been dead already. If they find out where dear old granny is, we'll all be fucked. It's your turn to come up with a plan now." The lady damn near *whispered into her phone.*

I looked at 12 confused. He shook his head and I could see the anger building in his face. He grabbed me by the hand and walked me over further where she really wouldn't be able to see us. He took his hand and placed it on my forehead along with the hand he told me to not move. I felt my body shoot into the air, and when I looked around I was back in front of the funeral home. On the ground of course.

I looked up and Mila was standing in front of me. "So, this is that passing out shit Devon was talking about. Girl, I was about to throw your ass in the backseat and head to the E.R. Don't do that shit around me without warning."

I looked at her, really unable to say anything. I was still in shock. If it didn't make sense before, it definitely made sense now. There was a real–life war being waged against my family and I didn't know who other than this Jackie character was behind it. This situation made everything even more suspicious.

"So now that Sleeping Beauty is awake, are you gonna tell me what the hell that was all about in there?" Mila crossed her arms and waited. It was obvious she wasn't gonna let that go.

I came up with the most logical explanation I possibly could. "She was just asking too many questions. It made me mad uncomfortable. I don't know how to deal with this shit, I've never had to plan nobody funeral before. Something just didn't feel right."

Mila didn't look enthused. I hate how everybody around me can tell when I'm bullshittin. "Look, why don't we meet up with the other three and go ahead and get lunch. You can tell us what really happened cause you trippin'."

We got in the car and I called Ky. Her, Andre, and Devon had already finished their tasks and wanted to meet at Tony's Pizza on Ireland Drive. I told her we were on the way. When we arrived at Tony's, I felt my anger bubbling up again. More than ever, I really felt like this nigga Andre was on some shady shit. I felt like the only reason he was "helping" us was to keep an eye on what we were doing and how much we knew. As hateful as it was, I already knew I was gonna enjoy watching him reap whatever was coming his way.

We walked into to Tony's to Ky and Devon sitting alone with no Andre in sight. That calmed my nerves a little. Now however, I wanted to know where he kept disappearing to. I greeted my sister and Devon, and while the two of them and Mila joked around I sat, confined to my thoughts. I really felt like I had to be Inspector Gadget out this bitch.

Kyleena interrupted my thoughts. "Sol, you ok? You haven't said shit since y'all got here."

Before I could answer, Mila answered for me. "She timeline jumped again at the funeral home. That was after of course she damn near ripped the ladies head off that was trying to help us."

I stared at Ky for a minute and hoped she caught my drift. Clearly, she didn't and I would have to say it. "She wasn't trying to help us. She was trying to gather information. When I time jumped, 12 showed up. We heard her on the phone with somebody saying that we should be dead already and we were getting in the way of whatever who the fuck ever is trying to pull off."

I looked around the table at my sister and my friends. If I knew nothing else at this point, I knew shit had just gotten real. There was no more guessing as to what happened to my parents, they were killed because of our gifts. Everybody silently ate as I talked to my brother inside of my head.

"So, I'm goin' out on a limb and saying shit just got really real, huh?" I asked, already knowing the answer.

It took him a while to answer me. "Chill. We can't talk about it right now, they could still be listening. I'll talk to y'all when you come back to the hotel. By the way, bring me a blunt please." I rolled my eyes at my brother.

Kyleena broke her gaze with a look of confusion. "So what do we do now? It's like we're hiding but we don't know who we're hiding from. Nobody got time for that shit. If I'm marked I wanna know who the hell got a price on my head, at the very least." I could tell she was mad irritated. I didn't have the answers for her, but I was ready to get back to somebody that I knew could help her.

I exhaled before I answered. "Twin is waiting back in our hotel room. I was telling Mila on the way to the funeral home that me and him talk to each other telepathically. I was trying to ask him some questions a few seconds ago but he thinks we're being watched and our thoughts are being listened to so he'd rather wait until we got back to the hotel to talk about everything."

Kyleena looked at me annoyed. "Speaking of the funeral home, besides you passing out did you get anything accomplished? Any arrangements made?"

I didn't understand where her attitude came from, but whatever. I didn't have time to worry about to her temper tantrum right now. "No, and I wanted to talk to you about that. I don't know how far this person's reach is and I really don't want to go talk to another funeral home because of that."

Kyleena looked at me like I had snakes coming out of my head. "Before you start actin' all fuckin' stank, hear me out."

I wasn't in the mood for this shit. I don't know what Ky's problem was, but she needs to keep it all the way cute. "I think we should do something in the backyard. Do something like set Momma's garden area up really nice, and do something intimate and private."

"Why would we have a memorial service in the back of a burned down house Solelil? You the one who wants to keep all this shit a secret, but you want them to see the crispy ass remains of a house like they're not gonna wanna ask questions. You sound stupid as hell." Ky spat.

I was really tryna keep my composure, but I was really like five seconds off of her ass. I didn't do anything to her for her to be acting like this. If she had something on her mind, she needed to say it. Once again though, we were out in public. I wasn't tryna draw no more attention to us.

"We could do something to keep them away from that area, Kyleena. What do you think we should do since my idea stinks so bad? While you over there throwin' shade I would hope you have some other ideas, because if not, you're just doin' what you're always doin' and throwin' your unwanted ass opinion around." I glared at her.

Mila sensed the tension and tried to diffuse the situation. "Alright y'all, chill. Fuck. Ky, did you get the pictures and stuff blown up? How did that turn out?"

Kyleena mean mugged the shit outta me before rolling her eyes and looking in Mila's direction. "Yea, they'll be ready to be picked up in two days. You know, because I know how to take care of shit."

FOOLISH

I had enough. "What the fuck is your problem Ky? Is there something you need to get off of your chest? Something I'm not aware of?" I damn near yelled loud enough for all of Fayetteville to hear.

Kyleena smirked and scrolled through her cell phone. "Nope big sis. You got it all under control, right?

I felt myself wanting to lunge across the table at her, so before I did, I got up and excused myself. As I stood outside smoking a cigarette, Devon joined me.

"It's not you girl. I don't know what the hell is wrong with Ky," he mentioned. "She was fine before we left the hotel but by the time we got to the lady's house to discuss the pictures she was on full bitch mode. Oddly enough, the only person she was cordial too was Andre."

"So, why his dumb ass not here? I gotta bone to pick with his ass, too. It's just not the right time, I don't have all the facts yet." I rolled my eyes.

"He said he had some meeting to go to or some shit like that, I don't know. You know I don't pay attention to his existence. But yea, ever since we left the hotel she been on ten. Spilled a drink in my damn truck and told me if I want it clean to clean it myself and everything. I'm over Ms. Ky for today. She need to get it together." Devon retorted.

I stared in space for a minute to just let my mind wander and not think about anything. I was tired of thinking, constantly trying to piece shit together. There were so many components to this whole situation and that crazy bitch at the funeral home just added one more. I really hoped that Twin had some answers. Mila and Ky came walking out of the restaurant, and I silently made my way to Mila's car. I was over talking for the moment.

Mila unlocked the doors and we got in, driving away in silence. Mila tried to hold a conversation with me about work, and I felt bad giving her short answers. I just wasn't in the mood. I feel like nobody around me understands what the hell I'm going through. What I've BEEN going through. This shit may be new to everybody else, but I had the pleasure of experiencing this my whole life. It doesn't get easier. It's as though just because now everybody is seeing the real full picture in the wake of my parent's death it somehow gives them the right to gauge how I handle shit.

Fuck that and fuck them.

We pulled up at the hotel and I walked to my room without saying anything to anybody. I assumed Ky was coming in the room and we would talk, but I heard her tell Mila she was coming to their room for a while. I walked into the room to see my brother laid across my bed propped up and watching TV.

When he saw me walk in, he sat up in the bed. "Do y'all argue like this all the time?" Not saying anything I tossed his blunts on the bed and kicked my shoes off. I sat beside him scrolling on my phone when I got a text from Danny, a DJ at Henny's. I was going to it ignore until I actually read the preview of the message that popped up.

"Somebody been in here looking for you. I didn't tell them any of your information because they looked suspect af. Hit me back when you get a chance."

I wanted to scream at this point out of frustration. Who the fuck would be looking for me at Henny's? Only a few people knew I worked there and they knew better than to come to my job looking for me. Everybody who was important enough to know me like that knew that I was out of town.

Twin sat at the desk rolling up. "You wanna know what I think? Of course you do. I think it's somebody connected to Momma and Daddy's murder. I told you I think Andre is playing both sides. Kinda got a confirmation today."

This nigga and the invasion of my thoughts bruh. My eyebrow raised at his last sentence. As much as I wanted to forget about all this shit, that statement intrigued me. "Continue," I prompted him.

He sealed the blunt and sat it on the table. "So, you know how I told you that I killed two of Andre's brothers, right? Well, what I didn't mention is there's another brother. An older one. He's been ducked off for some years now and nobody's heard from him. I jumped timelines again today and guess who I saw talking to the lady from the funeral home?"

I sat in silence, waiting for him to answer his own question. "You're no fun girl. It was his older brother, Amir. So when we jumped earlier today, she was either talking to Andre or Amir. I really think that Andre is the go between for the two of them, so it won't look obvious."

I thought about what he was saying, and a thought hit me. "Devon did say that Andre left early to go meet up with somebody today, but he didn't tell them who."

Twin shook his head. "See. I told you man. Ya'll can't trust that nigga and the quicker you let me take care of that, the quicker we get some answers. Make an example outta his bitch ass."

As I looked at my brother I could see the anger in his eyes, and he had every right to be mad. He was snatched away from his family by some jealous, psychotic, immortal woman who wants our family power. I'd be a tad pissed too. I remembered that I was in the process of texting Danny back.

"Thanks for the lookout. The next time they come in, take a pic and send it to me."

I wrote him back.

Twin took a pull of the blunt and passed it to me. I hadn't smoked in a couple days and realized that could be the source of my bitchiness. I took a long drag and let the smoke fill my lungs and immediately felt less tense.

"So what the fuck is up with Kyleena? Why she been snappin at everybody today? Is she normally like that?" Twin asked, switching the subject.

I rolled my eyes as I blew smoke into the air in front of me. "No, and I don't know what her problem is. Devon said she's been acting like that all day today. I guess reality is setting in and that's just how she's handling it. I need her to get it together though because my nerves can't take that shit. I be done snatched her ass up before thinkin' twice."

Twin laughed and coughed. "So this is what I'm walking back into? I'll beat both of yall asses!"

As we sat laughing and catching up on the last decade or more, there was knock at the door. Realizing it was probably Ky, I rolled my eyes as I pulled myself off the bed to answer it. I peeped through the peephole to see Mila and Devon standing there instead. I let them in, and Devon walked in while Mila stood at the door, staring.

"Freddy." Mila damn near whispered.

I turned around to see my brother twisting back and forth

in the computer chair and smirking. The look in his eyes made me want to throw up every hot wing I ate earlier.

"Twin, stop being rude." My brother said while twisting one of his locs in between his fingers. "I believe you know my ex–girlfriend, Camila."

CHAPTER 9

Hunted

What the fuck?

I felt like I was in the twilight zone, and I wasn't sure if I heard my brother correctly, yet I didn't want him to repeat it. I looked at Mila and she refused to make eye contact with me. Devon's eyes bounced from one end of the room to another, and I knew his messy ass wanted to know just as bad as I did. I felt that rage I've been suppressing raise up in my throat again. This is why I don't trust people. I knew Mila knew something she wasn't telling me, but this? This crossed the damn line. Ten times over. I swear if her and I didn't have a long history and I would have dog walked her right there in the hallway of this hotel.

Twin laughed and shook his head. "She didn't know I was your brother until long after we broke up Sol. Don't blame her. It was me."

I glared at my brother waiting for him to explain himself.

"So basically what you're telling me is you had contact with her, all this time and never ONCE thought to make yourself available to me? But you were 'thinking about me' and you were 'with me' all the time though right? Man I swear, you can't trust nobody these days. Not even ethereal niggas." I ranted.

I sat on the bed staring at my brother. I wanted to throw something at him. He walked over and sat on Ky's bed facing me. "First off, you not about to throw shit at nobody, so chill out. There's a reason for everything that I do. If I woulda came to you before you were mentally strong enough to handle it not only would you have thought you were crazy, but Jackie woulda caught me. I couldn't risk that. I'm not gonna sit here and lie to you and say at one point I didn't love Mila, but it didn't start out that way. She was just my connection to you."

Twin stared a hole in my face while waiting for me to respond. Truth is I didn't have shit to say. I was at a loss for words, and that didn't happen often.

He grabbed my hand as he began to talk. "Now, if you want me to tell you why I did what I did, I can do that but you gotta chill. Not everybody is against you. Mila is your best friend, always has been. She had no clue I was your brother. I couldn't risk telling her either. She's just finding out."

Mila finally made eye contact. "He's telling the truth Sol. I found out the same night yall met. He made me promise to wait to tell you together. It was hard for me, I felt like I was betraying you. As much as I felt like that, once he explained everything I felt like it was best option. You or I knowing beforehand woulda put you in more danger than you're already in."

I laughed to myself. Protecting me huh? Everybody was

so worried about protecting me, but nobody thought to protect my parents. I finally felt the need to speak. "Let's call it what it is. How long were you using my best friend to spy on me?"

Twin shook his head. "You don't get it, do you? You don't even know how powerful your friend is. I had to reach out to Mila in order to help her build her gifts. Me helping her allowed her to help you. You think y'all were brought together by mistake?" He asked as he nodded in Devon's direction. I looked at Mila as tears streamed down her face. I didn't wanna be mad at her, but I had no idea who to trust.

As usual, my brother answered out loud the questions I asked in my head. "Nobody here should be on the questioning end of your loyalty. I didn't have contact with you but best believe if I thought at any point they were on some fuck shit I woulda stepped in. This is your tribe, WE are your tribe. You can't do everything alone, that's what Jackie is banking on. Getting you alone so you're more vulnerable. There's power in numbers."

I looked around the room at the people I loved the most, minus Ky not being there. I knew deep down they had my best interest at heart, but this shit was personal. My parents were killed. Nobody knew my parents better than me. Their death felt like a personal attack that I had to take on by myself. I had to figure out how to maneuver around them. First thing on the agenda was trying to figure out how to block my brother from hearing my thoughts. I needed some time to myself.

I grabbed my jacket and my room key and headed to the door. Before I walked out, I turned to look at my family. "I just need a minute, don't follow me."

FOOLISH

~~ * ~~

The Uber I ordered pulled up 10 minutes into me waiting in the lobby. I hopped in and in about 10 minutes I was at one of my favorite hangouts when I lived here, The Coffee Scene. I ordered a mango and green tea smoothie and sat curled up in one of the plush sofas they had near the window looking out onto Morganton Rd. If anybody would have told me this would be my life, I woulda laughed in their faces. What the hell did a girl from the hood know about magic? This shit just kept getting more and more weird. I felt like I was living in some ghetto ass version of Harry Potter or some shit.

I had to come up with a game plan, but I didn't even know where to start. My brother was sure that if I decided to move on my own Jackie would eradicate me. I didn't know if I agreed with him. At the same time, I'm very much aware of how powerful Mila is, so I don't even know why he would assume I didn't. She taught me everything I know.

I would be lying if I said that the two of them...dating...if that's what you wanna call it didn't leave a sour taste in my mouth. It felt like everybody is in on this big joke except me. Everybody is laughing except me. I thought back to the timeline jump earlier. If Andre indeed was working with Jackie, how much was he telling her or his brother Amir? Where the hell was Amir? Would Jackie come after me in this timeline or another? As bad as I wanted to 86 Dre from the equation and let him know the jig is up, keeping him around might come in handy. With Twin being able to track him, we could keep tabs on him and be one step ahead at all times.

The trunk. I had forgotten all about the black trunk that Twin found in Momma and Daddy's attic. I hadn't been alone long enough to even look in it. I wondered what was so important in this trunk. I decided when I got back to the room I would look in it before Ky came back to the room, if she even decided to. Ky. I really wanted to know what's going on with her. She's always been a little temperamental, but she's never acted like this to me of all people. Part of me felt like this was just her way of dealing with everything, but something deeper in me told me otherwise. The Dupree girls were not a sensitive, emotional bunch. We pride ourselves in not letting our emotions show. Got that from our Momma. Yet and still Ky was acting like she was on her period until further notice. While I was deciding on whether I should confront her or not, Devon's car pulled up to the front of building. I knew it was him because well, not many people in Fayetteville was pushin' the kinda whip that he was. To my surprise, I watched as Jr. hopped out the driver's seat and put his blunt out before walking in.

When our eyes met, I squinted at him like a child who couldn't follow directions. "I coulda sworn I told you not to follow me Jr." I rolled my eyes as he continued to walk up to me. Without saying a word, he pulled me up by my arm and started walking me to the door. I watched his jaw clench as he looked around before we walked out.

Before I could get the chance to ask what his problem was, I heard his voice inside of my head again. "Don't say shit until we get in the car. Just shut up and get it."

He walked around to my side of the car and opened the door. When I was safely in the car, he walked around the perimeter before he hopped in himself. Once inside, pulled a beeper like thing out of his pocket, sat it on the dashboard and pressed a button. He closed his eyes and started to whisper lowly to himself. As he was whispering, it felt like my energy was draining out of my body. Trying not to freak the fuck out, I looked over at him while he continued to do what he was doing. After about two minutes, the contraption on the dashboard flashed a light and Twin placed it back in his pocket. He lit his blunt back and up and threw the car into reverse.

Speeding down Morganton, we got to the stop light and whipped a right on to Skibo. We drove for about 5 minutes until we pulled into the parking lot of a closed auto repair shop across from Wal–Mart, but deep enough in the woods that you had to be looking in order to find it. He left the car running but put it in park.

He sat there for what seemed like forever, to the point where it was getting awkward. I had to break the silence. "How much did you have to beg Devon to give you the keys?" I joked, trying to lighten the obvious tense mood. He looked at me out of the corner of his eye, still clenching his jaw with his face bright red. Yellow niggas always turnin' red when they're about to throw a temper tantrum.

He took a deep breath and grabbed me by the neck of my jacket, scaring the shit out of me. "Why is everything a joke to you Sol? I told your ass that all Jackie was waiting for was for your dumb ass to be alone to try and pull some shit. Do you know how close you were to getting touched just now? Do you know how hard it was for me to sit there and watch that shit unfold HOPING that you were smart enough to be paying attention to your surrondings? DO YOU?!" he screamed in my face. I felt the heat coming off of his body.

He let go of my jacket as I went flying into the car door. He stared out the window to try and gain his composure.

When he turned back around to face me, he had tears in his eyes.

"You didn't even look in the trunk. Did you?" he shook his head. "Your silence answers my question. I'm doing everything I can to protect you Solelil. I really am, but you won't even fuckin listen to me. This is deeper than just Momma and Daddy dying Sol. Stop tryna figure out who was behind it, it was Jackie. Momma and Daddy were marked for death the moment our yellow asses took our first breath. You gon' lose a lot of people in this game Sol, get used to it."

I looked out the window to control my laughter. "Nigga this aint a fuckin drug beef. We're not in the streets." I said with a smirk on my face.

He wasn't enthused. At all. "What's the difference? Instead of niggas tryna take you out to take over your block, they tryna take your ass out to take your gifts. It's the same damn thing, and it gets just as fuckin real. I've been in the streets. I've killed niggas with my bare fuckin hands over something simple as looking at me wrong. You my little sister, imagine the blood that would run through these streets if these niggas blink at you wrong. Andre is going to get his, and so is Amir but Jackie? Me and Jackie have a personal beef. You think Griselda Blanco and Thelma Wright was bad, imagine them combined and throw magic in the equation."

My brother stared off into space. I could tell that something was bothering him, and he was hesitant to tell me. There had to be a reason he looked so rattled.

I put my hand on top of his. "Jr, what's really going on? Why you so hype right now?" He turned and looked at me slowly, still teary eyed.

"I didn't think you were gonna actually leave the hotel

considering what I had just told you. One of Jackie's workers followed your ass and was waiting for any chance that you were all the way alone. Something as simple as you going outside to smoke. He woulda snatched your ass up and took you to Jackie, and I don't know where the fuck Jackie is. Do you not understand–" he screamed as he punched the steering wheel, causing the horn to blow. I jumped in my seat. I wasn't used to someone being this protective over me other than Momma.

Twin turned his body to face mine. "From here on out, you will have security. 24/7. I need to know where you are and what you are doing at all times. You will not eat, you will not piss, you won't get your back blown out by one of these ho ass niggas out here without security being present. DO YOU UNDERSTAND?!" he yelled about an inch from my face. "We tried doing it your way, now do this under my direction. When we get back to the hotel, we will go through that trunk. Together. If you even THINK about thinking about having an attitude, I will take your gifts from you myself. Understood? We are going to war and I don't think you quite understand the shit that's about to happen. Let me put it in perspective. They killed Momma and Daddy as a warning. Momma is the most powerful Oracle Women out of New Orleans. People feared her. There's no way she shoulda been able to get killed that easily. They killed Daddy because of his knowledge, and because they couldn't leave witnesses. If they can kill Momma, what the fuck makes you think they can't get to you? Use your fuckin head Solelil. I will NOT be separated from you again, not by Jackie and especially not because of your own stupidity."

The look in his eyes let me know he was far from playin.

It honestly scared me a little bit. His eyes glowed in a hazel hue as he waited for me to respond. I couldn't do anything but shake my head. At that moment, I started to piece together the chain of events that lead up to not only my parents being killed, but the events that will happen after. Twin was right. We were at war. I knew it all along, I just didn't want to accept it. I didn't want to be held responsible for any of this. This meant that I was carrying my entire family on my back. I wasn't a bad ass bruja like Mila. I was just a regular girl from the slums of Fayetteville, and I'm supposed to protect the magic of an entire bloodline. I didn't know if I had it in me. I was sure about to find out, whether I wanted to or not.

PART II

The Fool's Journey

CHAPTER 10

Freddy

My eyes were getting tired from lookin' through this damn trunk. Sol had already fallen asleep, so I decided to take a break and get some fresh air...in another timeline. I prepared my body to jump while I held the place I wanted to go in my mind. Since my job is never done, I ended up back in my old hood in New Orleans. I walked in the sticky ass humid air that surrounded Cleveland Ave. This area had been my hideout spot from Jackie because I knew her ass wouldn't dare come here. No matter how magical you think you are, somebody was always gonna see your ass. Being seen in this neighborhood when don't nobody know you was never a good idea. I walked up to a yellow house and banged on the door. I looked around at the dingy neighborhood that was my home. I felt a little more at ease than I had felt in the past couple of days.

A bloodshot eye stared back at me through the dirty

peephole as I waited for this dumb mu'fucka to open the door.

"12? Is that you?" Deon's hoarse voice croaked through the door.

I shook my head. "Deon how many light skinned niggas with dreads and face tattoos do you know? Open the door nigga."

The door creaked open and Deon's face appeared in front of me. One of the local crackheads, Deon was a lookout at this trap house one of my mans was in charge of. Instead paying him in cash, he paid him in crack. Even trade.

"Where you been at nigga? Yo ass been gon' for weeks. Niggas thought you mighta caught a charge or some shit." Deon prodded. I pushed past him and walked into the dirty kitchen.

"Nigga I catch bodies, not charges. Don't ever forget that shit. Where Dirt at?"

Dirt was my ace that ran the trap house I was standing in. He got the nickname Dirt because there wasn't nobody walking the streets of New Orleans dirtier or grimier than this nigga. If there was some shit poppin off in this neighborhood, you could bet your bottom dollar he was behind it. I had known him since I was a youngin'. He was the first one to take me under his wing. There was 5 of us who hung together, ravishin' the streets of New Orleans and raisin' all types of hell. There was me, Dirt, Legend, Hussein and Marcus. We were all fuckin' crazy, and best believe we were untouchable. We all had the same thing in common. Our magic. It wasn't until we all found each other that we found out that our families were considered the Five Sacred Families of New Orleans. Our parents knew each other and ran together, just like we do. All of our bloodlines held special magic with one thing in common, Jackie wanting it.

They all hid it well. Niggas always wondered how they did the shit they did but never did no time. It wasn't luck, I can tell you that. We all came from different timelines and made this one our safe haven. Niggas didn't ask too many questions here. Dirt's parents magic drove them crazy. His momma ended up committed somewhere here in Louisiana, and his daddy shot himself right between the eyes. He don't talk about them. Ever. It was fly to know I had somebody that understood my plight though.

"He downstairs. You might wanna make yourself known though, he handlin' some business." Dirt added. I knew what that meant. One of his workers had violated somehow and he was bein' dealt with. I opened the door to the basement and hollered down.

"AYE YO DIRT, IT'S 12 MAN," I listened to my voice echo off of the cold brick walls as I waited for him to respond.

"MYYYYY NIGGA! BRING YO ASS DOWN HERE MAN! GOTTTT DAMN!" he yelled back, happy that I was back in town. I jogged down the stairs and met him at the bottom where he was standing with his Glock in his hand with blood splattered all over it and him. I shook my head and chuckled.

"Man what the fuck you got goin' on here? Every time I come through this bitch you crackin somebody shit open. You bored or some shit man?" I laughed as we dapped each other up.

He laughed along with me. "Well man if these niggas stop actin like they don't know what's good, I wouldn't have to. I'm not a mean person man but these young boys out here don't know nothin' bout no respect." He was right though. A majority of the shit we dealt with was pure disrespectful shit. You give these young boys a chance and they wanna run shit. That's not how this shit works.

"Come on down here man. Roll up, have a drink and tell me where yo ass has been. You been jumpin again huh?" He quizzed me as we walked toward the den area. I sat down in front on the couch and poured a drink before I rolled one up. I couldn't lie and say it didn't feel like home here, or as close to a home as I had gotten. Dirt looked out for my ass when I was runnin' and duckin from Jackie and taught me how to do it better. If that's one thing Dirt knew was how to stay in the shadows. I felt the shot make its way through my body and loosen me up a little bit. I didn't realize how stressed I had been tryna keep Sol ass alive.

Damn. Sol.

"What's on yo mind bruh? You knew this shit was comin. We all did. I been tryna prepare yo ass for years," Dirt asked bringing me back into the moment. I didn't even know where to start, so I just started talkin.

I took a sip of my drink. I didn't even know where to start. "I been dealing with my sisters man. My parents got murked so I been havin' to watch out for em, you know? My younger sister Kyleena on some sneak shit, and my twin Sol don't realize the severity of the situation man. She just out here like with her head in the clouds or some shit. I don't man. This shit harder than I thought it was gonna be. Niggas almost took her out a couple of times and she ain't even know."

Dirt sat listening, rubbin his beard. That means he was puttin' two and two together from what I had told him the last time we spoke. "So that's why you had me send you some niggas for security? Sis whylin like that? Damn man. Women folk I tell you."

He ain't never lie. "Man she ain't even really whylin so to speak, she just don't want the responsibility. I mean I get it, shit. I don't want it either but the fuck we supposed to do with it? We can't act like the shit ain't there, that shit will get us killed man." I responded. The truth is, I really didn't know how to move at the moment, and that's what was stressing me out. I ain't the one for hidin' so that wasn't an option I even considered, but I had to protect Sol somehow.

Dirt cleared his throat. "I ain't wanna tell you this man and add insult to injury but Amir ass been lookin' for you. Said he wanted to talk, no funny shit. He been comin' round here a couple of times a week and shit. I don't know what his deal is and you know me, if I don't know you I ain't tellin you shit. Hell, even if I do know you, I still might not tell you shit." He laughed as he lit up a blunt. I wasn't even surprised. I had been expectin' that shit, especially dealing with Andre.

"What he been askin?" I held my head in my hands because I just had this feeling this shit was about to piss me off.

"He been askin' bout Andre man. I told him I ain't seen him in a year or so and didn't tell him nothin' more. Nigga, if you need mo' security just holla at me. You know I got you and shit." He nodded.

I sat there swirling my drink around in the glass. I know Sol thought I had all the answers, but I didn't. I was at a loss right now and damn sure didn't have time for that shit. I looked at my watch and realized I had been gone longer than I wanted to. I still had another stop to make, and I wanted to be back before Sol woke up.

I stood up and took my drink to the head, and took a

couple pulls of the blunt that sat in the ashtray. "Well man, lemme get the fuck up outta here. I got another stop I need to make at the warehouse. Imma need more protection."

Dirt looked up from cleanin' his gun and nodded. He stood up from his seat and dapped me up. "You know the drill nigga, just make sure that shit makes it back when you done."

They had a warehouse about 3 blocks away. We had this shit for a minute now. It held all the guns, ancient spells, herbs and tinctures and anything else we needed. We had built up a hefty little artillery for ourselves over the years. Dirt had a system for it and made sure it was out of view. Literally, he made this shit invisible. The only way you could even see it or know its there was by a spell he created. The five of us were the only ones who knew about it, so if some shit was missin' he knew where to look. As I walked toward the steps, Dirt called my name.

"My nigga, I'm serious about that help man. Just hit me up if you need me. Legend and them roamin' around the timeline you been in keepin an eye on shit. You might run into them. Don't let your guard slip. By the way, I can't wait to meet yo sister." He smiled that sick ass smile of his.

His greasy ass smile let me know what he was really sayin'. "Ayo Dirt, don't make me banish your ass somewhere you can't get out of you horny fuck. Don't even go there nigga," I laughed as I made my way up the stairs and out the door, headed to my next destination.

FOOLISH

I stood in front of the empty lot and chanted the spell that would make the warehouse appear. The dope thing about the house is even when it appears to us, nobody else can see it. So unless you had some magic, this shit didn't exist to you. The ops couldn't bust up in the shit. Shit couldn't get robbed, it was perfect. We did most of our dirt there too. Nobody would ever know. After the warehouse appeared, I pressed the code into the keypad and unlocked the door. As soon as I walked in I noticed some shit had been added to the artillery. Good shit.

I walked through takin' stock of what was new, what was checked out and what I needed. I headed to the library to look through some books for stronger protection spells. Originally, I thought I could trust Sol to be on her own, but that clearly backfired in my face. I knew our security would protect her, but I wanted to be sure. I would only break this shit out if I had to. These spells were heavy duty ass spells. I had gotten them from Marceline, and the rest of the spells came from Dirt and em'. That was the dope thing about it. All of our families intermingled and were close, so there was a little bit of every kinda spell in here. Different variations. I grabbed a couple of books and made my way to the herbs and tinctures. I grabbed a couple of oils and reminded myself I needed to come back here and make some more, just to keep the stock up.

Next, I moved on to the gun room where I collected a couple burners. I know pops had taught Sol how to shoot, but it was evident she needed to brush up on some lessons and I'll be damned if she jammed up my guns. After collecting everything I needed and puttin' it in my backpack, I looked at my watch. I had just enough time to snatch up some food. I had been missin' some good ass creole food. I locked up and made my way into the city. I walked into Café Creole, a dope little hole in the wall spot on Esplanade Ave. This placed had the best food, but if you blinked you'd miss the building. One of my past flings worked here, along with a couple niggas I ran the streets with, so I knew they'd hook some shit up for me.

I peeped shorty behind the counter cleaning up. It was closing time, but I knew that wouldn't matter. Just as expected, without turning around to look at me I heard her voice. "Sorry, we're closed. We open back up at 10am tomorrow," she said in a tired voice. I smiled. Shorty ass was still pokin out just right. Damn.

"So you gon' turn down a hungry soul? That's not right love," I said as I hopped my ass up on the barstool. She stopped what she was doing and whipped her head around.

"12?! Where the hell have you been?!" she screamed as she ran around the counter. She gave me a hug and just touchin' her made my manhood rise. She took a step back and looked at me with a smile.

"Nigga don't just sit there smilin'! What chu want to eat? Derek! Mike! Look who here!" she called for my niggas in the back. They peeped around the corner and came around and dapped me up.

I looked over the menu and decided to get a nice sized order of Jambalaya for me and Sol to share, some fried pickles for her weird ass and some Crawfish Étouffee for me. I made sure they threw in some extra french bread too. After chattin' it up for a little bit, I looked at my watch. I had been gone later than I wanted to, and I needed to be there when Sol woke up. I said my goodbyes to everybody, promisin' I wouldn't stay away this time. I walked around the block and closed my eyes, focusing on the hotel room. When I opened my eyes, I was back standing in the room surrounded by papers from the trunk.

Twin was still fast asleep, mouth open and everything. I looked at my watch and realized it was around 5am and I was too tired to eat. I moved the papers off of my bed and flopped down. The tv was just like I left it on ESPN. Had to keep an eye on them Saints. I laid there watching tv, until I felt my lids getting heavy. I closed my eyes and listened to the sound of my sisters snoring and smiled. I was gonna protect her and Ky at all costs. I had been away too long, and I'll be damned if another living being makes me miss out on another minute with them.

I turned over and looked at her face. She looked so much like Momma, and for the time being she was the closest I would ever get to her. She was beautiful, inside and out, and I made it my mission to keep her that way. I didn't want the life we were living to ruin her like it had ruined me. It fucked with me because I know she thought I was the best thing since sliced bread, but that's because I'm her twin. To her I could do no wrong as far as she was concerned. For people who knew me though, they could tell you some stories that would fuck your head up. I chalked it up to the hand I had been dealt in life.

People don't realize that this magic shit ain't butterflies and candy canes and shit. This shit has the potential to ruin your life. I was happy Momma decided to shield Sol from a lot of it, but she couldn't hide no more. I just didn't want this shit to do her how it had done so many people. Dirt's parents for example, this shit drove them niggas crazy. They blurred the lines too much, couldn't tell what was what and who was who. They were so powerful that even though they didn't want the responsibility much like my sister, it chased them down. That's what it does. You can't hide from it. You can't ignore it, that shit will engulf you. I saw it happen to my mans Legend before he finally accepted it. It'll scar you and turn you into a whole 'nother person.

I wasn't gonna let that shit happen to Sol.

She was gonna jump on board whether she was ready to or not, and I was gonna be there every step of the way.

CHAPTER 11

Sol

I woke up covered in a pile of books, news articles and pictures. Jr and I had started going through the black trunk from Momma and Daddy's attic, but we hadn't found anything mind blowing. We must have fallen asleep while doing it, because Jr. was lying on his bed passed out too. I got up and made my way to the bathroom to wash my face and brush my teeth. I needed coffee and this watered down shit in the room wasn't gonna work. I slid on my Nike slides and went to open the door when Jr's voice scared the shit outta me.

"I'm gonna assume you're taking one of the security guards with you, right? I got you some food by the way." The fact that he phrased it like a question, but really meant it as a demand caused me to roll my eyes so hard I thought they'd get stuck.

"Yes Jr. I'm taking one of the guards." I sighed. Don't get

me wrong. I understood the seriousness of the situation, but where the fuck did he get these security guards from? He must have some pull or some niggas that owe him a favor from somewhere. With him, the possibilities are endless. One thing I've learned is to stop asking him questions, because the answers were usually laughable.

I opened the door to two chocolate security guards standing at attention on either side of my door. I chuckled to myself. I could only imagine how they looked to people walking past the room. I examined them both, deciding which one I was gonna take. I didn't wanna look obvious, so I took the one that was less buff with long dreads. Mmm. Dreads. I don't know where this obsession with dudes with dreads came from, but the universe was def looking out when they created them.

The security guard walked behind me as I made my way down to the lobby of the hotel. After making some real coffee, we made our way back up to the room. I realized I hadn't updated my Snapchat in couple of days, so I pulled out my phone and opened the app. To my surprise, thanks to my front facing camera, I peeped the security card zoomed in on my ass as we walked. I chuckled to myself until I realized how long it had been since I had my back blown out. No wonder I was so grumpy.

We made it to the room and I thanked him for following me. He nodded his head as he looked me up and down before I walked in the room. I made a mental note to get to know him better. I walked in the room to my brother sitting on the floor smoking a blunt, going through the trunk and watching ESPN. Men. I plopped down on my bed, letting the first few sips of coffee wake my body up. I noticed he had separated things into piles. I came over and sat down on the other side of him.

"Find anything interesting?" I inquired as I picked up some of the piles and started going through them. He scratched his head as he looked through some papers.

"Nothing to really jump up and down about. I started to separate everything by dates. There's some shit in here dating all the way back to the 1800's. It looks like Momma or somebody had those older things preserved at some point." I decided to leave what he was doing alone and pull some more stuff out of the trunk.

There was some of everything in this trunk. There was my Momma's, grandma's and her grandmother's Book of Shadows, birth certificates for Jr and I, ritual jewelry, spells, mason jars filled with herbs and more. I was honestly amazed at the condition of all this stuff. Like Jr said, some of the dates on this stuff dated all the way back to the 1800s. There were pictures of my great great grandmother Marceline. She looked like a powerful woman. I shuffled through and organized all of the things I pulled out until I got to the bottom of the trunk. As I went to close it, I noticed that I had missed something. There was something wrapped in what looked like some type of brown paper bag, tied together by some Devil's Shoestring.

I undid the wrapping to find an old, and I do mean old deck of tarot cards. They had to have been special made, because I had never seen a deck like this before. The writing on the cards was of old Kreyol language, and the illustrations were all of black people. I shuffled through the cards in amazement. After looking through them, I unfolded the paper that was attached. It was actually two pieces of paper folded together. The first one was a letter.

To my dearest granddaughter,

If you're reading this letter, I have to assume that your parents are no longer amongst the living and for that I apologize. Please know that I've done everything on my end to prevent that, but your mother is much like me, hard–headed. I also must assume that you've found the trunk that I put away for you, and you've found the tarot deck. I put a spell on the deck so that nobody will be able to untie and use these cards but you and your brother, if you find him in time.

Considering that you've found these things, you must know that the fate of our bloodline lies in your hands. It is your time. Your birth was written about long before your mother and I were even conceived. It will be you who will rid the world of the evil that is the Moreau family and take your rightful place in the lineage of the powerful Dupree women. Lucky you to have your twin brother on your side. He's more powerful than even he realizes. Our magic is a special type of magic, and our family has been hunted for years for it. Our magic dates all the way to the original settling of what is now Haiti. Its been said that it was our magic that defeated the French Colonists during the mighty Haitian Revolution. Because of this, our magic was deemed holy and sacred. You must protect this.

We cannot let this get into the hands of Jaqueline Moreau and her family. Jackie and her two children are the last remaining limbs of their family tree, and if they get our gifts not only will they do greedy and evil things with it, they will then have the power to resurrect their family back from the Ether they've been waiting in. If that were to happen, the world as you know it will never be the same. Jackie and her family will drain the magic from every source on this planet for their own use and kill the ones she takes it from.

No one person should have that much power. Attached is a map of where you can find me. I was banished to another timeline for trying to assist your mother in finding Freddy Jr. I've been stuck here for as long as you have been born, unable to warn you of the danger that lies in front of you. If you find me, I can help you. Should you find Freddy Jr, allow him to be your support. Unbeknownst to your mother, he is alive and well. I've seen him bouncing from timeline to timeline here and there along with the sons of our friends from the Five Sacred Families. Ask your brother to explain that to you. Your mother at some point (I hope, knowing that daughter of mine) should have let you know what gifts you and your siblings possess. If not, Freddy Jr. has the innate gift of using his words. Anything he speaks out of his mouth with intent manifests in record timing. He's able to speak any language. The power of life and death truly lies in his tongue. Your sister, Kyleena has been gifted with all seeing. She can see things before they happen. She can change the outcome of anything just by picturing it in her mind, but she's also prone to nightmares. You my dear, you have all of the gifts of every Dupree woman that has ever existed.

I'm pretty sure Marceline has made herself known to you by now. She can be a lot to digest, but she means well. Listen to her. She will also be around to help guide you.

I know you don't know much about me, and your mother never spoke of me. I don't know if it was out of shame or because she just couldn't live up to the fact that her disobedience caused my banishment. Either or, if you find her on another timeline, tell her I love her, and I don't blame her. It was hard to trust anybody at that time, and I know she felt like she did what she had to do to protect you and your brother.

SAI MECCA

These tarot cards I'm including along with the map of where you can find me will be your guide. I enchanted the archetypes of the cards. They will present themselves in your reality to help guide you to me. Read up on the Major Arcana to help you understand what purpose each of them serves to start and then pay attention to those around you. Once you find them, they are your tribe. DO NOT TRUST ANYONE OUTSIDE OF THESE PEOPLE. No one, and I do mean NO ONE is to be trusted Solelil. These people that are supposed to help you will be unmistakable. Once you find each of the archetypes of the 6 cards I've enchanted, the corresponding card will disappear. You are included in this embodiment of archetypes also. It is up to you figure out what you represent.

Use these people and the map to find me. Once you find me, I will be able to help you further. The rest of the cards I will explain later. DO NOT LOSE THIS DECK SOLELIL. It is your guide. Like previously stated, I'm in New Orleans, but in a different timeline. Your brother will know what I'm talking about. I've hidden different clues for you in different timelines to let you know you're on the right path. I have hidden a Pentacle Coin, a Staff, a Sword and Golden Chalice. They will also help you along your journey. There's so many other things that I want to tell you, but it's not time for you to know them yet. Be the alchemist I know that you are. Give your siblings my love. I love you, and I look forward to seeing you.

With all my love,
Granny Odessa

I finished reading and picked my jaw up off the floor. Jr. was in the corner doing push ups and I came and sat in front of him. "Jr, you will not believe what I just read." He continued doing push ups and looked up at me.

"I was snatched away from ya'll by a psychotic voodoo priestess and I jump timelines, there's not much that shocks a nigga anymore Twin. Try me," he laughed. I read the letter out loud to him. By the time I finished, he was sitting in front of me with a confused look on his face.

"So…we basically just got hooked ALL the way the fuck up by our grandmother," he yelled jumping around the room. "Where's the deck, lemme see it, lemme see it!" he shouted plopping down on my bed. I pulled the deck out and he sorted the cards out, separating the Minor and Major Arcana. He then put the Major Arcana in order and spread them out.

I had to call Mila, Ky and Devon. They had to know this. I grabbed my phone and sent Mila a text to come to my room with the other two. About 5 minutes later, Ky let herself in along with my best friends. Ky rubbed her eyes as she laid down on her bed. "What's so important that you had to drag me out of bed Sol."

I took a look at her and noticed the dark circles and bags under her eyes. "Yo, are you aight? Why you look like that Ky?" She rolled her eyes and sat up.

"I'm fine, I'm just tired. Could you please make your announcement or whatever it is you called us over here for?" she asked waving her hands. I decided to let it go, but I made a mental note to talk to Mila and Devon later about it. I ran the whole situation down to them and watched their eyes bug out of their sockets as they looked at the tarot deck.

"So basically, a bitch is about to go on one of those old timey magic quests huh?" Devon joked. I laughed at his goofy ass.

"I guess so man. Like she laid everything out. The letter

said that she has more to tell me but she wants to do it face to face. So right now, the most important thing is finding her."

Jr. nodded his head. "That AND flying under the radar while you do it. That's gonna be the hard part. If grandma doing what I think she's doing, you're being tested. She's making sure you're strong enough to do this and making sure you can follow directions."

Mila stood with her head cocked to the side. She slowly walked over to the table where the cards were. "You said when the people who are supposed to help you are close, the cards would glow right?" Wondering what was so confusing about what I said that she needed to ask twice, I confirmed. She pulled six cards off of the table and held them up.

We all stood there in amazement staring at the six glowing cards and looked around at each other. "Bitch, I think you found them."

Just like that, my tribe was formed.

Mila held the cards in her hand as we all looked in silence. Even Ky, who was obviously disinterested in what I had to say a few minutes ago, had even perked up and was now at full attention. Mila looked frozen in place as I slowly walked over to her. As I got closer, one of the cards started to glow even brighter. The amber colored glow intensified as I waved my hand in front of it. I pulled the card out of her hand and read it aloud to myself. "The Fool".

As soon as I read the marking on the card, it disappeared out of my hand. I gasped and jumped back, not expecting that. Twin sat in the desk by the window, chuckling. "Well, that makes sense." I had no clue what he was talking about.

FOOLISH

By this point, Ky and Devon were standing around Mila also. Two more of the cards began to glow brighter.

I was hella anxious to know who went with what card. "Ky, you next." Ky looked at me and walked over closer to Mila. She did what I had done before, and waved her hand in front of the cards. She pulled out the card that lit up the brightest.

The Empress.

Just as before, once she read it out loud, the card vanished. She slowly sat her ass back on the bed, looking puzzled. Devon stepped up next and did what the rest of us did. He chose his card and read it out loud.

"The Hermit." He announced. Again, another head shake and chuckle from Jr.

Jr. stepped up and waved his hand in front of the cards. "Go figure," he chuckled. I didn't get a chance to see what his card said. He turned to walk back to the desk. "The Magician," he laughed as he sat back down. Mila did what we had all done before. She picked the card out and half chuckled and half gasped before she read her card. She lifted up her sleeve to show a tattoo on her forearm. It was a picture of a girl holding a scroll and a skull.

"Alta Sacerdotisa," she whispered. "The High Priestess," she smiled. Even though all of us had chosen cards, there was still one card glowing. We all looked at the card, confused as to why there was one left.

Devon stood up and broke the silence. "So you mean we have to invite some stranger ass ho into our tribe? Sol you know I don't like new bitches."

I couldn't hold my giggle and busted out laughing. "And you think I want some stranger ho in my business?" I retorted.

Mila did that head tilt thing she was famous for. More often than not that meant she was either thinking or had just came to a conclusion.

"What you got in mind Mila," Jr asked before I could get the words through my lips. I looked at him and squinted. I didn't wanna witness any of that lovey dovey 'I can read your mind, I know what you're thinkin' Avant ass shit in my presence. He looked back and me and smirked.

Ho ass.

Like a lightbulb exploded in her head, Mila got mad excited. "Sol, come here. Walk over here and wave your hand in front of the card. I did what she told me to, and the card lit up brighter. How the hell did I have two cards? I know I say there are several version of me, but damn. She told me to step back across the room as she called Jr. over. He walked over and waved his hand in front of the card and it did the same.

"I knew it," Mila laughed. I looked around the room, glad I wasn't the only one confused at this point. All of a sudden, Devon's face lit up. "The Lovers card! The Twins! Its yall dummies!!" Me and Jr. both looked at each other. "That's not what I would interpret that card as, but ok. I'll take it." Jr. laughed. Ky sighed in the background.

"The Lovers isn't just about sex and romance and shit. Y'all need to read. For us to be a family of fuckin oracles and shamans y'all really don't know shit. The Lovers card can also represent something that can make you feel a sense of completion. Balance. Something that you have like a magnetic pull to. Oh I don't know, souls? The other half of you maybe? Twins?" Kyleena waited for us to make the connection.

"Reading is fundamental y'all. Seriously," she said as she plopped back on the bed. We all sat down and passed a blunt around to take in what had just been made clear to us. Jr. was dead on when he said that these people are my tribe. It made me excited to want to know about the rest of the cards. I wrapped the cards back up and Jr. and I put the stuff back in the trunk. I took the letter and the map and tucked them in my purse.

For whatever reason, I felt so much safer knowing these crazy niggas were sent to me for a reason. It felt like a weight lifted off of my shoulders knowing that I didn't have to go through this shit alone. I thought about my life before all of this happened. How carefree I was living in Brooklyn, doing what felt right to me. The whole time, the universe was setting all of this up. That's when the thought hit me. I hadn't felt carefree in weeks. I hadn't painted. I hadn't sang a note to not one song. I hadn't danced. I need to let some of this stress melt off.

We needed a night out.

Before I could even utter the words, Jr. looked at me and nodded his head in agreement. "What you got in mind stank," he asked scrolling through his phone. Everybody in the room looked at us in confusion.

"Yall, we need to get out and relieve some stress. I know we're these "shamans and oracles" but damn it I'm still a damn human with needs, and I needs to shake my ass. A bitch all bound up, and up tight and shit. Let's go out tonight. We haven't been out in Fayetteville together in FOREVER." I stressed.

Devon open the door to the bathroom and poked his head out. "Bitch I'm down. All this shit got me ready to shake a couple tail feathers," he yelled as he flipped his imaginary ass hair. We all busted out laughing.

"Mila, Ky, y'all down? You know y'all can't say no to me," I teased as I twerked on the both of them as they sat beside each other on the bed.

Even though she didn't want to, I got Ky to laugh. "Uggh ok I'll go as long as you get your overly juicy ass off of me, shit." She giggled.

I moved on to Mila, still shaking my ass in her face. "Girl do you forget where we work at? I see asses every night and yours is one of em, that shit don't phase me no more. You know I'm going. We strippers bitch, us not shakin' our asses is like a talent that you don't use, and you know what they say." We laughed together.

Jr. was waiting for the rest of the sentence. "Well? What the hell do they say? I know whoever 'they' are didn't just laugh, if so that was a sorry ass punch line," he added as he rolled up another blunt. Mila and I looked at each other as we walked over to him. "IF YOU DON'T USE IT YOU LOSE ITTTTTT!" We screamed as we danced all over him.

We all agreed to get dressed and meet down in the lobby. As per usual, Devon was the last downstairs. "I will never understand how he started getting dressed before everybody but was the last person ready," Mila murmured as she rolled her eyes.

Devon came and squeezed in between Mila and I. "Because bitch, when you're beautiful like this shit takes time," he said rolling his eyes at Mila.

Jr. was by the window, dressed in all black like we were about to run up in somebody shit. Leave it to him to want to blend in. Old habits die hard I guess. The adrenaline was pumping through my body the way it did right before I get on stage. I hadn't been out in so long. I didn't know when or if I would get the chance to again, so I had to make tonight epic. I checked my reflection in the large mirror they had in the lobby of the hotel to make sure everything was in place.

I was workin' the SHIT outta my outfit. I had on a red lace body suit with the back open, and a long black skirt that had high splits that traveled the length of my legs on both sides showing my thick thighs. On my feet were a pair of red, peep toe satin tie up pumps that housed my blood red pedicure. My highlight was blindin' anybody that dared to stare at me too long and on my lips, sat the color Crawfish from the Crayon Box line by Supa. My hair was in the perfect bouffant, with half of my hair down in the back. I was determined to wreck somebody's son tonight.

We all decided to pile into Devon's truck and get our night started. We rode around for a little bit because we had left early. We cruised around Fayetteville with the windows down enjoying the warm weather that had started to creep up. With the windows down, music up and blunts being passed around, I felt like myself again. We laughed until we couldn't breathe talking about old times where me, Devon and Mila would do this every weekend. We had some of the best times together, even if one of us got too fucked up leaving the other two holding their hair, face down in the toilet at the end of the night.

We pulled up to this little hole in the wall spot that was literally in the woods. Everybody in the car looked around at each other trying to figure out where the hell we were.

Devon hopped out of the truck, waiting for us to join him.

"Why y'all sittin' there like bumps on a log? Come on."

Still none of us moved. Devon sighed. "Stop being so scary. I used to frequent this lil spot back in the day. It's a cute lil reggae club, music is on ten and the drinks will fuck your soul up." I'm not gonna fake like I didn't get excited when I heard it's a reggae spot. I had unknowingly dressed perfectly for the occasion. I said "fuck it" and hopped out of the truck. As Devon and I walked up to the door, I heard the click clack of heels behind me from Mila and Ky.

As we walked in the small, smoke filled building I automatically felt my body loosen up. I could fuck with this. All you saw in every inch of the place was sweaty bodies grinding to the beat of the music. The bass was thumpin' so hard I felt that shit in my soul. The DJ had just started to mix "Romie" by Beenie Man and "Action" by Terror Fabulous and Nadine Sutherland. Even if you didn't know shit about Reggae, you at least knew those songs when you heard them. We walked over to the bar and ordered a round of double shots of Patron We all toasted, took our shots to the head and headed to the dance floor. I don't know what it is about "Romie", but that song puts me in my element every damn time.

I started to move my hips along with the bass line. Devon took my hand as we started to dance together. I didn't realize Devon was such a good dancer, he kept up with me better than anybody I had ever danced with. We were having a ball, laughing and acting a fool when I saw a familiar face tucked away in the corner. These eyes had been on me ever since we stepped on the dance floor, but I had only just realized who it was. The bodyguard from earlier today.

He wasn't dressed in uniform, so I assumed he was just

here for a good time like I was. He was surrounded by a group of niggas passing three blunts around, but his eyes stayed on me. After a while, I got so caught up in the music, he slipped outta my mind. The next time I looked over, he was no longer there. I started to get tired, so I copped a seat where I could still see the dance floor. Jr and Mila were laughing and dancing together, and Ky had taken my place and started dancing with Devon. I smiled. Everybody looked like they were having so much fun. Hell, I was just happy we didn't look like what we had been through these past couple of weeks.

I was glad we came out. That's one thing I didn't want to get caught up in. I feel like some people get so caught up in the Ether, they don't remember that even though we may be souls having a human experience, that doesn't mean we can't take time out to have fun. I've met people where all they wanted to talk about was spirituality and magic. Like sis, come back down to this plane real quick. Take a shot. Shut the fuck up. I was glad my tribe, to this day, knows how to let our hair down.

My thoughts were interrupted by someone pulling out a chair at the table I was sitting. I was about to start kirkin, but I realized it was Mr. Security Guard with The Dreads. He smiled at me and gave me the universal "nigga nod". I waved back at him.

He scooted closer to my chair and yelled over the music. "Whatchu doin' here unattended? You good?" I pointed at my brother on the dance floor with Mila. He nodded his head ok. "You need a drink or anything? You good?" I held up my water bottle. He started to get the hint and laughed.

He got up from his chair and started to walk away until

he suddenly stopped and turned around. "I'm not tryna be disrespectful and cross any line or anything because I know I work for your brother. But ma...you are murdering that outfit. I had to stop myself several times earlier from snatchin' you off the dance floor. Would you mind dancing with me? You think your brother would mind?"

I chuckled to myself. I actually didn't know whether he would or not, but part of me didn't care. He may have hired him, but he was off the clock. To his surprise, I stood up and walk toward the dance floor. He followed with a shocked look his face. "Fever" by Vybz Kartel started booming through the building as I started to grind against him to the beat. As he grinded back, I swear my blood pressure shot up through the roof. It didn't help that he smelled amazing. He spun me around and suddenly we were face to face. There's something to be said about a man who looks good in and out of his uniform. He looked me in my eyes for several seconds without even blinking. Its like he was trying to peer into my soul.

I don't know if was the alcohol or the fact that nobody had parted these thighs in weeks, but every time he touched me he sent shockwaves through my body. Even him just looking sent a chill up my spine. As I turned around to continue dancing, my eyes immediately met Jr's. He was damn near staring a hole in me while sitting at the table I had just gotten up from with the rest of the tribe.

"Sol, don't make me grip ol' boy up for mixing business with pleasure." I heard his voice echo in my mind. Ignoring him, I took a hit of the blunt Mr. Dreads was passing to me. After a couple hits, I felt like I was floating.

After dancing a couple of songs with him, I took his

phone out of his pocket and put my number in it. "Going so soon?" he asked, looking like a sad puppy. I told him my friends were ready to go. "I guess I'll see you tomorrow then, right?" he perked up. These dudes don't waste no time these days.

"Tomorrow?" I questioned, ready to come up with a whole slew of excuses on why I could see him.

He chuckled. "Yea, I'll be waiting for you by your door, standing beside that big beefy nigga for 10 hours." He joked. Damn. Just that quick I had forgotten that he worked for my brother.

I smiled and turned around on my heels and walked out of the club with the tribe in tow.

~~ * ~~

Back in the hotel room, Jr didn't seem phased at all. As soon as we got in, he hopped on his game and really tuned me out unless I spoke to him first. Men and their game systems. It wasn't until he got hungry that he decided to be a chatter box.

"Man my stomach is screamin' right now," he said, alcohol speaking through him.

"Well, the only thing open right now is Waffle House and Denny's." I replied. He started getting up and putting his shoes on. When he bent over, I saw the chrome handle of his gun sticking out from underneath his shirt. I hadn't noticed that before.

"I had to pick up a lil somethin'. You know, some extra protection. Can't be too cautious." He mentioned, a serious look on his face. In the same moment, a smile slide across his face. "You up for a late night dinner date dear sister?" he asked as he held his hand out for me to grab. He pulled me up off the bed and I put my Nike ACG's on and followed him out of the door. We got downstairs and hopped in Mila's rental. As we put our seatbelts on, I gave him a look.

"She knows man, chill." He laughed.

Just like the other night, he took the beeper looking contraption out of his pocket and pressed a button. Closing his eyes, he mumbled a couple of words and I felt that energy suction that I did before. It felt like all of the energy was draining out of my body. As he stuck it back in his pocket, I had to know what the hell that was.

"What in the 90s dope boy hell is that thing?" I asked laughing.

He chuckled. "It's an energy protectant. It drains a little bit of your energy out and reads it as like, one of those finger ID's you see in movies. It protects whatever space we're in as long as I have it on me. It also vibrates when there's questionable energy around that doesn't belong to either one of us. I copped it from a future timeline. They got some dope shit in the works."

I shook my head at him and laughed. We pulled up to the Waffle House and grabbed a table. The waitress grabbed our drinks and orders, and we chatted it up. "So what was up with you and Legend at the club?" he asked, changing the topic from what we were talking about.

"Legend? Who the hell is Legend?" I questioned him, honestly not knowing what the hell he was talking about.

He squinted his eyes at me. "The nigga I hired to protect your ass, not so literally." I squirmed around in my chair. Legend. Jr. noticed the look on my face and looked disgusted.

"You know what, I don't even wanna know. Just know

like I said, business and pleasure don't always mix. You grown. I can't tell you who to deal with, but don't get him distracted." Jr. warned.

That went better than I thought it would. Let me find out my twin wasn't a cock blocker. "So since you hired him, what do you know about him?" I grilled him.

He took a sip of his water and cleared his throat. "I know him from way back. He a aight dude. Really don't know much about him but I know he'll fuck some shit up if need be and that's all I'm really concerned about."

I rolled my eyes. I felt like he was holdin' out. "How the hell did you hire somebody to protect your little sister but don't know shit about him Jr.? That sounds real responsible big bro." I joked.

He shrugged. Our food came to the table and for the better part of five minutes we stuffed our faces before continuing to talk. I was getting full too quickly, so I broke the silence. "So now that we have the tribe and the map, where do you suggest we start at?" I asked him.

He finished chewing and took another sip of his water before answering. "We're gonna have to retrace some steps. Do some timeline jumping. Before we do that though, we need to make sure everybody is on the same page. You timeline jump differently than I do, you can't really control it. I can. Everybody's mind needs to be right before we go hoppin in other dimensions. Speakin' of minds, you check out Ky? What's going on with her?"

To be honest, I had been racking my mind tryna figure out what's going on with her. I would have thought her mood woulda changed by now. Whatever it was, she only showed her aggression toward me. She even went as far as getting her own hotel room. I shook my head. "I don't know man. She's never really acted like this before." I told him.

He lifted an eyebrow. "Do you know that for sure or did you just not pay attention when yall were younger?" he proposed.

I thought back to how much I really shrugged Ky off as a child. It wasn't purposely, but hell I was going through my own magical craziness. Like she said before, she used to think I was bat shit crazy until she went off to college, so as far as I know she didn't believe me up until all this shit happened.

Twin broke my train of thought. "If you're gonna be the HBIC you really need to start paying attention more," he shook his head and took another bite of his sandwhich. Confused as to what that had to do with anything, I waited for him to continue. "I think she got some side shit goin' on, personally. Think about it. She changed rooms. That screams privacy... which screams sneaky shit. She's tired all the time, which could mean a couple different things like energy drainage...which could come from being around energy vampires aka lower vibrational beings...and last but definitely not least," he uttered, "hatred of yo' ass at the moment. She's jealous."

I took a sip of my fruit punch and tried to stomach what he said. I mean in all realness, it made sense even if I didn't want to admit it. What I couldn't understand though is why she would she be jealous? I didn't give myself these gifts nor did I put myself in charge. I'm on the same path everybody else is on. Shit. Twin shook his head as he put a huge piece of waffle in his mouth.

"No, you are not on the path that everybody else is on. You're making the path, that in itself puts you on a whole different threshold. Yea, you got some powerful niggas in your tribe, dare I say the strongest of this current generation but this is all up to you lil sis. You were chosen. In essence, you are in charge." He replied to my thoughts out loud.

"So me being chosen means I have to deal with being hated?" I questioned.

Twin laughed hard and loud as hell. "Uh, yea! The fuck kinda question is that? Think about it. Before you caught your glow up, was anybody hatin on you? Your ass was a recluse in high school outside of Devon and Mila. You ain't have no haters. I know, I was watching. What happened when you moved to Brooklyn and started making guap? Your ass was beatin the shit outta somebody every other night because those bitches was mad at you. Those are what we call haters. You usually don't have them until you're doing some shit that they wish they could do."

He was right, but Ky was the last person I wanted hating me. That was my blood. When it came down to it, she's one of the only people I got. I really needed to talk to her. Jr. got up to pay the ticket for our food. Standing above me, he kissed me on the forehead.

"Sometimes, the people that you think have your back are the very ones plottin your take down. Let her come to you." He winked as he walked up to the register. What the fuck does that even mean? I was honestly too tired to think about it.

We pulled up at the hotel and I was more than ready to wobble my tired ass into the bed. I went to get out of the car and the beeper in Jr's pocket started blaring this annoying ass noise. He pulled it out his pocket and it was glaring red.

"Fuck," he muttered. Before I could ask him what's going

on, he told me to stay put. He got out of the car and walked around to my side and stood in front of my door.

I tried to listen to what he was saying but it was really muffled so I gave up. About two seconds later, Mila and Devon came walking down and got in the car. Confused, I needed some answers, and now. I was tired, cranky and ready to scream if I didn't find some sleep.

"Um, what are yall doing?" I asked them looking in the rearview. Devon's face was planted against the door and Mila was in the middle of a deep yawn.

"Bitch, I don't know. Your security guards came banging on our door telling us that Jr. wants us to evacuate the hotel and to come down to the car. I'm too tired to ask questions," Devon said, now also in the middle of a yawn. I attempted to open the car door just for Jr. to slam it back closed with his foot. He turned around and gave me a look.

About a minute later, he got back in the car. "Where's Ky?" he quizzed.

Mila of course answered. "We don't know, security said she wasn't in her room. They said she left a little while after yall went to Waffle House. Thanks for asking me by the way, because you know, I didn't want anything to soak up all this liquor or anything." She teased.

Jr. shook his head. Reading his thoughts, his mind was bouncing all over the place trying to figure out where Ky could be. He turned the car back on, and two security trucks pulled around. One went in front of us, while the other waited for us to pull out in order to follow us. I snickered. I felt all presidential and shit. Twin looked at me and rolled his eyes. We drove for about ten minutes before everybody pulled off to the side of the road and threw their hazard lights on.

FOOLISH

Twin got out and was met by the whole security team, Legend included. I spotted his sexy ass as soon as he hopped out of the truck. I wondered what he was doing here seeing as though I had just saw him at the club. He had a serious look on his face as he listened to my brother giving him orders. Once everything was understood, everybody hopped back in and pulled back on to the road. Twin got back in and immediately pulled his gun that was tucked in the back of his pants. He turned to me, holding it out for me to grab.

"I need everybody to listen to me, and listen to me very well. Solelil, you're being tracked, like a muthafucka right now. The only thing that is stopping whoever the fuck this could be is the fact that they keep picking up my energy near you." He grabbed my hand before he continued. "I know you're hurting and I know giving Momma and Daddy a proper burial is important to you, but right now, the best thing I can tell you is to schedule a memorial service for this Friday because I'm sending you back to Brooklyn until I tell you to come back."

I looked at him in disbelief. It was Wednesday morning. How in the fuck was I supposed to plan a Memorial Service in less than forty–eight hours?

He rubbed his beard. "We will figure it out. Hop on social media later and make a post about it. It'll get passed around. Devon, Mila I'm sending y'all with her for comfort and I'm sending security with you too. None of y'all and I mean NOBODY is to go ANYWHERE without security. That means to work, to the bodega...nothing. If your body is there, security needs to be with you. Don't tell nobody shit, and if Security gives you directions don't question it because it's coming from me. Got it?"

I nodded my head trying to soak up everything he had just said. Who the fuck or what the fuck I should say, was tracking me? "Wait a minute, where the fuck are you gonna be?" I questioned him. I hope he didn't think I didn't notice him not including himself in these plans. He busted a left and pulled up at the Extended Stay on Owen Drive.

"I got some shit to check out, so I'll be jumping but im not gonna start until yall leave. We're gonna stay here for the next couple of nights until the service is over and I get y'all a flight outta here. We'll talk some more tomorrow, right now everybody needs some sleep.", he assured us. A security guard tapped on his window, letting him know he had booked two rooms and they were locked, loaded and ready to go. He slid the keys in the window and Jr passed one to Mila.

"Mila and Devon, y'all will be sharing a room, I gotta stay with Sol," he mentioned as I looked at the disappointment on Mila's face. I know her too well. She was really hoping that somehow, they would get stuck in the same room.

I couldn't contain myself. "Ugh bitch please stop. He can blow your back out another time but right now he has a twin to protect, please fix your face," she busted out laughing as she punched me in the shoulder.

We got settled in the rooms and before long I couldn't hold my questions any longer. I knew it was about 3am and I needed to get some sleep, but my mind wouldn't shut the fuck up with questions. Before I got the chance to ask them, there was a knock at the door. Twin pulled the door open and stepped outside. I listened through the crack.

"Yo boss, there's some dude out here named Andre that said he needs to holla at you." The security guard tried

FOOLISH

horribly to whisper. I rolled my eyes so hard I think I saw the back of my skull. Twin instructed the guard to let him in.

Andre stepped in the room, looking horrible. Before I could hurl any insults, he spoke.

"We need to talk. It's about Kyleena."

CHAPTER 12

My heart stopped, or at least it felt like it did.

Jr. stood with his arms crossed in front of Andre. "You have a lot of balls showing your face here right now. Matter of fact, how the fuck did you know where we were huh?" Jr. took a step closer to Andre. Andre looked like he was un–phased by the fact that he just walked into the lion's den. He either didn't realize or didn't care that Jr. was prepared to rip his head off at any given moment. Whatever he had to say better be important.

"I just told you I had something to tell you about our sister and you ready to peel my scalp back. Dude, you really need some anger management and fuckin focus." Andre stammered.

Jr. glared at him. "Our sister? Nah nigga. That's my sister. Say what the fuck you got to say before I beat your ass into another timeline."

Andre sat on the edge of the unoccupied bed and cleared his throat. "I know y'all noticed Kyleena has been acting kinda weird lately, and I know y'all have been being tracked.

I also know y'all think that I have something to do with it, but I'm telling you right now I don't. I don't even know where Jackie is right now." He stuttered. He turned and faced me. "Look Sol, I know you think you can't trust me, and you have every reason not to. I know I lied about a lot of things, but even Luna said that I can be trusted until I prove otherwise. I realize what my mother did was wrong, really wrong. I'm here trying to make it right. Y'all don't have to tell me any plans or details, but I want you to know that I'm here to help. I'm not playing sides."

I stared a hole into his face, trying to resist the urge to hop over the bed and strangle the shit outta him. At this point, I didn't give a fuck what my Momma said, Andre and trust didn't belong in the same sentence.

"And what the hell would make you think just because my Momma co–signed you brings me any comfort? She co–signed your Momma and look at what the hell that got us. Nigga, the best thing you could do is tell me what you need to tell me about my sister and hope that Jr. keeps his finger off the trigger," I shouted.

Andre ran his hand over his face. "So, I think Jackie has gotten her hooks in her. She's been keeping in contact with me, and she's been acting really strange, being really secretive. I don't know what happened between y'all, but one thing she made sure of was to let me know how much she's really not fuckin with you right now. If we–" Twin raised his eyebrow.

"If y'all don't figure it out and catch up to her before Jackie really goes in for the kill, you're gonna lose her for good and Jackie doesn't do give backs." I looked over at Jr. He had this real convenient way of making it so I can't read his thoughts sometimes, so I had no idea what he was thinking. He started to pace in front of the door.

"So if what you're saying is true, why the hell would Ky switch up like that? Especially with somebody that is responsible for the death of our parents? As loyal as Ky is that just doesn't make sense," Jr. stated as he turned in my direction. I didn't have any answers. My mind was just as blown as everyone else's. Andre walked over to the window and stood looking out of it, like he was searching for an answer that I'm pretty sure he already had.

"The only thing I can think of is she promised her something, she dangled something of importance in front of her and she bit. I just don't know what that could be. You have to think also, she doesn't know what you and Jr know," He replied.

I rolled my eyes. "You know your momma better than anybody Andre. Don't feed us that 'I don't know' shit." I yelled. Before I could stop myself, I was on my feet and headed in his direction. The next thing I know, I have him pinned down on the bed with a gun pressed to his cheek with somebody banging on our hotel room door.

I had about enough. I was at the boiling point. Andre knew more than he was letting on and I knew it. You don't live around someone for 16 years of your life and not know the ins and outs of them. Twin opened the door and stepped out to see who was banging. Mila and Devon ran in and closed the door. Before it closed, I could see the security ready to ride with a signal from Jr. Jr. knocked on the window to tell them to stand down.

"Sol, Dios mio... pero qué coño?! Have you lost your mind?!" Mila screamed. As she tried to position her body in between me and Andre, I gave her a look.

"Mila, I love you with my soul, but move. Now." I quietly demanded, not taking my eyes off of Andre. Catching the hint, she slid from in between us but stayed close. I looked at Jr. who stood not too far away arms crossed, smirking playing with a toothpick hanging out of his mouth. I cocked the gun back and placed it back on Andre's cheek.

"Now, I shot you before just to scare you. You keep fuckin' with me your momma will be searching for your soul for eternity. I am NOT the same Sol you knew. What the fuck is going on with my sister?! If I even think you're lying I'll blow a fuckin hole right through your face. Try me nigga," Andre's eyes were as big as golf balls and he was sweating like a ho in a church house.

I raised my eyebrow waiting for him to speak. "Andre, don't make me wait," I warned him.

Stuttering, he finally started to talk. "Your parents. She told her she knew where your parents are and if she told them what y'all were up to she would bring them back. She's been telling her everything, she even knows that Jr. is back. That's how Jackie has been able to track your movement." I looked over at my brother who was staring off into space. All I heard from Devon and Mila were "oh my god's" and deep sighs.

"What makes you think he's telling the truth though Sol? This could just be a ploy to through you off. Think about it," Devon commented.

He had a point. I couldn't see my sister doing that, but it would explain why she's been acting so out of character. I had to consider all options, because either way we were kinda fucked.

Jr. spoke up. "He's telling the truth. The real question

is..." he damn near whispered as he walked over to the bed I had

Andre pinned down on, "what is his real motive? Why are you tellin' us this shit? You know just as well as I do if Jackie knew you were flip floppin your ass would be a mere memory. So what's your angle?"

Andre looked up at Jr. as he stood over the bed. "You're right. I do have an angle. The magic in the Moreau bloodline is supposed to belong to me. I'm supposed to be the chosen one in this family. She knows that once you all take your power back, she'll die because the only magic she has left is the immortality she stole from Marceline. When she dies, I'm supposed to be her successor. Word on the street is she's giving it to my brother, Amir. I want what's mine, I want my throne. I want to take them both down. If I have to use her enemy to do it, so be it."

Fifty million thoughts ran through my head. It's like the deeper we dug, the more complicated shit got. As much as I still didn't trust him, I kinda felt bad for Dre. He lived his life as a fuckin pawn for everybody's game. I knew how I felt to not be taken seriously. I sat the gun on the table by the bed and lit a cigarette.

"Jr, game plan?" I asked, hoping he had come up with something.

Jr. helped Andre up off the bed, grabbed a chair and sat in front of him. "I'm not gon' go as far as to say I trust you, but I understand you nigga. I do have to say thank you for tellin' us about Ky because you didn't have to."

Andre nodded his head. "Look, I know y'all think I'm a piece of shit, and I can be but I didn't want none of this to happen. I was taken against my will just like Jr. was."

FOOLISH

He turned to look at me. "I begged Luna to let me go, if she woulda let me go I woulda brought Jr. back, I swear I would have. Luna was too afraid of what might happen. She didn't want to put you in danger after already losing another child."

My bitch ass eyes started to tear up as I felt Mila wrap her arms around me to console me. Deep down inside, I knew Andre was telling the truth. I knew my anger toward him was misplaced, it was really myself I was mad at. Even though I knew things had turned out the way they did because of fate, I still couldn't help but think had I known sooner I could've saved my parents.

The sucky part of that realization was intuitively, I had known all along. I just wasn't payin' attention. I didn't want to. I didn't want to accept this gift and anything that came with it, so I ran from it. I'm not going to say I knew my parents were gonna die, or that I knew any of the history of my family. What I did know is me having these gifts was no mistake, and I had been using them for my selfish wants for years. The reason I stayed with money? Magic. Sex magic. Glamour magic. Its not hard to be poppin' when you have magic on your side.

Just looking at me with plain eyes, you'd never know that with a simple flip of my hair I could make you give me whatever I wanted. Niggas thought my pussy was just A1 but it wasn't just that. My pussy casts spells. Simp ass niggas can't help but to give me what I want after a taste. They didn't understand why as badly as I treated them they just couldn't refuse me. These hoity–toity white men didn't understand why they felt the strong urge to throw me the equivalent of their mortgage payment night after night as I slid up and down the pole, really doing the bare minimum.

Now it was time for me to use my gifts for a purpose. I had to find Odessa. I had to harness and save my families magic and take down the Moreau's, or we all would be fucked. We all sat in silence trying to figure out how we could use Andre to our advantage. Devon spoke up first.

"Why don't we just let him in, try him out. If shit gets back to Jackie, we know who it came from. Have security with him at all times," he suggested.

Jr. rubbed his chin. "The only thing wrong with that is he's gonna have to still play it smooth with Jackie. If she suspects anything, there goes our mole. If he pop up in a timeline with security she gon' know something is up. We're gonna need something only traceable by the people in this room. Some type of magic I don't know nothing about."

Mila chuckled as she walked over to Andre. "Jr, I really can't believe you sleep on me the way you do. And to think you're the one who taught me Mole Magic."

Jr. looked confused. "Girl what are you talkin' about? I mean, I taught you some things, I taught you a lot of things–" he smirked, "but I don't remember nothin' called Mole Magic." I wanted throw up in my mouth. This nigga had the nastiest mind ever in life.

Mila rolled her eyes as she turned to face Andre. She took her blade out of her bra and pricked his finger with it. She took her finger and pressed it into the blood that had formed on his fingertip. "Now, I need you to take your shirt off and take a deep breath, this is only gonna sting a little," she instructed Andre as she smirked. Such a bitch. Even I knew that whatever she was about to was gonna hurt more than a damn little sting.

FOOLISH

Andre took his shirt off and started taking slow breaths as Mila drew a sigil on his chest with the blood. She went over the sigil a second time, this time chanting and whispering with her eyes closed.

When she was done, she stepped back. Andre look scared and mad confused. "I thought you said it was gonna sting a little." He retorted.

Mila chuckled. "Don't worry, give it a second."

Devon leaned over and whispered in my ear. "So he does know this shit about to hurt right? Like he has to know that," he commented as we both chuckled. Andre started to look a little worried.

"Nah Mila, why they laughin though?" he asked. Before Mila had the chance to answer, the sigil that Mila drew started to glow a bright red.

Andre looked down at his chest as the smell of burning flesh filled the room. Andre started to scream as the sigil burned a branding like mark into his skin. Almost like it had never happened, the sigil disappeared. Andre stared at his chest then back at Mila.

"Mila man, what the fuck was that?!" he screamed as the rest of us laughed so hard I thought we were all gonna piss on ourselves.

Jr. answered for her. "Mole magic. Now anywhere you go, we have access to your thoughts. We'll know where you are, what you're doing...who you're talking to. We'll be able to hear your conversations. Its like a magic wire tap."

Mila looked at him and smiled. "I knew you'd remember." I looked back and forth between them. Jr. rolled his eyes at me because he knew I wanted the story behind that comment. "Your friend has trust issues. I'll leave it at that," he replied.

Andre put his shirt back on. "So does this mean I'm one of y'all now?"

Jr. looked at him with a raised eyebrow. "Nigga what do you think this is, Captain Planet? The Power Rangers? You not one of shit. You just helpin', so don't get comfortable and forget that shit. We only workin' together for one common goal and that's to take your ho ass Momma down. We not friends nigga." Andre nodded.

Jr. got up and started pacing. "Aight, so check this out. Andre I'ma fill you in on some shit. I'ma send the three amigos back to Brooklyn this weekend after the Memorial service. Speaking of the service, you need to be there to show face. Act normal, we don't need nobody askin' questions. If they do, tell them as part of the investigation you can't tell them shit. You also need to convince Jackie to let Ky come to the funeral. We need this as normal as possible. You think she'll let her?"

Andre thought before he spoke. "I doubt she wanna blow her spot so I don't see why not, but she'll probably have some of her guys watchin' her in case one of yall try and snatch her."

Jr. rubbed his chin hair. "Nah, I'ma let her think she can have her for the moment. Let her think we don't know shit. Anyway, make that happen." Andre nodded in agreement. Jr. looked at me before he continued talking. "You think you ready for this? Can you really handle this shit sis? I mean if I need to stay out there in Brooklyn with you for a couple days—" I interrupted him by putting my hand up. I know I needed to handle this on my own. I knew he couldn't be around me all day every day, so I needed to go ahead and get used to it.

FOOLISH

He kissed me on top of the forehead. "That's my girl" he smiled as he dapped me up. "So like I was saying, I'ma send them back to Brooklyn. Make it look like life is going on as normal. Dre, you gon' stay here in Fayetteville and make sure shit don't get outta line here. Also, you'll be the contact for the Detective handling their case. We don't need them because we know that this shit is far above the law, but just make them think they're doing something."

He turned to look at Mila, Devon and me. "Y'all, when you get back to Brooklyn, it's life as usual. Go back to work. Do the shit you normally would do, just with security. Devon, you're just a friend visiting them if anybody asks you. Nothing more, nothing less. We'll have a more formal meeting about this after the memorial service, because I wasn't expecting all this shit tonight and I need some time to sort some shit out in my head."

We all looked around at each other in silence. Even though none of us were talking, you could sense all of our minds were racing. We were officially at war and there was no turning back now. Our name and our magic had to be protected, no matter what. It made me hella mad that we were in this repetitive cycle of black people having to protect what's ours. It seems like on this plane we have to protect our very existence and identity, and in the Ether, it was no different.

Our magic is what gets us through, ya know? I can't imagine growing up not having it. It protected me. It guided me. It understood me damn sure better than I understood myself. Don't get it fucked up, magic isn't just about spells and being able to do mad dope shit with your mind. Magic lies in the ability to create when you feel stifled. Its in the bars rappers spit, the notes singers sing...the ill ass paintings artists dream up. Its in my body as I twirl and snake around on stage. My magic isn't no different than anybody else's.

Jr. cleared his throat as he sat there wide eyed. "Uh, yall are dismissed. A nigga needs his handsome rest. Can't be out here wit baggy eyes and shit. Andre, call Sol's phone in the morning and I'll have her give you details about the service."

Andre, Devon and Mila dragged their tired bodies to the door, but Andre stopped before he got there. He turned around and pulled me into a hug. I wasn't quite sure how to take it, but for once in my life instead of being a bitch I returned it. As he pulled away, he whispered "I love you" and made his exit.

Too tired for conversation, I turned off the lights and let the glow from the tv light up the room. I opened up Facebook to make a post regarding Momma and Daddy's service. The nutty ass events of the day did the Running Man through my mind on repeat, it felt like. I just wanted things to go back to the way they were, but I knew better. I was always saving everybody, and this was no different. Now my sister was added into the mix. I save everybody, but is anybody ever gonna save me?

"I'll save you. I've always saved you. As long as I'm breathing, you're safe. I love you Solelil, now close your eyes and get some sleep." Jr. spoke softly as he stared into the tv, watching highlights from the Saints game.

The last thing I remember seeing before I closed my eyes was the red tip of my brother's blunt before I slipped into sleep.

~~ * ~~

FOOLISH

I woke up to the sound of Jr. rappin', echoing through the room from the bathroom. Steam floated from under the door, and the smell of fresh man came along with it. Thank god the sink was on the outside of the bathroom because my breath was hollerin' and I needed to brush my teeth. As I walked past the table, there was a breakfast platter with a bow and the words "Other Half" written on it with a freshly rolled blunt sitting on top. I smiled at how thoughtful my brother was. In just these few short weeks, he had learned more about me than anyone I know just by paying attention.

"Well thank you for giving me credit for paying attention, but girl that's 27 years of watching your ass. I know your hungry ass ready to eat as soon as your feet hit the floor in the morning, and everything is better with a blunt" he laughed as he stepped outta the bathroom in some ballin' shorts.

I rolled my eyes as I continued brushing my teeth. He stood beside me in the mirror to put lotion on his face, and for the first time ever, I saw how much we looked alike. We were nowhere near identical, but I saw Momma in both of us, strong. I smiled at him, thankful that I now had access to him. I think I felt so reckless lately because I knew he was around, and he'll be damned if something happened to me on his watch. He is the brother that I always wanted, and thinking about not being around him while I'm in Brooklyn made me a little sad.

"Imma miss you too twin, but I'll be around. I'll be poppin in and shit." He responded to my thought. I finished rinsing out my mouth and chuckled.

"You might wanna knock before you just be appearing places, yo ass might pop up on some shit that scars you for life," I joked.

He shook his head. "Nigga, ew. All I know is you better not have Legend ass in there breakin headboards when he should be breakin necks. Shit." He muttered. I stopped in my tracks.

"So you're sending Legend to Brooklyn with us?" I asked tryna hold back my excitement.

He rolled his eyes. "Don't get that excited. I'm not playin Sol. He's not to be distracted during work hours. Y'all can chill and shit when his shift over, but when he on the clock his one and only duty is to protect you. He gets distracted and that could cost your life, which would cost him his. Don't get ol' boy fucked up." He warned. He grabbed the car keys off the table and headed to the door.

"Um, where are you going?" I questioned.

He pulled his hoodie over his head and pulled his long dreads out. "I'm going to the house to set up for the memorial service. You said you wanted to have it in the backyard right? I gotta go pick up the pictures and obituaries. Andre is gonna meet up with the pastor and meet me over at the house to get the backyard situated." I looked at him waiting for him to tell me what my instructions were for the day, but they never came.

"Soooo, what am I supposed to do? Stay in the room all day?" I questioned, in between bites of avocado toast topped with a fresh, cold tomato.

He pulled open his wallet and put his credit card on the table. "You, Mila and Devon go have y'all a day. Hit the spa, get your nails done, find something to wear to the service...or whatever y'all do when y'all hang out. Solelil Marceline, don't run up my mu'fuckin credit card. This ain't 1999 and my card is not a fuckin No Limit Soldier." He walked over and kissed me on the forehead. "Keep security with you," he reminded me as he walked out of the room.

I had so many questions. How the hell does he have so much money? Let me find out Ethereal niggas be caked up. Finishing my food, I couldn't hold in my excitement. You know it was gonna be a good day when you could get pampered and NOT spend your money. I shot a text to Mila and told her and Devon to get ready as I hopped in the shower. After a light face beat courtesy of my Fenty by Rihanna products, I danced around the room to my favorite song of the moment, "Plain Jane" by A$AP Ferg as I put lotion on. By the time I was sliding on my flip flops, Mila was knocking on the door.

After a day full of full sets, a bomb ass massage and shopping, I had worked up quite an appetite. I shot a text to Jr. asking him if he wanted to take a breath and meet us for lunch, but he was hell bent on the backyard being perfect for tomorrow, so he passed. I decided I was gonna bring him food instead. Waiting in Kyoto Express for our food, I think the purpose of the day kinda hit everybody at the same time.

"I can't wait to see what Jr. did with the backyard." Mila mentioned as our food came up and Devon went to grab it.

I nodded, not because I didn't wonder the same thing, but because I realized that all the emotions were hitting me at one time. Devon walked over with the food and sat it on the table.

"I'm sure he hooked it up, you know his ass is full of surprises. I feel like he has an event planner tucked away in there somewhere," Devon agreed.

Before I knew what was happening, my face was glossy and wet. Mila looked at me with empathtic eyes as she held my hand across the table.

"Sis, I know. I know it's hard. I can't sit here and lie and tell you I know how it feels, but we'll be here every step of the way with you.", Mila assured me.

Devon sat digging into his food. "Can I take my steps after this steak bowl because bitch, this shit is just what my life needed," he muttered with a mouth full of food. We all laughed at his greedy ass. "Y'all laughin', pop a piece of that steak in your mouth and tell me that cow wasn't marinated by God and seared to perfection."

My phone buzzed and I looked down to a text from Jr. asking me to come to the house, alone when we got done eating. I shot him a text back to confirm and finished up. We got back to the hotel, and security was waiting for me, to take me to my brother. I hopped in the tinted out Suburban. As we drove toward my parents' house, my mind raced trying to figure out why Jr. wanted to see me. We pulled up at what used to be the front of the house. The demolition team that Jr. hired a few weeks ago had already torn down the house, and seeing that made me want to break down. The lot looked huge compared to what it did when the house stood there. Now it just looked black and empty.

There was a trail of roses leading from the driveway to the backyard. As I walked with one of the security guards, I felt like I was going to collapse. I still couldn't process the fact that my parents were gone, over something so stupid as magic. Jackie was gonna pay for what she did, and the longer it took the worse it would be for her. I got to the entrance of the backyard and walked up on a sign asking for shoes to be removed. I slid off my flip flops and let my freshly manicured feet marry the damp, glistening fresh cut grass under them. As I walked into the backyard, there were pictures everywhere. Pictures of Mommy and I, pictures of Daddy with all of us...pictures of them when they were children...just pictures.

The life–size pictures were hung up by twine with fairy lights around them. Momma's man–made pond was glowing with the same fairy lights around it, and rose petals floating around in it. The chairs where the guests would sit were situated in front of the pond. Behind it, The House that Roses Built had been repainted white with red and green trim and looked beautiful. Pictures hung there of Momma in her garden. Momma and Daddy's favorite song, "Just My Imagination" by the Temptations was playing in the background.

Jr. was sitting in one of the chairs when I walked up. I pushed the back of his head and he turned around and smiled at me.

He patted the seat next to him and told me to sit. "So twin, whatchu think? How did I do?" Before I could get the words out of my mouth, the tears fell. For once, I didn't want to control them. My soul needed this. Jr. took me in his arms and let me cry.

I felt his face get wet as we sat there in silence, hugging. "Momma and Daddy would be so proud of you Sol. Don't think anything other than that. I'm proud of you. It takes a hell of a woman to carry a whole bloodline on her back and you do that shit gracefully. Crazy at times, but gracefully." He chuckled.

I playfully punched him in the arm. "I couldn't do it without you though Jr., know that."

He turned and looked around the backyard. "Well, go take a look. Take some time for yourself before you have to deal with guests tomorrow. I'll be here finishing up."

He kissed me on the forehead and walked away singing along with the Temptations. I got up and the first place I wanted to go was Momma's greenhouse. The doors were already opened, so I just walked in. Walking in felt like at any moment, Momma could pop out and greet me. The inside of the greenhouse was so Momma, Jr. had captured her perfectly. Even little things, like her scent. Momma always smelled like rose water and vanilla. Always. I took a deep breath and inhaled that now foreign scent. There were pictures of Momma in her garden plastered all over, and all of her roses had been repotted into red, white and green pots. Jr. really put some thought into this. All of her mason jars, full of herbs, sat on a rack that Jr. must've just built.

I sat on Momma stool, listening to the music that hummed through the speakers. No wonder Momma loved her some R&B from the 50s & 60s, this shit was mad soothing. I sang along as I kicked my feet back and forth through the dirt floor. I missed living in the country sometimes. It had been a long time since my bare feet touched the earth and it felt amazing. I remember being teenagers, and Mila telling me that I needed to ground myself.

She told me I could do that by doing something as simple as walking barefoot on the ground and connecting with nature. I had done it so much before I left Fayetteville, and here I was doing it when I needed it most. Crazy how things come full circle that way. Remembering I had half of my blunt left over from earlier, I took it out of my satchel and lit up. It was only right. Anybody that really knew Luna Day Dupree knew she smoked her some green. She used to say the roses appreciated her for it. I chuckled. Visions of smelling her weed floating through the kitchen while she quietly cooked crept into my head. I would come in the kitchen and she would be whippin' up something delicious, hummin' along to her music and smokin'. I would watch her in amazement and awe. She was such a beautiful woman.

I closed my eyes and let the effects of the weed settle into my body as I sang along to Stevie Wonder's "Isn't She Lovely", another one of Momma's favorite songs. I heard footsteps coming toward the greenhouse, and I knew that could only be Jr, so I didn't budge. It was so crazy how much I felt her presence around me right now, and I hadn't felt that before. I continued singing along to the song. "I never thought, true love could bring…"

A soft voice began to hum along with me. I stopped singing, kinda afraid to open my eyes. The voice sounded just like my mother, and I knew that couldn't be possible. I didn't want to open my eyes and be disappointed. Tears streamed down my face as the footsteps got closer. I felt two hands gently touch my face and I knew that soft touch could only be Luna. I opened my eyes to see her and Jr. standing in front of me. Stevie was wrapping up the song.

"Isn't she lovely, made from loooooveeee". Momma smiled as she gripped my face.

"Yes. Yes she is…"

CHAPTER 13

Jr.

You coulda bought Sol for a penny.

She sat there, mouth open and not sure how to react. "Nah, you not dreaming. I had to go through a lot of shit just to get her here. This real ass life my nigga," I answered, reading her mind.

Momma turned around and gave me a look. "Boy watch your mouth," she chuckled as she reached for my hand. "Here, come stand beside your sister. Let me look at yall." I hopped off of the table and came and sat beside my sister. Momma's eyes got all misty.

"If you woulda told me the day would come that I would see my twins together I woulda laughed. Now look at the two of you. Jr. I swear you got hands just like your daddy. Tellin' by the looks of this backyard you sho' know how to use em too." I held my Momma's hand, tryin' not to tear up.

"Listen baby," Momma said turning to Sol. "It's so good

to see you but I need you to listen to me ok? I'm just a holographic image, but my thoughts and soul have been programmed into it. I might not be here in the physical right now but trust me, my soul is what's standing in front of you. I don't know where I am right now, I couldn't give you a description if I tried to. Jackie has me locked somewhere on a plane I've never heard of.

"If you want to find me, you have to find your grandmother. That's the only way and that needs to be your concentration right now. Listen to your brother. He's been around, and he knows how to navigate this thing. The two of you together will be a force this world and others have never seen before, this is your purpose in life."

Looking at Sol trying to soak in everything she was telling her, I felt her getting overwhelmed. It was becomin' more and more clear to her that this shit was serious business. As much as she told herself she was ready, she still didn't feel like she was capable enough to pull this off.

Momma smiled. "You're ready Solelil. You can't keep running from who you are. I know it's a lot, but every woman in our family before you had their own feat they had to conquer. You just have the biggest one, and you can do it. You have more help than you know but be careful about who you trust. Most of the people coming to the service tomorrow hold magic in them too. Oracles, Shamans, lightworkers. They all know, that's why we surrounded ourselves with them. Nothing is too crazy for them. Make sure you connect with them tomorrow. They know how to handle certain things, they've been prepped for this because we knew this day would come."

Momma looked over at me. "Make sure you protect your

sister. Above all else son," I nodded. Momma turned and looked around the greenhouse. "Beautiful, just beautiful. I have to go now, but I'll be waiting. I'm so proud of yall. I love you both."

Momma walked through the open double doors of the greenhouse and toward a light shining between two trees. Right before she got to the light, she stopped and turned around.

"There will be a man by the name of O'Mere at the services tomorrow. He will make himself known to you. Get to know him," Momma winked as she continued to walk toward the light. Once in front of it, the light engulfed her, and just like that she was gone.

I sat in pleased as fuck that had just happened. I looked at my sister, waiting for her to tell me what she thought.

She didn't say anything, so I started talking. "Just like I can hear your thoughts, I can hear Momma's too. It started happening a couple of days ago, that's how I knew even though they are physically dead, her soul wasn't at rest. If it was, I doubt I'd be able to hear her. Anyway, there's this dude I know that specializes in holographic images. Real dope dude. I went to see him last night after you went to sleep and told him what was up and asked if he could help out...and bam."

She sat there, not knowing how to feel. I know how I felt. Just knowing she was out there somewhere made me wanna slit Jackie's throat that much more. But what about Daddy? Through all of this, the focus had been on Momma.

"Now Pops, that's a whole different situation. I haven't heard him like I heard Momma. I don't know if its because he wasn't technically part of our bloodline or if it's just another one of Jackie's games. I'ma find him though Sol. We gon' do this shit together. Don't worry." I assured her.

"Now, you need some rest before tomorrow. Go head back to the hotel and I'll catch up with you later. I got some more shit I wanna wrap up before the service." I walked her back to the truck and made sure she was in safe before they pulled off. I walked backed toward the pond a popped a squat. I was proud that I had pulled that off, my mans Legend and Hussein really came through for a nigga. Speakin' of the devil, I saw Legend walkin toward me comin' from my pops shed. I had him freak that for me but I didn't want Twin to be overwhelmed so I held off on showing her that. I had set the backyard up like a museum dedicated to my parents, my fallen soldiers. I tried to incorporate them into every aspect off the backyard, and I think I did a bang-up job if I gotta say so myself.

Legend came and sat down in the row of chairs in front of me. "You good my nig? How your sis like the set up?" He asked taking his garden gloves off. He the only man I knew that didn't like his hands dirty.

"She really liked it man. She loved the hologram too. Thank yall for pullin' through on that for me." I dapped him up.

"Anytime man, you know us Ethereal niggas gotta stick together," he chuckled. He looked like something was on his mind.

"What's up man, you takin a break?" I asked, waiting for him to say whatever he had to say. I had a feeling it had something to do with my sister.

"Yea man, you out here workin' a nigga like a field hand," he laughed. His face got real stern.

"But nah though, I know you saw me talkin' to your sister at the club last night." He mentioned.

I played with the toothpick hangin' outta my mouth and nodded. "You know I peeped that shit nigga, that's my sister. Even if she wasn't being hunted I woulda peeped that shit."

Legend looked caught, like he was expectin' me to swing off on em or somethin'. "I just wanted to be up front with you because you sendin' me to Brooklyn and you know I got her number. You been around me for a minute, so you see how I've treated females in the past," he stuttered, avoiding eye contact.

I flexed my jaw. Hell yea I had seen it. Legend was a ho if I ever saw one. I was givin' him the benefit of the doubt with my sister. He done seen me get down and he know I don't play about mine, homie or not.

I just wanted you to know it ain't like that. Not only outta respect fo' you, but I'm really feelin' yo sister man. I'm not gon front. I haven't hit her up yet or nothin because I wanted to talk to you first fo' I made another move, but it's just somethin' about her. She seem mad different than a lot of these chicks out here and I'm at that age where I'm tryna move kinda different," he staggered.

I looked at him and chuckled. "You? Movin different? Man get the fuck outta here. I've known you since we were youngins man, you always had the same approach, stick and move. I just would hope you aint that stupid," I mentioned as my face got serious.

Legend studied my face. "Man, I got you. Now I ain't sayin' ima change overnight and marry her or no shit like that. I ain't perfect man," He laughed.

I kept a straight face. "You better try your hardest my

nigga. If I even think she hurt, you gonna have to see me. Straight up. Don't be up there in Brooklyn distracted and shit. What yall do outside of your work hours in on yall, but don't have my sister up there wide open man. I'm not payin you to fuck my twin," I smirked.

I looked around the yard and noticed Andre pullin up. "Look my man, do you. I gotta go holla at this nigga Andre real quick, I'll get up witcha later."

We dapped each other up and I waited for Andre to come over. He came over and sat down exactly where Legend had been. "You wanted to talk to me?" he asked.

I nodded. "So a couple of my niggas been tellin me that word around the street is Amir been lookin for me. Whatchu know about that?" I asked him as I crossed my arms and looked dead into his eyes.

He didn't flinch whatsoever. "Jackie got him watchin' you. She wants to know if yall about to make some moves or not. She don't think I'm up for the job, she think I'm too attached to the situation, you with me being raised with them and shit. She don't think I'll tell the truth," he muttered.

Sounds like some typical Jackie shit. "So let me ask you this. I been doin' a little jumpin or what not and the other day I heard Jackie talkin to somebody on the phone. Later on that day, I saw her talkin' to Amir. You mean to tell me you ain't have nothing to do with that?" I was waiting for him to lie so I could have a reason to jump on his ass. We may have a common goal, but one thing I know is not to trust anybody, especially somebody I once considered an enemy.

He still held his stance. "Jackie don't trust me, I didn't say that Amir didn't. Amir has the same goal I do, he wants to take down Jackie. He just don't know that I wanna take him down too. The more I play it like I'm on his side and I'm the outcasted son, the more he tells me because he knows I want her outta there. Its all a front my G," he assured me.

I studied his face. "So what have you heard about Ky? Have you talked to her?"

"She'll be here tomorrow. She still mad at Sol. Like I don't think yall understand. Jackie is really making her think Sol has something to do with your parent's death. Jackie has this sick way of brainwashin' mu'fuckas." He shook his head.

If anybody knew that shit it was me. Jackie damn sure made me think I was evil and my parents didn't want me when she first kidnapped me. That's honestly why I stayed gone for so long. It was part of her plan. By the time I had realized the truth, it was too late. She had already set her plan in motion and there wasn't shit I could do about it without getting Sol hurt. So I sat by. I waited and plotted for the perfect time. When I found out my parents were dead, all bets were off. She gotta go, just off GP.

I was getting tired and still had some shit to do back at the hotel. "Aight man. That's all I wanted. We'll talk some more when I need you. I'll see you tomorrow."

I walked toward Mila's car and got in. I know Sol thought she was the only person that was hurt over this shit, but at least she got to spend sometime with them. I missed out on a lifetime with them, and here I was planning to say goodbye. It wouldn't be for long though. If I could get Sol to really tap into her magic, we could really reverse some shit.

~~ * ~~

I walked up to the hotel room door and heard Sol singin'

FOOLISH

"Broken Clocks" by that one chick SZA. I stood at the door as she belted the song out better the orginal. That girl just don't know. She's one of the most talented people I've ever witnessed in life. If only she really tapped in to all that shit, couldn't nobody fuck with her. I opened the door to the room and found her folding her clothes up and putting them in her suitcase.

"Well damn, tell us about them Broken Clocks girl!" I yelled over the music. She looked up at me and smiled, still not missing a note. She turned the music down and gave me a hug.

"Thank you, for everything today. You really did a dope ass job with the set up and everything, and I just wanted you to know I appreciated it," she looked up at me and smiled. I could tell she had been cryin. Her eyes were puffy as hell an red as ever. I winked at her. I sat laid back on the bed to relax my sore ass body. Damn I was hungry as mu'fucka.

"I got you a shrimp bowl from Kyotos with extra veggies. I know you don't fuck with red meat all like that," Sol smiled as she walked over to the microwave and heated up my food. I shook my head and her and laughed. The only thing missin' was a nice, cold ass beer.

She giggled as she walked over to the fridge and cracked open a 12 pack of Colt 45 and handed me one. We both died laughing.

"Now who been payin attention?" I teased her as I took a gulp of the beer. I ate and watched tv while she we talked about her plans, what she wanted to do when all of this was over.

"I hope you not plannin' on stayin at the strip club too much longer. You too creative for that shit." I mentioned. She rolled her eyes.

"I'm dead ass man. You could be ownin' some type of business. You hella talented and creative. On the real though, I've been thinkin' about openin' up a couple of businesses myself." I taunted. I knew that would bait her in.

She raised her eyebrow. "You? Own a business? I got hear this one, Trap King of New Orleans," she teased.

I threw my empty beer can at her. "Nah, dead ass though. I wanna build a studio. I don't wanna charge no outrageous ass price for studio time though. I want it to be for all the niggas that I know are talented but can't afford it, ya know? I think that would be dope."

She nodded as she thought of the possiblites. "So, where would you put this studio? Would you have just one or like a couple of em?"

I had hooked her. HA! "A couple of em. One here. One in NOLA of course. Maybe one up by you in Brooklyn. See how they do before I expand."

I could see the wheels turnin' in her head. I knew by me having plans she would want some of her own. Sol don't like nobody outdoin' her. Just like I knew she would, she started spillin.

"Man I wanna do so much. I wanna open up a salon. I wanna open up a after school spot for creative kids…gifted kids really, but we're gonna cover that up with creative," She laughed. "I've been tryna to decided how to invest with Momma and Daddy's insurance money."

I hadn't even thought about the money. I know I wasn't left shit, so I wasn't too much worried about it. I knew though, whatever Sol wanted to do with it, she wanted to honor Momma and Daddy and I respected that.

"Jr...Momma and Daddy did leave you money, you do know that right?" Sol asked, invading my thoughts like I usually did hers. I looked at her confused.

"Sol, how Momma and Daddy leave me money and they thought I was dead? What sense does that make?" I asked.

Sol chuckled. "A mother knows. Honestly, I think she knew what was about to happen Jr. Ky told me not too long after she got here that Momma was coming back and forth to NOLA the months before she died. She told me that one of the times she came, she had Ky look over her and Daddy's will and insurance policies. She had Andre on there, but changed everything over to you, me and Ky."

My mind started racing. She never gave up hope, even after all those years. Kinda brought tears to my eyes, but I couldn't deal with Sol crying too so I sucked that shit back up. "Well damn. What a plot twist," I laughed.

"So you ready for tomorrow, gon' head and get this out the way so we can really fuck the world up on some twin shit?" I asked changing the subject. I walked over and put my arm around her.

"Look, Solelil. You can do this shit. Ima be right here. I'm not gonna let you be out there wide open. Yea we got our tribe and everything, but when I tell you that you have some of the deadliest niggas ridin' witchu, I mean that. Nobody gon' let shit happen to you. When you get back to BK, I need you focused. Studying. Gettin' your skills up. Findin' grandma not gon' be easy at all. You gotta be sure and ready, if not I can do this shit." I looked her with all the seriousness I could muster plastered across my face.

She stared back, not blinkin an eye. "I just need to get this service out of the way so I can concentrate. I'll be good, I promise. I want them back just as bad as you do."

I looked at her outta the corner of my eye. "Whatchu mean want them back?" I hadn't said shit to her about that, I didn't wanna get her hopes up.

She smirked. "I don't tell you everything Freddy Jr."

CHAPTER 14

Sol

All of this felt so surreal. There was a mix of anger, hurt, and pain from missing my parents all caught up in the mix. I closed my eyes and tried to mentally prepare myself for the next day, but thoughts kept rolling in.

Knowing what I now knew, I wondered how hard the police station was looking for their bodies. Fayetteville ain't but so big. I was so suspicious of everybody, but I had to be. I felt like I had to pay attention to every little tiny detail. Momma just kept throwing curve balls. I had no idea that most, if not all, of my parents' friends knew about their lifestyle. Here I was tryna hide it when it was already out in the open. I was curious to what O'Mere had to say and was actually kinda looking forward to meeting him.

When I got back to the hotel that night, all I wanted to do was lay down. Clear my mind before Jr. got back. Usually, I would bolt to Devon and Mila's room and tell them what had just happened, but I felt this was something special I needed to keep to myself. Once I got in the room, I texted Jr. to let him know I made it back okay, and shot a text to Mila saying the same. I told her I really wanted some time to myself before tomorrow, and that I would talk to her first thing. I laid across the bed and just let my thoughts filter through. I missed Ky, and I hated Jackie that much more for taking her away from me like this. I was also a little salty with Ky for falling for that shit. It made me wonder honestly. There had to be another piece to the puzzle that we weren't looking at. Ky has never been the dingbat type, and she knew all the details.

My phone lay beside me buzzing every couple of minutes with people sending their condolences. I know it was what people are supposed to do and they didn't mean any harm, but damn. I just wanted them to stop. I had to drown out the noise. I opened my laptop and hopped on Youtube to catch up on some of my subscriptions. I looked at the cosmic forecast from Tatianna Tarot, and also checked out the new video from Amber from Quietest Revolution. Before I knew it, my eyes were getting heavy and I was knocked out.

I sat up in the bed, letting my eyes focus to where I was. My laptop was still open showing an old Quietest Revolution video. The rest of the room was just how I'd left it, a clear indication that Jr. hadn't came back yet. Hell, for all I know he was next door with Mila. Ick. I headed to the bathroom, took a piss, and splashed some water on my face. The video playing on my laptop got louder and louder on its own, scaring the shit outta me. It was clearly time for a new one.

As I walked over to shut it off, Amber started talking about The Fool card, so instead of pressing pause, I turned it down and watched.

FOOLISH

"The Fool card coming up in your reading for this month doesn't surprise me based on the energy surrounding your reading, Aquarius. When I see The Fool card, I think of it as a card of new beginnings, and intentions...something is in the midst of STARTING. Keyword here. Let's look at the imagery of the card. There's a man who's clearly about to walk off of a cliff and not really too concerned about it. He has his little knapsack. White rose. Yellow background. White dog nipping at his heels like "dumb ass, watch where you're going"...but he doesn't care. He may not even have a destination at this point. He's blissfully ignorant because he hasn't endured all the hiccups of life yet. He's still wet behind the ears. (giggles) Martin reference for those of you who love that show the way I do, anyway.

"Let's look at the yellow background. In tarot, The Fool card is connected to the planet Uranus. Very mental energy, right? In this case, the yellow is representing mental clarity. He knows what he's doing even if he don't know what he's doing, ya know? He may not have a clue what he's doing, but he's very clear that it's being done for a reason. His gut is guiding him. His intuition is, that internal knowing.

The white rose symbolizes purity and the black in his outfit indicates ignorance...the balance. So he's off into the unknown, right...that new beginning I was talking about? It's all about risks. That's how I feel about this card in relation to the rest of the cards in your spread. Right now, people may not understand the journey you're about to go on, but its okay. People may not understand you. Hell, you may not completely understand yourself. You could have people telling you that it's dangerous and you shouldn't do it...but it could also be something beautiful, that you need on the other side. Now is not the time to listen to the fears of others or even yourself. Now is time for you to step into your power and let the universe take *you where it will..."*

I pressed mute on my laptop and laughed at the irony. The Fool. I decided I wanted to step out for a minute to grab some fresh air and smoke a cigarette. I opened the door to step out of the room, and to my surprise, I found myself free falling off the edge of the sidewalk. The deeper I fell into the darkness, the more scared my ass got. I landed with a thud, into what looked like a cemetery.

I got up and brushed myself off. My skin was crawling, because one thing I do not do is cemeteries. As I was brushing myself off, I looked down at my sleeves and noticed I wasn't dressed in what I left the hotel in. Instead, I had on this flowy yellow skirt with a white, off the shoulder top with black trim around the collar.

The Fool.

I looked around and heard what sounded like a bell being tolled somewhere in the distance. I walked toward the noise. I know, very white girl of me. As scared as I wanted to be, I felt very protected. I felt my hand to make sure the black tourmaline ring my brother had given to me was still on me. You could never have too much protection. As I continued to walk toward the tolling bell, I made out a shadowy figure in the distance. Not knowing exactly what I was walking up on, I stopped a few feet behind the figure.

Sensing my presence, the figure stopped what it was doing. I could see the black hooded cloak of the figure begin to form a golden hued outline around it. To my amazement, several other hooded, glowing figures came walking out of the shadows all around me.

Now a bitch was gettin' scared.

The first hooded figure I saw started walkin' toward me slowly. I wanted to back up, but there was so many others around, it would be pointless. The figure walked up to me, and got close enough for me to feel the heat from their nostrils. Slowly, they removed their hood.

FOOLISH

Marceline. She's so fuckin' dramatic!

Smiling, she fixed her hair. "So, you came. Wasn't really exepectin' that. Us Durpee women can be stubborn and hard headed."

She walked around me, looking me up and down. She stopped and took my hand, looking at my ring. "So, I see you've connected with your twin. You couldn't have gotten this from anywhere else. I gave this to him myself during his travels. I'm glad you found each other. Everybody needs somebody on this journey, and you just happened to be born with that somebody. How is he?"

I eyed her like she was insane. "He aight. Why you got me in the woods though? We couldn't have talked about this somewhere else?"

She chuckled. "And break tradition? Why would I do a thing like that? There is power in our traditions. Our traditions have gotten us through some tough times, to break them would mean to risk losing...and Duprees do not lose chile."

I looked around at the other hooded figures, now standing in a tight circle around us. Air could barely get through that bitch, it was packed so tight. "Sooo...we couldn't have talked alone either?"

She shook her head as she sat down in the middle of the circle on a fallen tree. "These are the people you want around, trust me. I brought you here for a reason Solelil. By now you're very aware of the journey you're about to go on, I would hope. I'm coming to you just like I came to Luna, just like I came to Odessa and so on and so forth. There's no more room fo' games and second guessin' ya'self and all that nonsense. Time is tickin'. Either you own who you are, and what you've been put in this realm to do, or continue doubting yourself and be the reason this whole bloodline disappears. That's not even the worst part. Do you really want somebody like Jackie Moreau runnin' thangs? Chile, I know I don't."

SAI MECCA

She lit a cigarette before she continued talkin'. Guess I know where I got that from. As she took a puff and exhaled she walked around the circle of hooded figures. One by one she revealed them by removing their robes. I was amazed. I stood among women with the same features as me. Damn, Dupree genes are strong. She walked over to the last woman and stood in front of her. She motioned for me to walk over.

I walked over and stood beside her. "Grab either side of the hood," she instructed. I did as I was told. She stood behind me.

"There are times on this journey that you're preparin' to embark on ,that you will feel alone, misunderstood...alienated even. That should not stop you. You have looked in the faces of the women folk in this circle and you see that they look like you. They have been through the same, yet different struggles you find yo'self in. They carried the same blood as you do. Every one of these women paved the way fo' you. Their memory and their essence deserve to live on. Live on through you, your sister, your daughters. They fought, so you don't have to feel alone. They were once you, standing in that very spot. They are with you, they will be with you. So when you feel alone, remember the words your brother spoke. You have a whole team of Dupree's behind you. Any of these women will be available to you when you need them. Just call on your ancestors."

She came and stood on the side of me and smiled. "Remove her hood," she instructed. Carefully, I pulled back the hood of the last woman.

Luna.

It was not my physical mother, but a statue. I ran my fingers over the wood that it was made of and fought back tears. So many times in the last 24 hours I've come in contact with her essence and not her. I just wanted to touch her, smell her scent...something. I wanted the real her.

FOOLISH

"If you want the real her, you have to fight. Anything worth having, especially your Mother, is worth fighting for," my great, great–grandmother responded.

"Listen to the people who are trying to guide you. Pay attention to everything, nothing that has happened to you or that will happen is by mistake. It was all intricately planned. It is you who is supposed to reign, and I have all faith that you will, alongside your brother." She continued.

I looked around at my great great–grandmother. She was right. I've always known I was special, and I've always run from it. I couldn't anymore, too many things were hangin' in the balance. I didn't have time to be scared anymore. My great great grandmother smiled, and took my hand. She led me down a wooded path, with me shakin' the entire time. I said I couldn't be scared of my journey, woods were still a whole 'nother thing. The only thing that lit the path was the moonlight, until we got to what I assumed was the bank of a river. My grandmother and myself, with the ten ladies behind us, walked onto this bank. The ladies walked out into the river and positioned themselves in a straight line.

My grandmother took my hand and lead me to edge of the water. "Here, you are going to be given the rest of your gifts, and I will awaken and strengthen the ones you already have. Once you partake in this, you cannot go back Solelil. Make sure you understand what you're doin'. If you think Jackie crazy ass is after you now, wait until your magic is totally activated. You're gonna have no choice but to fight. Life doesn't go back to normal after this."

I thought about what I was about to do. Honestly, I had no choice but to fight either way. I had nothing in this life. My parents were dead, my sister was being manipulated. All I had was my brother, and I knew I would continue to have him, but I missed my parents. Nothin' in this grimy, dark ass life could ever replace them.

If I had to give up my old way of livin' just to get them back, I could live with that.

I took my great grandmother's hand and she lead me deeper into the water. She positioned me in front of the first ancestor. My ancestor stepped forward. Cupping water from the river in her hands, she poured it over me. She placed her hands on my chest and chanted. I started to get warm the longer she chanted, and eventually that warm turned into a damn burnin' sensation. Tryin' not to ho out, I grabbed my great great grandmother's hand tighter. I felt my ancestor's magic course through my veins like hot sauce. Every part of my body burned until she took her hands off of my chest. When she did, I felt stronger. It's hard to explain, but I knew something else lived within me now. I did this nine more times, each ancestor giving me their particular gifts to help me along my journey.

After they were done, my great great grandmother walked in front of me. The ten ancestors gathered around me, slowly chanting while my grandmother chanted with them. When I least expected it and without her ever touchin me, I felt this burst of energy that brought me to my knees. Like, that shit knocked me all... the way... the fuck... down. I don't know what my great great grandmother was holdin' but shit. After she was done, she walked me up to the river bank.

"You now have everything you need, no more excuses. Life as you know it has changed. Flow with it like the stream of a river. The more you fight it, the better the chances are you will drown. If you ever need me, ever need any of us, summon us. Instructions on how to do that are in the black book in your trunk. I love you"

She pushed me forward into the water, and the next second after that I was standing in my hotel room over my sleeping body. Why did I have to travel so fuckin' weird sometimes? Like, it was a struggle to take my body with me. Shit. I lined up with my body and laid down. Other than being tired, I felt no different. I decided to get some sleep, because tomorrow is just the start of the madness to follow.

CHAPTER 15

Sol

The sun peaked through the curtains of the hotel and interrupted my sleep. Even though I was annoyed, I couldn't lie and say I didn't get some good ass sleep. I got up and made my way to the sink, to brush my teeth, when I heard my brother in the shower. I don't know how he always got in that bitch before me...how could one man be that dirty? As I brushed my teeth, I heard him rappin', which wasn't unusual. What was unusual was the volume that I heard him at. It was like somebody had stuck my head in a Beats by Dre headphone speaker, and that shit was crisp and clear.

> *Mama said don't be no fool boy...*
> *You better find your way...*
> *So I walked into the jungle*
> *Looking for a lion, who wants to play...*

FOOLISH

Gold in my heart, silver in my veins
Can't be torn apart, by these demons and this pain
Still on my path, I could never walk away...
Stay trill keep it 120 till my dying day.

I continued brushing my teeth as I smiled. So this is what it must feel like to hear someone's thoughts clearly. I had heard his thoughts, but they always come in fuzzy and jumbled like I needed to clean my ears out or some shit. I heard him cut the water off. Finally. As I splashed water on my face to wake up, I heard him open the bathroom door. I finished and dried my face off.

"Soooooo what color are you wearin' today? I think my fly should match your fly, ya know? Standin' in solidarity and such," He asked as he put his fist up. I turned around to answer him, but before I had the chance, he fell back against the table, looking at me like I had three horns and shit. I stared at him and walked around to lay out the clothes I bought.

"Yo, what fuck is up with your eyes? You smoke some bad shit? You good?" he asked, walkin' toward me. I raised my eyebrow, confused as fuck.

"Nigga, what are you talkin' about? My eyes are fine...fuckin' creep."

"Nah..." he slowly walked over to me and started sniffin' around me. He placed his hand on my chest, and I started to feel that burnin' sensation all over again. I jumped back and slapped his hand down.

He nodded his head while he stepped back. "Uh huh. So you just was gon' skip the fact that you got initiated last night, huh? You thought I wouldn't know?" he asked, now with his back to me while he put on deodorant. I tried to figure out how he would know.

"Because I smell it on you, and after you get initiated your eyes change color temporarily. Marceline, huh? You met the Ten Ladies? It hurt, didn't it? HA! Did you cry? I know ya bitch ass cried cause I know that shit hurt! Ahhhhh shit! My lil nigga official now! Ahh fuck!" He danced around the room while he put his pants on.

"By the way, you know there's no going back now, right? You literally have no choice but to kill Jackie. I'm hypin' security up because I know she can smell you too now." He got serious for a minute.

"Smell me? What is there to smell, am I funky or some shit?" I asked, preparing to be offended. I knew I had been in the woods but damn.

He chuckled. "No dummy. When a new Oracle, witch, whatever you wanna call yourself, gets their ancestral magic other witches can smell it. It's like a…new baby smell. That's the best way I can describe it. It can be a good thing because it lets other witches know that you cool and shit. Every bloodline has a different scent. Like I said, it can be a good thing, but that shit can also put new witches in a bad situation."

I tried to take this all in. "But I'm not a new witch though, I just have more gifts now."

"To them, you are new. Before you was out here undetected because you just had your magic. Now, you're carrying generations of magic with you. Magic that a crooked mu'fucka would kill for. Remember that night we were in the car and you were like 'This ain't the streets'? My nigga, consider this the ethereal streets. You gotta move the same way. Ain't no lettin' your guard down." He warned.

FOOLISH

This was too much for one morning. I pulled the rest of my clothes out of my suitcase. "By the way, I'm wearing rose gold," I mentioned.

He looked at me and scruntched his nose up. "Rose gold nigga? Seriously? Who randomly owns rose gold clothes?"

I shrugged. "You can match Devon and Andre. They're wearing black and gold."

He nodded. "That's more like it, I can swing that shit. Black is like my signature color."

I rolled my eyes and walked into the bathroom. I hopped in the shower and let the hot water run over my body. The day was finally here. Granted, I wasn't technically putting my parents in the ground, nor did I have access to them right now. I had to go through the motions of being reminded they weren't here. That was the hard part. I went through about thirty different emotions including sobbin' in the shower. By the time I actually washed and rinsed, the water was freezing cold.

Out of the shower, I realized that all that cryin' had made my eyes puffy. I wanted to go Au Natural to the memorial but that wasn't happenin'. I pulled out my makeup bag and lightly beat my face. Nothing too major or showy. I moisturized because nobody had time to be getting ashy in this humid Fayetteville heat. If you know anything about Fayetteville, there is no such thing as Spring. It gets cold, and then you sweat your ass off for a good 7 months of the year. I slipped my clothes on and opened the door to Legend sittin' in the chair. I was kinda shocked. Once he heard the door opened, he turned around and smiled.

"What's good ma? Your brother sent me here to escort you to the services. He wanted to go over and make sure everything was alright before it was time." That smile. I looked him up and down. He had his long locs pulled up into a bun with a gold scarf wrapped around them. I hadn't talked to him since we left the club that night because so much was going on. I was wondering why he hadn't texted me and then I remembered...my brother.

I sat on the bed and slipped my heels on. I watched as he moved his eyes up and down my legs. When he caught me watchin', he chuckled and I smiled back.

"I'm sorry, I know this is a tough day fo' you and shit. I'm not tryna be rude," he stated.

"I don't remember sayin' anything about you bein' rude, did I?" I joked. He walked over to help me up, and there was a knock on the door. Jumpin right into bodyguard mode, he answered it, gun tucked in the holster for easy access. In the doorway, Mila stood lookin' mad confused.

He opened the door wider to let her in. "Good mornin' Mila," he offered as he closed the door behind her. Her eyes bounced back and forth between both of us.

"Ohhhh okay!! I see what's goin' on! Ya'll finally hooked the fuck up huh? Bout time, all the damn sexual tension in the air every time y'all around each other was killin' me," She smiled. I rolled my eyes. Just as she started giggling, Jr's voice came over the Push–To–Talk speaker connected to Legend's shoulder.

"Nobody better be hookin' shit up but shoe straps. Y'all runnin' late, lets go." His voice boomed through the little speaker.

"10–4. We on the way my nigga," Legend responded with a laugh.

I looked around and noticed Devon was missing. "Umm,

where's Devon?"

Just as the last word slipped outta my mouth, he knocked on the window. Ready to go, Legend and the other guard, Hussein, walked us down to one of the shiny black Suburban's. They hopped in the front seat and Legend picked up the walkie talkie to let the other guards know it was time to go.

A few minutes later, we arrived at my parents back yard and I couldn't believe my eyes as we turned on to my street. There were what looked like HUNDREDS of people sitting in our backyard. Cars lined the driveway and streets in front of the house. There were some of the guards directing traffic. Legend pulled up to one of the guards and let his window down. Without even sayin' anything, the guard directing traffic nodded and Legend whipped into the yard and parked the truck.

He helped Mila and I out, and we waited for the other guards to park. Once we were all out of the truck we made our way to what used to be my Daddy's shed. All of the things my Daddy worked on were perfectly positioned in his shed, and the attached garage had been turned into an open bar. I laughed because that's exactly what Freddy Monroe would've wanted. I spotted my brother with his arms folded standing by the bar, smokin' a blunt. I asked one of the guards to take me to him. As I walked up to him, he handed me the blunt.

"You're gonna need that today. My nerves all over the place and I know yours are too." He assumed. He assumed correctly. I hit the blunt a few times and felt my body mellow out. There was still a tinge of something I couldn't put my finger on. I felt off. Jr. placed his hand around the small of my back.

"It's all the energy you're not used to, it seems overwhelming at first with all this magic around, but you'll get used to it." He mentioned.

I wanted to believe him, but it was something else. I didn't know why, but I felt the need to stay close to my brother. Legend turned around and looked at me and smiled. He mouthed "You good?" and I shook my head yes with a smile. At least I knew if anything came of this dreadful feeling I had, I was protected. Jr., Mila, Devon, and Legend especially didn't take their eyes off of me the entire 15 minutes we had been there.

I spotted Mila's parents and sister sitting near the front behind the empty chairs reserved for my siblings and I. I saw old friends of theirs in the crowds, neighbors and the likes. Most of the people there I didn't recognize, but I figured they were more part of the magical side of things. Jr leaned forward and whispered.

"Most of the people here are from the Five Sacred Families of New Orleans, that's why you don't recognize them. I'll introduce you after the service." He added.

I was getting nervous. Where was Kyleena and Andre? We were literally waiting on them to start the services. I knew Kyleena was mad at me, but if she missed this service I would never forgive her. I know that sounds selfish seeing as though Jackie was holding her captive, but it was her greed and dumbness that got her in that situation. You never ride against family, period. I heard the click of heels behind me, and felt a hand on my shoulder. I turned around to see my sister standing there. She looked different from the last time I saw her, but I couldn't put my finger on it. She didn't smile, just looked and nodded her head and put her over–exaggerated glasses back on. I shook my head and turned back around.

In the distance, I heard music start to play. It was "Pass Me Over" by Anthony Hamilton. My eyes immediately started producin' tears. My parents always said that when they passed, this was the song that each of them wanted played at their funerals. Creepy because I doubt they knew they would die together. I felt Jr. tug the back of my dress and pull me off to the side.

"I'm not gonna sit with y'all because that would raise too many questions to people outside of the Five Famlies. They know I'm back, but it would freak everybody else out. I'll be back here in the cut if you need me, just make eye contact. You got this, I have all the faith in you." He kissed me on the forehead, and I got in front of the precession line with Andre and Kyleena.

We all locked arms and proceeded to walk to the front together. The pastor that was officiating the services stood at the front, and hugged each of us before we took our seats. I spotted Mila and Devon in the row behind us sitting with Mila's family. They were the closest thing to family we had since Momma and Daddy were only children, no aunties or uncles for us. I also spotted our Godparents at the end of the row that Mila and her family were seated in. My Godmother Nairobi blew a kiss at me from where she sat. It was good to see her, I hadn't seen her since my high school graduation.

I stared at the front where the pastor stood as the music came to an end. He walked up to the microphone and started to speak.

"We are gathered here today, to pay honor and tribute to

two amazing people in our community. Anyone who knew Freddy and Luna knew love. They were pillars in our community, and the love they spread can still be felt and seen today. Luna was a gentle, quiet woman who spared no expense when it came to the children of this community. She opened her arms and her doors to any child in need. She not only tutored children, but she instilled in them self-confidence, and taught them important lessons like how to be self-sufficient, often having them help out in the beautiful garden you see to the left of me.

"Freddy stood proudly beside his wife, also helping raise the children of this community. Freddy took many boys under his wing and protected them from a life of crime and unwise choices. Any boy you ran into was excited to work back there in Freddy's shop, learning to work with their hands and walking in the ways that a man should walk. Joining us today, we have their three children; Andre, Solelil and Kyleena. Before I open up the floor for others to share their memories of these two wonderful people, I would like to give their children a chance to speak."

I looked at Ky and Andre. I wasn't prepared for this, at all. All three of us sat there, before Andre grabbed my hand and pulled me up, and I did the same to Ky. Hell, if I had to go, so was everybody else. We walked up and stood beside Bishop Matthews, a long time family friend. He hugged us again and handed the mic to Andre as he stood off to the side. I looked out into the crowd and was speechless. There were so many, I'd say about 250–300 people packed in this backyard to say goodbye to my parents. Some faces in the sea of faces I recognized, others I had never seen before. One thing that stood out was I could definitely tell who was part of the Five Families and who was just regular people. Must be part of all my new gifts. People who were part of the Five Families had this glow to them, their auras. Blues, purples, Oranges and other colors lit up around a lot of people.

I listened to Andre speak. "I don't have much to say, as many of you know me, I'm not a man of many words. I do want to thank you all for coming here and paying your respects to my parents. I wasn't around during the last days of their lives as I was out doing my job in the Navy, but I'm proud that I have a lifetime of memories to remember them by. Once again, thank you all for coming, I'm going to turn it over to my sister Solelil."

He handed me the mic. I froze up because public speakin' isn't my forte. I'm not scared of crowds, clearly... I just didn't know what to say. I stood there tellin' myself not to cry.

"Alright Sol, you gotta say something. Don't start cryin'. Open your mouth and speak. Say thank you or somethin' bitch, damn." Before I knew it, I opened my mouth to speak and instead tears started to roll down my face. Andre pulled me closer to him, while Kyleena gave me a few stank ass pats on the back. Once I got myself together, I started to speak.

"Like my brother said, I want to thank everybody for coming to show their love and support to my family. None of us were expecting to lose our parents in such a fu–" I stopped myself. "In such a horrific way. I remember being little and having this back yard filled with kids from our neighborhood helping my parents and learning so much. My parents were huge on bringin' kids up the old school way, switches included when necessary," I mentioned as the crowd erupted in laughter. I spotted Jr. in the back as well as security placed in strategic spots around the backyard. I saw Legend standing behind the last row of chairs. I couldn't see his eyes because of the dark Aviators he wore, but just seeing his face made me feel safer.

I finished speaking and passed the mic to Kyleena. As she was speakin', this wave of nervousness crept back over me. I looked at the back again to make sure my brother and security were still there. Something wasn't right, and I felt it in my bones. I looked up toward the sky while Kyleena spoke, and the sky had went from beautiful, warm and sunny, to kinda overcast and a chill fell through the air. I peeped my brother whispering somethin' to the second chain of command in security after Legend, Hussein. I noticed their stances changed and that confirmed what I felt in my body. Up until this point, I wasn't really paying attention to what Ky was saying, until Andre nudged me.

He bent over to whisper in my ear. "Where the fuck is she goin' with this? If she start talkin' crazy, take the mic from her." Andre instructed.

Kyleena continued talking. "I know all of you here think my parents were "Pillars of the Community", but the truth is my parents were into some dark things, and it was these dark things that got my parents killed. My brother and sister seem to be following in their footsteps. It will end the same way for them if they don't stop. My parents were sacrifices, they passed their dark magic to myself and my siblings and because of that, we're being hunted. I'm being held captive, and if somebody doesn't stop Ja–"

Legend came out of nowhere and snatched the mic from her. I looked at Mila and Devon and their mouths were gapped open, not believing what Ky just said. I looked over at Ky, but by the time I turned my head, she was no longer there. I heard gasps from the crowd and as I looked to the back for my brother, I noticed Marceline sitting in the back. She looked pissed. The next thing I know, Andre, Mila, along with her family, Devon, my godmother Nairobi and I were being snatched up and taken towards my Daddy's shed. Once inside, Jr. came from the back and told me not to move, no matter what happens. He whispered something to Legend as he stood guard and nodded.

The wind was picking up and the sky was damn near black. The same chills I felt in my body at the beginnin' had intensified. I saw a woman walking from around the shed. It turned out to be Detective Moreau. I was kinda happy to see her. When she cut the corner, I spoke.

"Detective," I said gently grabbing her by the arm.

Legend pushed me back with a crazy look on his face. She turned to look at me with a fucked up look and walked off. That shit caught me off guard and I wondered what that was about. I heard screams come from the crowd. The next thing I know, the people who came to pay their respects to my parents were locked in invisible cages screaming and begging for their lives.

They had all been gathered with no way to escape, except for a man with long grey locs dressed in white linen, outlined with gold trim. He lowkey looked like a magical OG of some sort. He had to be of some importance. Detective Moreau walked through the center aisle, and as she did, everything that she walked by died. Plants, fish in my mother's pond...the grass even went from a beautiful green to brown and dead. I couldn't believe my eyes. Uncontrollable anger built up in me from nowhere, and I needed my brother. Almost as soon as I thought it, he came running into the shed.

"Chill out, O'Mere is here. Don't make a move unless he tells you to," Jr. mentioned to the guards who were surrounding Mila's family, Nairobi, Devon and myself.

I noticed that Andre had disappeared also. I was kinda taken aback that my brother was telling security to listen to the command of someone else. That's when I put two and two together. The dude with the grey locs had to be O'Mere.

All of a sudden, I heard my name being screamed across the backyard.

"SOLELIL! COME AND FACE ME! THIS IS YOUR ONE AND ONLY CHANCE TO TURN OVER WHAT BELONGS TO ME BEFORE I'M FORCED TO TAKE IT!" Detective Moreau stood in the middle of the yard lookin' in my direction.

Trying to figure out what the fuck she was callin' me out for, Jr, Legend and Hussein closed in on me, shielding me from her sight. I peeked in between their arms to see what was going on. A streak of what looked like light purple dust snaked from a necklace that the Detective was wearing in my direction. I felt myself being drained of my energy, kinda like how it felt when you were in the sun all day, and that shit felt like it just drained all your life force out. I grabbed on to Jr. as he turned around and looked at me. His jaw clenched as he grabbed me and backed me into a corner, shielding me with his body. Just when I thought I couldn't take it anymore, Nairobi jumped in front of the purple wave and sent it flying back to the Detective. Nairobi ran out into the middle of the yard and stood beside O'Mere.

As if shit couldn't get any crazier, a grey funnel cloud appeared in the middle of the yard surrounding the Detective. O'Mere, Nairobi and Marceline joined hands and chanted as the funnel grew stronger and stronger, and the Detective grew more pissed. The people locked in cages were still screaming. As they completed their chant, the funnel created glowing gold chains and locks around the Detective. O'Mere walked toward the Dectective who was kickin' and screamin' to be freed at this point. With a lift of his hand, O'Mere lifted the Detective's body off of the ground and balanced it in midair. I stood behind my brother with my eyes poppin' out of my head. I had seen some crazy shit in my day, but this shit took the cake.

I heard O'Mere's thunderous voice shake the shed that we were secured in. "JACKIE MOREAU, THIS IS WAR!!" he yelled as he thrust his arm and sent her spinning into a vortex, and into another timeline.

CHAPTER 16

Freddy Jr.

Yo.

I don't even know where to start. THAT. SHIT. WAS. CRAZY.

I looked back at my sister to make sure she was good, and the little bit of heart I have left sank to the floor. My sister was slumped over and pale and it freaked me the fuck out. I let out a scream and O'Mere came runnin'. He lifted my sisters limp body up and told me to point him in the direction of some privacy. I pointed him towards Momma's greenhouse. Nairobi stayed back with Marceline to comfort the guests. I know they asses was traumatized. As they worked to get everybody seated, I gathered security and ran toward the greenhouse.

O'Mere laid Sol on a table in the greenhouse surrounded by Mila's family, Devon and myself. He took her hand into his and felt for her pulse. "She's hangin' in there man, but we gotta get her blood pumpin' or she risks loosing her gifts.", he stated. Just as I was about to lose my shit, Dirt and Marcus walked in. I was glad to see them. Dirt's expression told me he was ready for war and that's something that I could appreciate. We were gonna need all the help we could get. Dirt walked over and asked to speak with me for a couple of seconds, and O'Mere said by the time I got back he would have my sister good as new. I walked off surrounded by Dirt, Marcus, Legend and Hussein. Everybody's expression looked like they were ready to kill the next thing walkin'. We stopped in front of my Pops shed and began talkin'.

"Man what the fuck was that?!" Dirt asked. I shook my head, not really knowing what to say. I was looking for answers just like he was.

"Man, look. I don't know. I do know that Sol got initiated last night, and maybe that's how Jackie found her so quick. Regardless, we don't have time to spare. I'ma talk to O'Mere because I wanna know where he put her. Like, it's game time!" I yelled.

I thought we would have a little bit of time after I sent them back to Brooklyn, but hell naw. Somethin' gotta shake now. All I kept thinkin' about is my sister laid out on that table, and how close Jackie got to her. If it wasn't for our great great grandmother, O'Mere and Nairobi, I don't know what the fuck would've happened.

"Did you stop by the warehouse man? Please tell me you did," Dirt mentioned.

I nodded. "Now I'm wonderin' if I took enough, fuck.", I responded as I lit a blunt. My nerves were on 1000. I hadn't been near Jackie in years and being that close to her made me hate her that much more. She came at family, but not just any family, she came at my twin. My other half and the person who I shared a womb with. That's violation at it's finest.

"Look, I know you gon' send Legend and Hussein out there, but I got a spot in Brooklyn set up real nice to watch her. I can be up there in a matter of hours, just let me know.", Dirt suggested.

I thought about it. Instead of getting them flights out, I could have security ride up with them. I knew Dirt wouldn't let shit happen to my sister. I needed to talk to O'Mere and Nairobi first.

"Let me clear my mind first man, so I know exactly how to handle this. I know time is of the essence, but I wanna move smart. We can't afford not to. Trust me when I tell you, Jackie Moreau is good as dead. All in divine timin' my nigga." I dapped them up and told them I'ma go check on sis. I walked out of the shed to Nairobi and Marceline speaking to what was left of the crowd.

"We sincerely apologize for what has happened here today. This was supposed to be a celebration of two lives who were very important to us. Instead, greed and jealousy of others ruined what could've been a beautiful day. To the Five Families, please hang around for further instructions. Other friends of the family, please enjoy the music for about ten minutes while we gather security to get you to your vehicles."

I shook my head and laughed. The music that Nairobi was referring to was "Forget Me Not", which did the exact opposite of the title. They created that shit centuries ago to make civilians not affiliated with the Five Families forget the things that took place that they weren't supposed to see. The singer of the song was an ancient Siren who was damn good at her job. I watched as the civilian guests sat, eyes glued to the Siren that stood in front of them. Damn.

I made my way back in the greenhouse, hopin' like shit that my sister looked like herself again thankfully. When I walked in she sat cross–legged drinking a bottle of water and eating pineapple chunks.

She perked up when she saw me. "I was wondering where you were. Pineapple chunk?"

I laughed and took a piece of pineapple and hopped up on the table beside her. "You know you can't scare me like that, right? You almost had a nigga set this whole backyard on fire," I chuckled more out of relief than humor.

O'Mere walked in the greenhouse and sat in one of the chairs. "And exactly what would that solve youngin'?" he smirked. "Y'all young boys always wanna fuck some shit up before finding a smarter solution. That's what worries me, and that's why your Momma sent me. We gotta think strategically."

Before I knew it Legend, Dirt, and Hussein walked in followed by Mila and her family, Devon and Nairobi. Everybody stood on guard as O'Mere got up and pulled the doors to the greenhouse shut before Nairobi stopped him.

"All of the civilian guests are gone. It's just the Five Families here." O'Mere nodded as he stood in the middle of the floor.

"What happened here today was no mistake. It was planned. In order for it to be planned, it means we're being watched. Most importantly, it means that Solelil in particular is being watched. She's being hunted. Many of us standing here right now have been through it. The Five Families are who we are for a reason. It's because of our magic and the power that lives in it." O'Mere turned to look at Sol.

"You dodged a bullet today. One that I'm almost sure that, as much as your brother loves you, he couldn't protect you from. You're lucky we were all here today. This is just one of the examples of what can happen when greed overtakes someone outside of this family." O'Mere sternly stared at Sol.

I'm not gonna lie, that comment rubbed me the wrong way. I had a lot of respect for O'Mere, but one of the things I hated was how much he slept on me. Yea, it was good they were here, but don't doubt me and my soldiers couldn't handle that shit. I'ma always protect my sister, even if it costs me my life.

Nairobi came and stood next to O'Mere. "Don't scare the damn girl O, shit. She's new to this thang. Break her in easy," she mentioned as she put her arm around Sol. You could tell there was a lot of love there.

O'Mere shook his head. "We don't have time for that Nairobi. Breakin' her in easy could mean her death. We didn't break Luna in easy, now did we?"

Nairobi chuckled to herself. "No, no we didn't, but Solelil is not Luna. She's Solelil. You don't know what Solelil can handle yet. So my vote is to break her in easy." I sat back listening to them go back and forth about the old days, with Mila's mom Luci chimin' in every now and then. Evidently all of them were some hard-headed asses back in the day.

Dirt spoke up. "With all due respect Nairobi, I have to agree with O'Mere. Jackie was bold enough to show her ass up here today, so she has to know there's gonna be some push back for what she did. Believe me when I say she's preparing for it. You're right. Sol isn't Luna, she's more powerful, she was born for this. I say we hit the ground runnin'. Get her trained and ready. Her brother and I have plans to ship her back to Brooklyn tonight, and I have a location where she can do her training. The quicker we get her trained and get her on the path to find Odessa, the quicker we can get Jackie the fuck up outta here. We all know this can't be done without Odessa. She has her tribe, she has her brother, and she has us. We'll get her straight."

O'Mere looked around, deep in thought. "Nairobi, what do you think?"

Nairobi smiled that warm ass smile. "I think you should give 'em a chance O. I mean you trained everybody standing in the room from the Old Family. Let these kids forge their own path. You knew this was comin', you just havin' separation anxiety. Get your emotions under control old man. You knew a hundred and some odd years ago these kids were gonna take over. You can't fight destiny O'Mere, we tried that before. Need I remind you how that turned out?"

O'Mere stood there in thought. I had some questions, how old were these niggas? How much about the Five Families did I really know? I had some diggin' to do. O'Mere jolted me out of my train of thought.

"Jr," his voiced echoed through the greenhouse. "A word brotha?" I followed him out of the greenhouse and sat by the pond. He stared off for a while, getting his thoughts together. As much as I wanted to heed his words, Nairobi was right. We were a whole new generation of magic. That's not to say we were just gonna abandon the old ways, but sometimes the old ways don't always work. It was time for some new ways of doin' shit.

O'Mere looked at me closely before he started speakin'. "Youngin', I've had the pleasure of trainin' Odessa, Luna, you and coulda trained ya Daddy if the church hadn't sunk their claws into him," he laughed. "I've trained a hell of a lot of people man, this has always been my jig, ya know? Its hard to turn that over to some knuckleheads that once looked up to me. With that bein' said, I have to trust that I trained y'all right. You, Dirt, Legend and Hussein were some of my strongest students. I can see y'all initiating the takeover. Y'all just gotta be smart dude. Y'all can't be out here whylin' out like y'all did in NOLA. You gotta be strategic."

I nodded my head. "Man, we can do it. My motivation is my sister. I know what she's up against. Jackie gon' have to lay me down before I let her get anywhere close to her, even then I'll be taggin' her ass from the Ether." I joked. The truth is, while I was more than ready, I knew that if I wanted to be able to protect Sol I would have to train along with her. Don't get me wrong, I'ma bad mu'fucka, but a smart mu'fucka knows learnin' never stops. Even when you're dead.

O'Mere nodded. "I'm going against my better judgment and givin' y'all my stamp of approval. Now don't go getting' big headed on me and forget the chain of command. I need to know about everything, every phase of training. I need to know a plan of action before you leave off to go find Odessa. I'll be checkin' in with you every week, pop ups and shit. If I feel like some shit ain't right, I'ma work with y'all to get it straight. I'm gon' send Nairobi with y'all to get her settled back in Brooklyn for a couple of days. Get her hipped to some things she needs to know."

He extended his hand and I dapped him up. This was big. I had even more elbow grease behind me now, and that calmed my nerves a little bit. I knew sis was shaken up, so I needed to go talk to her. O'Mere read my mind as I got up and headed in her direction.

FOOLISH

"Hey Jr... let Nairobi do that, you know it might come out a little bit better from a female's perspective. You know how these womens is man." He chuckled. I nodded and walked over to join my sister.

Back over in the greenhouse, Nairobi was gettin' Sol's vitals and making sure she was okay for the ten–hour trek we had in front of us tonight. Devon and Mila stood around her jokin' with her to make her comfortable. I walked over and kissed her on the forehead. She had moved on from pineapple chunks to slices of avocado with salt and pepper sprinkled all over it.

That girl was gon' turn into a damn avocado as much as she eats them. I stood over to the side to let Nairobi do her thing while I just observed. That girl had no idea how strong she was. I watched her as she laughed and joked with her friends. I hadn't seen her smile like that since she got here. Her magic gave her a glow that added on to the purple aura that surrounded her.

Royalty.

I listened to her, Mila, Devon, and Mila's mom, Luci, talk about the shit they used to get in when they were little. "I knew y'all were some little witches and priestesses in trainin' when I found Mila's dinner on a makeshift alter in her closet." Luci laughed.

"Well I had to feed the ancestors Mami. Who was I to deny them your cookin'?", Mila joked with her mother. They continued to joke around while I watched O'Mere watch them from the pond like a proud Papa and shit. I could tell he had faith in us, it was just a matter of provin' it to him, and oh...I planned to. Nairobi waved me over to join them. I walked over toward them and she pulled me off to the side.

"Your sister is good as new, her magic is in perfect condition. I heard O'Mere say she got initiated last night, is that true?" Nairobi asked, looking confused.

"Yea, man. When she got up this mornin' her eyes were different colors and she smelled...different.", I agreed.

Nairobi continued to look puzzled. "Different how?"

This is gonna sound crazy, but almost like...peppery, spicy. You know how it smells when y'all got all the spices out and its smellin' lovely in the kitchen," I joked.

Nairobi laughed and started to sniff around me. I stood back kinda confused. I said SHE smelled spicy, not me.

"Hmmm..." Nairobi observed. "Then you should smell like that too. You're twins. Once one of you gets initiated, you both should be. It's your families special scent. Luna had it and I'm pretty sure when Kyleena gets initiated, she'll have it also...but for some reason...you don't."

"Is that a bad thing?" I asked, getting kinda nervous.

"No, not at the moment. The last set of twins we had initiated at the same time. That could be the culprit." She mentioned.

"But I've already been initiated, years ago. By O'Mere."

She shook her head. "You were initiated into the Five Families son, you were never given your magic. You already had some magic because of your sister, Solelil. You were lucky, some of hers rubbed off on you in the womb. There are different types of initiations. There's the initiation that Sol went through, that all heads of each of the Five Families go through. Its their Rites of Passage to get their Ancestral Magic. Sol is now considered the head of the Dupree bloodline. Then there's the initiation that males go through. That's what you went through. Bloodline magic only lives in women. Men are chosen. O'Mere simply branded you with the Dupree stamp so to speak so when you're around other families they know who you belong to."

She tilted her head to the side and looked. "Since you and Solelil are twins, I was expectin' you to have some symptoms. I know it sucks but take it as punishment. We have periods and menstrual cramps, males have initiation symptoms. Hey, fair trade ain't a robbery.", she joked. "If I'm right, you should be getting them soon. Your magic is activated through your sister and you're both stronger when you're together but you know that already. Hopefully I'm around when it happens, I haven't seen that in a couple hundred years, it'll be interesting."

I cringed at the thought of that shit. That shit wasn't funny at all. The things I go through for this girl, FUCK! O'Mere walked over and stood beside me, peepin' the scene. The rest of the Five Families remained strung throughout the backyard, catching up and enjoying the bar and food like nothing had happened thirty minutes ago. Damn they move on quick. O'Mere rubbed his beard as he watched the goings on. I prepared myself for whatever he was about to say.

"Ya know, Solelil is supposed to be trained before she takes her crown as the head of the Dupree bloodline, but today looks like a great day to do it. Its nice out, she's already initiated...we can bend the rules a little, right?", O'Mere asked my opinion.

The crowning he was referring to wasn't her actually getting a crown. The Crowning Ceremony is when the new head of the family takes their rightful place among the other heads of the Five Families. What he said was true, she was supposed to go through her trainin' first, but hell. Everybody was already here. New rules right?

"I say let's do the damn thing, one less thing to do.", I agreed. O'Mere called out to Sol and went walking toward her. I stayed back and studied her facial expression. She went from "huh" to "OH MY GOD" in a matter of seconds.

I laughed as her, Mila and Devon hugged it out. Girls were so fuckin' dramatic. She locked eyes with me across the yard and I put up my fist and laughed. Nairobi took her to freshen up and O'Mere made the announcement.

"If I could have your attention and pull y'all away from the booze, the loud pack and food for a minute...", O'Mere laughed. "Just like black folks. All y'all need is one reason to have a cookout huh? But nah, seriously. I know today went a little bit to the left as far as the memorial service for Luna and Freddy Sr. I don't want today to be marked with the ugly stain that is Jackie. Because of that, myself along with Freddy Jr., decided that we're gonna step outside of norm and have ourselves a crowning ceremony." The Five Families cheered as O'Mere paused.

"The only reason y'all happy is because that means the party lasts a little longer. Some of y'all may be hundreds of years old but still love y'all a kick–back," he joked. "Today, we're going to be crowning the daughter of Freddy and Luna, Solelil. She has went through her initiation, and I think the actions of today prove that she is ready to take her throne as the head of the Dupree bloodline. If you all will grab your joints, your ribs and dranks and what not and take a seat, we'll be gettin' started in just a few moments. Thank you." He laughed as he sat the mic down.

I have never been through one of these, so I had no clue what to expect. "Freddy Jr?" I heard my name being called from behind me. O'Mere stood behind me smiling. "You're sister needs you bruh," he motioned toward my pops shed. I walked back there where my sister was getting her tribal markings placed on her face by one of Nairobi's daughters. Before saying anything I just observed her. She still had on her rose gold dress from earlier, instead of heels, she was barefooted. She wore a headband of flowers around her head that tied in the back. I watched as Nina, Nairobi's daughter put some sparkly shit on her face with this church fan lookin' thing.

She looked beautiful. Glowing almost. The tint of her purple aura snaked around her adding to what was already perfect and gorgeous.

I walked over to her and kissed her hand. "What you need me for, my make–up skills need some work, Nina look like she got it under control." I joked.

She punched me in the shoulder, laughing. "I need you up there while I'm being crowned. It's supposed to be Daddy you know." My face started to get hot. Those were some big shoes to fill.

Nairobi didn't make it any easier. "Your Daddy woulda wanted it, Freddy. You know that." She smirked.

She knew I wouldn't be able to resist that. I agreed and asked Nairobi what I needed to do. After she explained I would just stand there and be a witness, that took a little pressure off. I kissed my sister on the cheek and jogged up the aisle to the pond where O'Mere stood. Around me stood O'Mere of course, who was head of the the Bordelon Family, and the heads of the LaRoix, Darbonne and last but not least, the Miliano family, represented by Mila's father. Once the heads of Four of the Five Families were in place, Solelil made her way to the front. Pictures snapped, and Nairobi and Luci looked like they were about to bawl their eyes out.

Devon and Mila stood off to the side, lookin' proud as fuck of their friend. Devon captured everything on his camera. Once she got up to the front, O'Mere kissed her on each cheek, and so did the representatives of the other three families. O'Mere grabbed the mic and started to speak.

"Now, I'm not gon' drag this out. I know it's been a long day for everybody, especially Luna and Freddy's children. We're here today, to crown Solelil Dupree...daughter of Luna Dupree and Freddy Monroe Sr. To bear witness, we have the oldest child of Freddy and Luna, Freddy Jr." O'Mere took a stick of Palo Santo and lit it and used it to light a candle that Sol held. She looked ethereal. I never thought that I would see the day that not only would I be able to be around my sister, but I would be here to see her take over our family bloodline.

Once the candle was lit, O'Mere continued. "It is my pleasure, to light this candle for Solelil Dupree. It is my wish that she uses the light inside of her to guide her inner wisdom. It is my hope, that the magic of the Dupree women that came before her finds a home within her. It is your turn Solelil. Make your mother proud. I introduce to you, Solelil Marceline Dupree, head of the Dupree Bloodline!"

The crowd clapped and cheered for my sister, as Nairobi and Luci ran up to hug her. O'Mere hugged her, as well as the other heads of the Five Families. I saw Legend bitch ass back there clappin' like he was about to bust out in tears and shit and I laughed. She did it. She now sat at the throne.

She walked over to me and gave me the biggest hug. As we stood there and embraced each other, "Back that Ass Up" by Juvenile started playing and we busted out laughin'.

FOOLISH

"These magical niggas really know how to fuckin' party," I heard Devon laughin' as him and Mila started dancing. In that moment, despite what lies ahead of us, everything was perfect. My sister took her rightful place among the family and it was our turn to do things our way. I watched everybody dance and party, turnin' what started out to be a horrible day into one that was for the books. I stood beside Dirt as he was scammin' on which broad he was gonna try to hook.

He leaned over and whispered to me. "Let the games begin my nigga. I'ma bout to have Sol out here whoopin' ass in these fucked up magical streets my nigga. Jackie better protect her neck, and that's word to my moms and pops."

CHAPTER 17

Sol

I took a minute to myself and snuck off into Momma's greenhouse. After everything that had happened today, mostly fuckin' unexpected, my emotions were all over the place. I figured I'd enjoy my last few moments of freedom before training began. I just hoped wherever Momma and Daddy were, they were proud. A couple of weeks ago, you could've never told me I'd be the head of the Dupree bloodline. I probably woulda called you nuts. Now I had to go back to Brooklyn and act normal. With the nosey niggas I worked with, it was gonna be kinda hard.

Every now and then people trickled in and out of the greenhouse, strikin' up small talk. If everybody was gonna be actin' intimidated I was gonna have to put a stop to that shit. I'm still the same ol' Sol, just gotta a li'l more magic. I really didn't want people treatin' me different. That was gonna blow my shit. I guess it's always different for people who don't want to be in the spotlight. You would think as much crazy shit that I do it would be the opposite, but I do crazy shit for my satisfaction only. I watched Mila dance with my brother and wondered when the hell they were gonna stop pretending like they didn't still love each other. The thought of that brought throw up to the top of my throat.

That made me start thinkin' about my own love life, and how non–existent it was before all of this, and how because of this it would probably continue to be. Who the hell was gonna wanna be with somebody like me? My mind floated to Legend. As fine and protective as he was, and even though he had seen all the craziness because he's my bodyguard, that doesn't automatically mean he's up for the weirdness in his personal life. My brother made it seem like he was okay with it, so why hadn't he text me? Just as soon as the thought left my head, I looked up to see Legend walking toward me. He had that sexy smile stretched across his face, and I immediately got moist. Standing at the greenhouse door, he waited until I smiled back.

"Why you sittin' in here by yourself girl? You should be out there enjoyin' yourself, you know Dirt about to kill you with this trainin' right? You better have all the fun you can while your body still allows you to," he chuckled. He hopped up on the table beside me and stared out into the yard.

"Aren't you gonna get in trouble for canoodlin' with me on the clock? You know my brother extra antsy after what happened earlier." I asked, half serious, half joking.

He took off his bullet proof vest and his shirt that had "Security" written on the front to reveal a wife beater underneath. Even though he wasn't the biggest nigga around, his arms and chest were huge. Shit.

He put all his gear behind him and smiled. "Is that better? For the record, I'm off the clock by the way."

I held up my hands in surrender. "Hey, I'm just tryna make sure shit cool, you know my brother a hot head. We don't need no more issues around here today. I've had enough excitement to last me until I'm fifty."

"Yes Ma'am HBIC." He joked.

He must have peeped my face because his facial expression changed too. I've never been one to be able to keep how I felt off of my face. "Please don't treat me like that. I hate that. I'm not different than y'all."

He shook his head. "Ma you gon' have to start acceptin' that you're different. I mean, I get it. At the same time, realize you aren't just another witch out here. Or another oracle woman. This was your path before you were even conceived Ma. There's only four, five if you count your brother, other people in this world that holds as much magic as you do. Once Dirt trains you, nobody gon' be able to fuck with you, and that's includin' the other four family heads. Why you think O'Mere was so hesitant to let Jr. loose and control shit? C'mon Ma, don't downplay yourself like that."

I'm not gon' sit here and lie and act like he didn't boost my head up. Yea, all that was true and everything, but shit. Where was there enough room for me to still be Solelil? Jr. came walking into the greenhouse followed by Mila and Devon, as expected. Cockblocker. I let him have his moments with Mila but I couldn't get a second alone with Chocolate Zaddy over here.

"Legend, Solelil. What ya'll over here chattin' it up about?", my brother casually interrupted.

I rolled my eyes. "Don't matter now, you killed that

whole vibe."

He smirked. "As an older brother should. We got bidness to handle." Dirt, Marcus and Hussein joined us. "Now, since all of us are here, we can get down to it. We'll be leavin' around seven tonight so we won't hit all that traffic. Sol, you and Mila will be ridin' with Devon. Mila, I'ma turn in your rental car in about a hour, so you don't have to worry about that. It's about five–thirty now, so everybody needs to make their rounds and say goodbye to everybody so we can get back to the hotel, pack, and load up."

He switched his attention to Dirt. "Y'all got the itinerary all mapped out right? Rest stops, food, gas, allat shit?"

Dirt nodded. "All of that is covered. We'll grab food and fill up before we leave Fayetteville and the next time we should have to stop shouldn't be at least until Virginia."

Jr. nodded. "I'll give y'all some more directions after we get back to the hotel and load up." Everybody peeled out to say goodbye to everybody we knew, while the security guards started the trucks. Legend walked over and put back on his gear.

"Well, guess it's time to hop back on the clock Ma. We got a long drive ahead of us, I'll hit you up, aight?" he asked while he got dressed back in uniform. I nodded my head and he winked at me on his way to the truck. He has no idea what dangerous waters he was in just now. Had jackass not interrupted, I coulda cured my dry spell. Niggas.

As I hopped off the table, I looked around at my Momma's greenhouse. This had been the craziest day, but part of me wishes my parents were here to see me at least get crowned. I know wherever they were they were watchin', and I hoped they would help a sista out with this newfound path.

O'Mere's voice startled me.

"They would be so proud of you Solelil. Don't you worry about that. If I thought you weren't up for the job, I wouldn't have turned your crazy ass brother loose in New York of all places." O'Mere chuckled. I hugged him and Nina, Nairobi's eldest daughter.

"Thank you guys for everything today. The funny thing is, Momma told me to reach out to you. Guess Jackie kinda did that for us." I smiled.

O'Mere nodded in agreement. "I'll be up in New York in a couple of days to peep the scene and make sure everything is smooth. Nairobi is gonna be up there with you until I get there. If you need me, don't hesitate. She knows how to get ahold of me."

He turned to walk away and stopped. "Remember, this is YOUR journey. Don't lose yourself tryna find Odessa. Always do what feels right to you. Your intuition is the most important thing that you have, use it." He turned and walked away into a crowd of people.

Nairobi stood there, smiling. "Well, I guess I have some packing to do, huh? I'll meet you guys at the hotel." I walked around saying goodbye to everyone, starting with the four heads of the families.

Everyone wished me well and told me how proud my parents must be. I held my composure for as long as I could. After saying goodbye to everyone, I had an idea. While everybody was loading up to head back to the hotel, I snuck away and grabbed a mason jar from Daddy's shed. With one of his tools, I cut a few small holes into the top of it. I put some dirt from his shed floor into the jar and filled it halfway. I ran back to Momma's rose garden and cut a few of her roses off of the bushes. I stuck the roses into the holes. I knew that wasn't gonna keep them alive long, but what the hell. I had a piece of each of them in one jar. I took one last look at my parent's yard. I felt their energy surge through me. It's go time.

~~ * ~~

Back at the hotel, everybody packed and loaded their things up. I put my things in Devon's truck along with Mila, while the rest of the team split their stuff up between the five security trucks. I sat in the truck waiting for security to check out and Jr. to come give us our "briefing". When everybody was ready and situated, Jr. stood in front of us with security. Me, Mila, Devon, Nairobi and security listened carefully as Jr. spoke.

"Aight, so we'll be travelin' about six deep. Five security trucks and Devon's truck. Nairobi and myself will be in the second truck. We all need to stay together. If somebody gets left behind, we pull over and wait for that other person. Nobody stops unless you clear it with me first. Period. We have scheduled stops, so if you a pissy ass mu'fucka, I suggest you limit your drinkin'." He stressed.

Everybody laughed, but Jr's faced stayed stern. This nigga was playin' no games. "Devon, you need to be in the middle of the caravan at all times. Don't be tryna race ahead of nobody, stay within security's range. Like I said, we have scheduled stops for food and allat shit, so if you know you be hawngry, I suggest you stock up on snacks when we get gas. We should arrive in Brooklyn around five tomorrow morning. Everybody is to stay alert, security you already have your driving shifts so y'all should be all set. Anybody got any questions?"

Mila raised her hand. "Umm, where is Andre?" I saw Jr's jaw clench when she asked.

"We don't know right now. We have a couple of people keepin' an eye out for him, but he dipped out when Jackie showed up. That's all we know about that right now." He responded.

He looked around the group. "The most important thing is that my sister stays safe. I will not HESITATE to stick my foot in somebody ass if she goes unattended. Got it? If nobody has questions, lets go. We fuelin' up and we out."

We all loaded up and made our way to the gas station. After buying what had to be about $200 collectively in snacks, we climbed back into Devon's truck. I wanted the backseat, and since we all agreed that I've slept the least out of all of us, they let me have it. I stretched out in the back while Mila played DJ and Devon made sure to keep up with the caravan. The first two hours were filled with jokes, memories and blunts. By hour three, we were all hungry as fuck and had torn through our snacks. I decided to take a nap before we pulled off to get food. Just as I closed my eyes, my cell phone buzzed. I looked down, and an unknown number popped across my screen.

"Yo, you up beautiful?"

The message read. I knew it couldn't be nobody but Legend. I smiled and wondered what truck he was in.

"Barely lol. What time are we stopping for food? My stomach

is touchin' my back right now..."

"We should be stoppin' in like the next thirty minutes. Yo brother and Nairobi been in here blowin' it down and your brother hungry too. We still on schedule to be stoppin' though. You good?"

"Yea I'm fine. I wish we coulda talked longer. You know how that go though..."

"Yea lol its cool though. He doin' what a brother posed to be doin. I'm the same way with my sister."

"So you have a sister? How old is she? You strike me as the big brother type. All those overcompensatin' muscles you got lmao"

"My sister 22. Hahaha you got jokes though. Ain't nothin over here to overcompensate about Ma."

"That's what they all say. Where you from?"

"I'm not the rest of these pissy ass niggas, but you know that. You wouldn't be talkin' to me if I was. I'm from Chicago. Born there anyway. Raised a lil bit of everywhere. You?"

"Born and kinda raised in New Orleans but grew up in Fayetteville. You can't trust my judgement when it comes to men. I've made more than a few bad judgement calls."

"Well I ain't one of em."

That's the last message I read before my eyes were like "fuck you" and closed on their own. I woke up to Mila shakin' me, tellin' me it was time to eat. That shit was like music to my ears. I threw my pillow on the other side of the truck and hopped out so fast you would think Anastasia Beverly Hills was havin' a 50% off sale. As I hopped out I was surrounded by security who stopped me before I could take a step.

Dirt walked over lookin' pissed. "Your brother just got a phone call about Andre. Evidently he was wherever Jackie is at, but he fell off the radar. I don't know what this nigga told y'all, but I been told your brother you can't trust a snake ass mu'fucka like him. No matter what he said."

"What about the Mole he has inside of him? Shouldn't that let y'all know where he at?" Devon asked.

Dirt shook his head. "Can't pick up that signal. My thoughts is, Jackie knew about that shit and took care of it."

Jr. came walkin back toward where we were gathered with Nairobi. "So this nigga Andre is on the run, from what or who I really don't know. Until we meet up with him and find out, he's public enemy number two."

Nairobi nodded in agreement. "In this line of work, you can't trust a flip flopper like him. I've seen it too many times. He clearly has his own agenda. Shit like that never ends well."

Jr. looked irked. "We're gonna have to tighten up security when we get to Brooklyn. If I come up with somethin' else y'all need to know, I'll let you know. For now, I'm hungry and I get irritated when I'm hungry. Let's eat."

We all damn near ran into Wingstop. After everybody ordered and got the first couple of wings down, we all joked and laughed but stayed together. Jr looked over at me smashin' my wings with hardly any breaths in between. "You might wanna slow down and savor that shit. It's the last time you'll have it for a while." He joked.

I hopped back in the truck, as we loaded up, and prepared myself to go to sleep. I knew that when I got back to Brooklyn, my time was no longer my time. I wondered what life was gonna be like from here on out. Would I be happier? Would I be stressed out? Could I pass this shit on to somebody else if it got too hard? The closer we got to Brooklyn, the more nervous and apprehensive I got. Play time was over and my brother made that very clear. I put my earbuds in and let Jhene Aiko sing me to sleep.

I sat in the living room of my apartment flippin through the black book that was included in my trunk. I was strugglin' to keep my eyes open as I tried to absorb what I was reading. Jr. sat behind me laughin'. He stayed with me three days out of the week and the other three he was doin' I don't know what.

"Jumpin'", he says.

Between training and work I was wore the fuck out. All I've been doing for the past three weeks is training, working and sleeping. Dirt said it was important to get my endurance up, so the first week we ran. And we ran. And we ran some more. Then he threw in some weight training...and we ran some more. Kickboxing. You guessed it, more fuckin' runnin'. My body was so sore I could barely climb up the pole at work. I was surprised I was still makin' money. I felt bad that I couldn't rip and run with Mila and Devon. I'd got so boring Devon been bouncin' from my house to Mila's. I don't blame him.

I gave up trying to read because my burnin' eyes were cussin' me the fuck out. I plopped down on the couch next to Jr, who was hoggin' my TV watchin' the History Channel. I curled up on the other end of the couch and watched the end of a documentary Jr was watchin' about Ancient Egypt.

"You know, you should check some of these documentaries out. A lot of our magic dates back to Ancient Kemet. Worth knowin' about." He suggested.

"I'll be sure to do that in between runnin' for my life and old white men tuckin' hundred dollar bills in my g–string. Thanks for the suggestion buddy." I humored him.

He got up and walked toward the kitchen. "Is that complaining wrapped up in sarcasm I hear? What you got to eat in here that doesn't have avocado in it?"

"Good luck with that. There's a Chinese spot down the street. Lo Mein actually sounds amazing right now," I suggested.

He sighed and threw his jacket on. "You're lucky I'm hungry. Veggie Lo Mein it is. Be back in a minute."

Once he left, I decided that I couldn't take enough hot baths with Epsom salt, and it was time for another one before I called it a night. I ran the water as hot as I could stand it, sprinkled some salt in and decided a bath bomb would be a nice touch. I looked in the mirror at my face, and realized my face looked slimmer.

"Hm, maybe all this training ain't all bad," I thought to myself. I lowered my achy body into the hot water and relaxed. I slid down into the tub until only my face was above water. It was way too quiet, so I decided to listen to a Podcast. I told my bottom bitch Alexa to play the latest episode of my favorite podcast at the moment, 2 Dope Queens. As I listened,

FOOLISH

I felt my body getting heavier and heavier and knew sleep was on the horizon.

I shot up from the water gasping for air. I looked around my bathroom, not knowing how long I had been sleeping. Judgin' from the now cold ass water, it had to be a minute. I hopped outta the tub and threw my terry cloth robe on, prepared to tear up the food that Jr. shoulda been back with already. Much to my irriated surprise, there was no sign of him or Veggie Lo Mein.

"How long does it take somebody to get some damn noodles and veggies," I said to nobody in particular.

I grabbed my clothes off the floor before I sat on the edge of my bed, slatherin' lotion on my body. You know that feelin' you have when you know you're alone, but you don't feel alone. I was havin' a huge dose of that. I decided to turn some music on to cure the quietness until Jr. came back from whatever black hole he had fallen into with my damn food. After gettin' dressed, I threw some clothes on, nothing fancy. Just some sweats and an oversized t–shirt. I laid back on my bed, listenin' to the music. I heard the front door open and close, and my inner fat girl leaped for joy.

"Fuckin' finally!" I yelled from my bedroom. "What the fuck bruh, did you have to make the people who made the food? Shit." After him not throwin' an insult back, I walked toward the kitchen to see what his problem was. I got to the kitchen to the surprise of...no one.

I knew I heard that damn door closed. I'm tired, not crazy.

I grabbed an iron pipe I kept in my hallway and walked toward the door. It was still locked. Oh fuck this shit. I walked through the house flippin' on every light, and turnin' on every TV. I was clearly tired, and my mind was getting the best of me. I sat on the couch and decided I wasn't gonna move until my brother was standing in front of me. Ignoring the TV, I flipped through my tarot deck and decided to get a little bit more familiar with the cards.

I shuffled my deck and decided that whatever card popped out, that's the card I would get to know better. I shuffled for what seemed like forever and nothing slid out. In one of our many lessons, Nairobi told me that sometimes it takes a while for the cards to warm up. They have to line up just right to give you the message you need, so I kept shufflin'. Just as I got tired and was about say fuck it, a card popped out and landed on the floor.

The High Priestess.

I opened my black book and flipped to her page.

"The High Priestess makes her appearance when you need to pay attention. Not just logically, but by using your higher self, intuition, dreams and signals. When you see this card in a reading, take time and meditate and tune in to your higher self, your subconscious mind..."

"Hmm." I thought to myself. "Interesting." Just as I was about to continue to read, I heard a crash in my bed room. Grabbing the steel pipe, I slowly walked down the hallway. Of course, somebody would wait until there was no testosterone in here to try and break the fuck in. I peeked into my bedroom to see everything in place except for my oversized mirror that sat in the corner.

"I really hope this shit ain't broke, I don't need no more bad luck," I said out loud to myself with a chuckle. Gotta thank Momma for all the superstitious beliefs I had. I put the steel pipe down and lifted up the mirror. The image I saw looking back at me almost caused me to drop it again.

Mystery girl dressed in red from the club WEEKS ago.

I walked closer to the mirror with my hand out. She looked just like me, hell she was me. I kneeled down in front of the mirror, trying to make sense of this shit. She decided to do it for me as she handed me a card through the mirror. It was the High Priestess card. That's when it hit me.

I was staring at my higher self.

CHAPTER 18

Freddy Jr.

"Magic in my blood
Swear if you blink you gone miss it...
Mama cooking that holy nectar while she up in that kitchen.
Being watched, they reading my thoughts...
Hope they don't hear it as I listen...
Watch and learn, try not to crash and burn...
Here's the pivot...
Broke outta the trenches, timeline jumping new dimensions..."

—Foolish x Freddy

You would think having magic would make life easier.
Don't let nobody tell you that lie.

This last month, there hasn't been enough of me to go around. Jumpin' here, jumpin' there... trainin' this day...bruh. My mind was shot. Let's not even talk about my physical. I swear I was comin' down with somethin' and nobody has time for that bullshit. We were about two weeks away from wrappin' up trainin' for Sol and gettin' ready to start lookin' for Odessa. She was out here beastin'. Dirt got her physical together, while Mila, Nairobi and O'Mere took turns with her mental. She has surpassed every test and trial in record speed. I was impressed. Because time is of the essence, we had to jam pack all of her training into a condensed, yet still potent version. What she learned in a month, it took others damn near two years to accomplish.

Did I mention my sister was a whole beast in this bitch?!

I planned on sittin' in on her session tonight, but first I had to find out what the fuck was up with this nigga Andre. Part of me feels like he got scared off by Jackie. The other half feels like he's hidin' some shit. Either way, I decided that's somebody we can't risk havin' around. Yea, he would be a good source of information in regard to Jackie, but to be real we got O'Mere backin' us. That and my niggas can find out anything about anybody so in reality, he's no longer needed. My mentality right now? If you ain't with us, you against us. If I gotta question your loyalty, you good as dead, just like Andre will be when I found him.

We hadn't had any contact from Ky either and that was kinda buggin' me. I mean, that is my sister. Regardless, Jackie was gonna pay for what the fuck she's doing. Point blank. When I catch her, she better be prepared. I sat on the ledge of the Market House in the middle of the square, lurkin' in the shadows of Downtown Fayetteville. I had got a tip from Dirt that Andre had been seen in the downtown area recently, and I wanted to peep the scene to see what was up. As I sat at this old market place, chills ran through my body. Not cold chills, energy chills. Up until 1865, in the very place I sat, slaves had been sold. I was pickin' up so much scared, uncertain energy I had to move even though I had a perfect view.

Right before I went to hop down, a black car pulled up and parked where the normal naked eye wouldn't be able to see it. I decided to stick around for a few minutes just in case it was somethin' I needed to see. I saw a dark figure come from the car and walk to the back of the trunk. They waited for about five minutes, and another car pulled up. They talked for a minute, and to my shock, they pulled a body from the trunk bound up and seemingly lifeless or at least unconscious. Even though I felt kinda weak and didn't wanna run myself down, I needed to use my magic to see what was goin' on. I closed my eyes and whispered "Speaker".

At first it came in kinda fuzzy, but within seconds I could hear the whole conversation.

"If you woulda did what the fuck you were supposed to do, we wouldn't be in this situation, so man the fuck up. I don't wanna hear your fuckin' excuses because somehow little brother, they always come back to me." I knew that voice. Amir.

"How the fuck do you think I'm supposed to keep this up Amir? Huh? She's gonna find out and when she does that's both of our asses. I want her gon' just as bad as you, but you gotta stop bein' a hothead. What the fuck comes back to you nigga, huh? You're the favorite. Let me play my role man." A second voice responded. I'm damn near certain that's Andre.

"Look nigga, just get her back to Jackie and meet me at the spot. I don't have time to be babysittin' nobody. You need to be preparin' yourself for her family comin' at somebody head about this shit. You better do this right. Let me know when you make the drop." Amir growled.

I had heard enough. It was like Nairobi said, this nigga was flip floppin' back and forth. You can't trust nobody like that. Even if he was helpin' us out, it's too risky. Andre had just signed his walkin' papers, I just had to be patient and wait for the right time. Believe me, nothin' would bring me more joy than to see his blood spilled.

~~ * ~~

I closed my eyes and when I opened them, I was back in Brooklyn in front of Dirt's trainin' warehouse. I walked in to Sol runnin' a hellish obstacle course that I used to be scared of and honestly had a hard time with, but she was killin' that shit. I didn't wanna break her concentration, so I just stood beside Dirt while I waited for her to finish.

I looked around the open layout of the warehouse, it kinda reminded me of like a gladiator ring. You had all the training equipment and course on the bottom level. The classrooms wrapped around in a complete circle, stretchin' about 4 stories high. His shit didn't look this glamorous back when I trained with him back in the old one in New Orleans. I was proud of the growth though. So many descendants of the Five Families trained with Dirt. Outside of O'Mere, Dirt was one of the most sought-after trainers. My nigga ill with a gun and with trainin' you to knock somebody's head off, magically.

"So how she comin' along man? You think she ready?" I asked Dirt.

"Man look, she ready. All the way around. Mentally.

Physically. She ready to go. The question is my nigga, are you ready? You look like you sick as hell my dude." He commented. I had already been feelin' sick earlier, now that I was standin' here I felt like my body was gonna shut down on me. I know I haven't been takin care of myself but damn. Maybe I needed to lay off the jumpin until it's time to train Sol.

"Yea man, I think I'm comin' down with somethin'. Fucked up time for me to be gettin' sick right?" I mentioned.

I watched Sol come to the end of the course. Dirt stood beside me smirkin'. "Man, watch this shit. This shit kills me every time."

Sol got to the end and stood there, body relaxed, and eyes closed. Sweat poured from every inch of her body as her chest heaved in and out to catch her breath. She stretched her hands out, almost touchin' the brick wall that was in front of her. The wall was the only thing that stood between her and the make shift finish line ribbon Dirt had at the end. Her purple glitter aura started to glow around her, becoming more intense with each second that passed. Leave it to Sol to have some sparkly, glittery ass color. Dirt pulled me by my hoodie sleeve and we ended up standing on the other side of the wall, a few feet back. I watched in amazement as a glowing purple circle formed in the middle of the wall. The remaining outside perimeter of the circle started to crumble. When the rest of the wall was literally brick dust, Sol closed her hands into fists, and started chanting. The chanting started off slow and she got louder. The louder she got, the more intense the purple color of her aura and the circle got. Sol let out a yell that shook the warehouse, and with the yell, the brick circle in front of her exploded. She opened her eyes, and her left eye glowed the color of white marble.

I stood there shook. Dirt was right, Sol was more than ready, and I was proud of her. I shot a thought over to her. *"Well damn. I shoulda wore some damn safety goggles. Good shit sis. Real good shit."*

She looked at me in confusion with her head cocked to the side. She shook her head like she was tryna clear it out and walked over. "So, what's next?" she asked, almost in a cocky manner. Dirt laughed at her.

"Girl you ain't tired yet?" Dirt joked.

She rolled her eyes and smiled. "You've pumped enough leafy greens in me to give me enough energy for the next six months, let's go!" She giggled as she kicked the punching bag.

"Well that's all I got for you today on my end. O'Mere and Nairobi just got here though. You can go see if they got anything for you."

"Let me find out I'm too much for you Dirt," she giggled and ran upstairs to check out O'Mere and Nairobi.

Dirt stood there laughin' and shakin' his head. "Man, she ain't lyin. I never trained somebody and ran out of stuff to train em. She literally demolished everything I put her through, I literally have nothin' left!"

I smiled to myself. She had only been training for a month at this point. When I was trainin' a month in, Dirt was still yellin' at me to push harder. This girl is breakin' down barriers left and right. I had no doubt that she was ready. Security been trainin' with her too. I'm kinda glad that her and Legend been kickin' it, he's pushed her a lot...trainin with her on her days off and shit. I could fuck with that. We were buildin' a solid ass team. While Dirt cleaned up what Sol had just destroyed, I looked over at the wall that housed the pictures of every person that Dirt ever trained. It had to be a good couple hundred of pictures up there. He had them all grouped into different cliques. On the far-right hand side, there were some empty spots.

"That right there belongs to y'all. Sol. You. Mila. Devon. Y'all are the first under this new regime, new way of doin' shit. What y'all are doin' now is setting the standard. I've trained a hell of a lot of people my nigga, you know. You one of em." Dirt walked around and stood in front of me. "My nigga, I have NEVER trained anybody like y'all. Nobody. Y'all are special. I'm not just sayin' that because you and me tight, blood couldn't make us any closer. I'm tellin' you the truth. You don't have shit to worry about. She's realizing her power and she's way more confident now. Jackie woke up that beast in her. That spot on the wall, that belongs to y'all. My young ones." He stood there lookin' like a proud father.

"The Young Ones. I like that," I agreed.

Nairobi cracked the door to the upstairs level. "Hey, you black faced nigga, do you still have some of that brick dust?"

Dirt chuckled and grabbed a mason jar filled with the left-over dust from the wall Sol destroyed and waved it in the air. "Of course, I do Nairobi."

She gave him the thumbs up and bounced down the stairs to get it. She took grabbin' the brick dust as an opportunity to holla at me. "Your sister man...she reminds me so much of your Momma. She catches on so quick. We've been trying simple spells you know, something to get her used to using her magic...boy lemme tell you. Two days. Two days is all it took. We already ran through every book she brought me from the trunk, and most of that shit is old world magic, that hard shit. She knows all of it. She's ready man."

FOOLISH

I shook my head. I was so glad to hear all of this. Mila and Devon had been training with Nairobi also, so everybody was on the same page. Nairobi's hands on my face shook me out of my thoughts. "You feel aight? You look a little paler than usual bruh."

"I'm fine. I think it's because I've been doin' too much jumpin. Wearin' myself out you know? I'ma take the next week to rest up, you know we leave the week after. So I'ma just kinda chill out. Nothin' major." I smiled to reassure her. I looked up at my sister who was sitting in the room waiting for Nairobi. She looked at me, cockin' her head to the side and squinting her eyes. I really wanted to know why she kept lookin' at me like that.

I sat down and waited for her to finish up with Nairobi and O'Mere. About an hour later, she came bouncin' downstairs. She grabbed some cut up fruit chunks from the fridge along with a bottled water. She grabbed the bottle of Bragg's Apple Cider Vinegar and some lemon juice and used a dropper to squirt a couple drops of each into her water. She grabbed her jacket and sat beside me.

I looked at her and raised my eyebrow. "You aight? You been lookin at me all fucked up all day. If it got somethin' to do with Legend I don't have shit to do with it, on Momma."

She looked at me and rolled her eyes. "Speakin' of which. I need to get home. I gotta shower and shit. Legend is comin' over to chill and shit."

"I mean, do I need to dip for the night? Just let me know cause..." she cut me off.

"Why every time a chick chill with a nigga they gotta be bonin'? Can we just chill and talk about some shit? Magic and shit? Damn. You ain't gotta go nowhere." She laughed.

We walked home, enjoying the warm weather and talkin'. I was glad to see her so much more confident. She still looked like something was bothering her. I listened to her talk and tried to pinpoint it, but I'll be damned if Sol ain't just like me. You won't know some shit unless she wants you to. I decided to cut the bullshit and figure out what was going on.

"Yo, what's up witchu? You been actin' strange all day love. What's goin' on?" I asked.

She looked at me and stopped walkin'. "You haven't answered me today. I've been talkin to you all day and you've been ignorin' me. Did I do something?"

I looked at her confused. I hadn't been able to hear her thoughts all day, but I mostly thought that it was because I really wasn't tryin' to. Her mind races constantly and I honestly didn't know how the hell she put up with it. She has the mind of a crazy person. I guess that's why she can manifest shit so quickly though. Makes sense.

"Sol, I haven't heard shit from you all day. When have you said something to me that I didn't answer?" I quizzed her. She looked at me confused. She walked into the bodega that we were standing in front of, while I stood outside tryna make sense of this shit. Maybe that's why she looked confused when I was tryna talk to her earlier back at the warehouse. She popped back out of the bodega with two blunts and started walkin. I jogged to catch up with her.

"Yo love, seriously. When haven't I answered you? I said something to you earlier and you didn't respond. I thought maybe you were just comin' down off your adrenaline high or some shit." I pleaded with her. I'm not usually one to give a fuck about somebody bein' mad at me but seeing her frowned up face hit me in a soft spot I didn't really know existed.

"I kinda heard you. It was like static. I couldn't even make it out." She wrinkled her nose and twisted her lips, a sign her mind had just shifted into overdrive.

We kept walkin' until we got to her apartment, where Devon and Mila were in the kitchen cookin'. Whatever they were whippin' up smelled amazin' and I had just realized I hadn't ate all day. I walked over and sat on the couch, rackin' my brain tryna figure out what the fuck was going on with our communication. I was starting to feel even worse. My head felt like it was about to pop from what I assumed was sinus pressure. Mila brought over some warm lemon water with honey and cayenne pepper.

"This should open you up and make you feel a little better," she added as she handed me the steaming hot cup. I took a sip and almost spit the shit out. That was the nastiest shit I had ever tasted in my life. I looked at her with a frown.

"Nigga I didn't say the shit was gonna taste good. Drink it," she giggled, kissed me on the forehead and bounced back to the kitchen.

There was a knock and before I could get off the couch Sol was at the door. Before he even cut the corner into the livin' room I heard my nigga Legend's voice, followed by Hussein. I dapped them up while they ran to the kitchen to be involuntary taste testers for what was bein' cooked.

"Nigga get your grubby little light skinned fingers outta my pot. This ain't yo Momma kitchen and I'll burn the shit outta them nubs." Devon threatened Hussein.

"Man, this shit shoulda been done already. You know niggas like some refreshments and shit." Hussein laughed.

Sol joined Mila and Devon in the kitchen, while my

niggas came and sat in the livin' room with me watchin' the Lakers vs. the Heat game and rolled up a couple blunts. I went to wet the blunt to crack it and Legend snatched it outta my hand.

"Nah nigga, you got the cooties and shit. Ain't nobody tryna get sick. It's bad enough I gotta smoke behind your ass. You look like somebody ran you over with a truck my nigga." Legend laughed and cracked the blunt open.

I rolled my eyes and grabbed the grinder and the bong. "That's aight, you ain't gotta smoke behind me. I know yo ass ain't talkin' about no cooties. Yo ass been layin' up with my sister doin' God knows what." Sol was about to comment until Lonzo Ball sunk the rock from the half court line and everybody in the house lost it, cheerin' at the top of our lungs. Devon came over with a bottle and six shot glasses.

"That shit right there is shot worthy with his fine ass," Devon laughed. We all took a shot to the head. Well most of us did. As soon as the shot hit my throat it came right back up again, all over my lap. Sol ran over with a towel to clean me up. The look on her face had went from mad to concerned. I can't lie, I was startin' to get kinda worried myself. We were scheduled to leave for New Orleans in two weeks, and I had no time to be sick.

"Man, what the fuck is that about?" Hussein asked.

"Man, I don't even fuckin' know. I jumped earlier to spy on Andre and ever since then I been feelin' like shit. Like my magic even fuckin up right now. A couple of times I tried to jump I couldn't even go no damn where." I responded.

"Damn man, that's crazy. You talk to O'Mere about it?" he asked.

"Nah man," I waved him off. "O'Mere got bigger fish to

fry right now. It ain't nothin but a little cold. I'll be aight in a couple of days." Mila stood there with her hands on her hips.

"So you went to spy on Andre and didn't tell nobody? What happened?" she questioned. I forgot all about telling them.

"Man, Nairobi right. I know we could use him for help, even for bait but I'm wonderin' if it's even worth it. I saw him and Amir in downtown Fayetteville earlier tonight at the Market Circle. They were talkin about pullin' a fast one on Jackie, but we already know that shit. What fucked me up is they had a body with them. Somebody tied up. I'ma go out on a limb and say it was Ky." I stopped and took a sip of the nasty ass shit Mila had mixed up.

"How do you know it was Ky though, like what could you see?" Sol asked, soundin' nervous. I know her and Ky were beefin, but she's still our sister. We still give a fuck about what happens to her.

"That's why I said I think love, I don't know if it was her. I just feel like it was. Anyway, they were arguing about some shit, I think Amir don't trust Andre too much as far as gettin' rid of Jackie goes. I think he feels like Andre gon' switch sides and ride with Jackie. My concern is Amir feelin' like that. He knows his brother better than anybody. Andre had to do something in order to make him feel like that." I reasoned.

"But what does that have to do with us?" Devon asked.

I shook my head. "A lot, man. We already know he wanna take em both down. That's cool and all. If Amir finds out that he's workin' with us too, which could be why he feel somethin' ain't right, it could fuck up everything and get us all killed. I'm tellin' you, fuckin with Andre ain't worth it. We gonna find some other way to get Ky and get to Jackie."

Everybody sat quietly trying to make sense of everything. "Look y'all don't get your respective undergarments in a bunch about it right now. Just don't fuck with Andre. We'll figure the rest out later." I added, tryna redirect the energy.

Sol spoke up. "So, we're supposed to leave in two weeks. When are we gonna talk about a game plan? Y'all know O'Mere ain't gon' let us walk up into New Orleans dumpin' and actin' all crazy."

Legend took a hit of the blunt. "That's where Marcus is as we speak, that's why he's not here. He's meetin up with O'Mere and Dirt and tryna scope some shit out. We'll be having a meeting closer to the departure time. Don't worry, we got you Ma. Everything is taken care of, y'all just keep up trainin' the way y'all have been and we good."

I nodded in agreement. I started to speak, but before I could get any words out, my entire throat started burnin'. I ran over to the kitchen and gulped down a bottle of water that was sitting on the counter, but that didn't stop shit. I started coughin' as Sol grabbed my arm and sat me back down on the couch. She pulled out her phone and dialed Nairobi's number while walkin' out of the room. All I heard was a bunch of "okay's". Sol came back in the living room and asked everybody to stand back.

Mila looked terrified. "Sol, what the fuck is goin on? Shouldn't we be gettin' him to the hospital?"

Sol chuckled, cool calm and collected while I'm over here about to die. "Nope. He's fine. I can handle it."

I didn't feel fine whatsoever. Whatever she was going to do she needed to do fast because at this point my whole body was lit up like the end of a blunt tip. She cut my shirt open and felt around my chest.

FOOLISH

"Yup. There it is." She confirmed the findin' of whatever the fuck she was lookin for. She took her pointer finger and middle finger and pressed it into the spot. That shit burned so much I wanted to back hand her across the room. I tensed my body up in response to the pain.

"Yo, look at me. You gotta chill. You're gonna be fine but the more you tense your body up the longer this is gonna take. I know it hurts but you gotta trust me. Chill out, breathe. Focus on me." Sol spoke gently.

Something about the calming sensation of her voice worked. I took slow deep breaths as she continued to press her finger into my chest. The area around my chest started glowin', outlined in purple. She was using her aura. She spoke softly as the richness of the color intensified. My whole body went from feeling like it was on fire, to a rush of energy radiating through it.

"Good, keep breathing," Sol mentioned, smiling.

I looked around at everybody and they all were glowin' also. I had never seen any of their aura's. Everything around me looked bright and vibrant as hell, like a blind person seeing things for the first time. Every sensation in my body, I felt ten times more. Sol took her finger off of my chest and it was as if nothing ever happened. I looked around at everybody, and they were calm too. Sol sunk down in the sofa beside me.

"Sooooo...how does it feel, DeAngelo voice?" she laughed.

"How does what feel? The fuck did you just do?" I asked her.

She smirked. "I just initiated you and gave you the rest of my magic. You know, the magic you were teasing me about the other day? The pain I had to go through? Nairobi told you this would happen. How does it feel to be a full on Shaman?"

Fuck. Nairobi sho' did tell me this would happen and I didn't even put two and two together. Legend sat there rollin' a blunt and smirkin. "What's funny nigga?" I asked as I threw a stem from the weed at em.

"Man, you ran to that faucet like a li'l ho my nigga." He died laughin' as he imitated me, and everybody cracked up laughin'.

"Now everything that happened earlier makes sense, you know...with us not being able to hear each other and all that and you feelin sick. Your body was preparin' itself for me to give you my magic. We have periods, y'all get initiation symptoms. Remember?", she reminded me.

I got up and went to the bathroom to look in the mirror. Nothing had really changed, except now I could see my aura, a nigga was lookin Golden as shit. I walked back into the living room and everybody had grabbed a plate and was sitting around eating and jokin' about the game like nothin' had just happened. My plate sat beside Mila, so I popped a squat.

"Hey y'all. This is probably one of the last times that all of us will be able to just kick back and chill before we leave for New Orleans. We gotta take pics," Sol jumped and got her camera.

"Man niggas can't even finish eatin' first? Got me lookin' all chubby and shit..." Hussein commented.

"Nigga wipe your greasy ass face off and come on." Sol pushed him into the frame.

She was havin trouble setting up the timer, so I got up and helped. After settin it, I squeezed back in. Sol was right.

FOOLISH

This was probably the last time we'd all be able to chill with no stress and sleepin' with one eye open. Shit was about to get real and there was no turnin' back, for anybody at this point. We had built a solid team of oracle, shamans and lightworkers, with the power of generations backin' us. I'm not worried in the least little bit. I'm proud as fuck of my sister. I looked over at her and noticed her beautiful smile...with her chubby ass cheeks. It was dope as fuck to see how far she had come from a scared little girl to a powerful woman, who just so happened to be the head of our family and my sister. I'm just ready to get this shit crackin', ya feel me?

We all counted down while we waited for the camera to snap the picture. When it got down to two, I told everybody to say "The Young Ones".

We finally arrived.

CHAPTER 19

Solelil

I sat at the bar, having a drink and waitin' to clock in. This would be my last shift here at Henny's until, hell maybe forever. I saw Danny, my favorite DJ, walk through the door. When he saw me, he smiled and made his way over.

"Sollllllll! So how it feel girl, this yo last hoorah. Graduatin' up out this shit!" he yelled over the music. Honestly, I didn't know how to answer that question. This place had been a stamp in my life for years. I always knew I would leave here, I just didn't think it would be like this.

"I don't know mannn... I'ma miss it!" I shouted as I poked my lip out. "You just make sure you set me up real proper tonight with the music list. You know my favorites and you know I gotta go out with a bang!"

"Oh but of course, anything for my favorite girl," he smiled as he pulled me into a hug. "Let me get my ass back here and set up. Tear that shit up tonight girl," he waved as he walked up to the DJ's booth.

I sat there watchin' the crowd. The girls I had seen so far seemed like they were tryna step it up tonight. They would wait until my last night to try and upstage a bitch. I laughed to myself. They musta forgot how Sol get down. Filled with liquid courage, I made my way to the back, makin' sure to switch extra hard because for one, I had to give these people a peek of what was about to hit the stage, and two to remind these bitches. Even on my worse night they not touchin' me.

I sat at my booth which had been decorated by Mila and a couple of the other girls. I had done the same to Mila's booth. I started to tear up a little bit. My booth was filled with bottles of my favorite liquor, Green Apple Crown Royal, balloons, cards and money. I can't say that I was tight or even friends with most of these chicks, but some of them I did hold close to my heart. I was attacked by hugs before I could sit down. I basked in all the love and then sat down and put my earbuds in. This may be my last night, but ain't shit change. I still had my rituals. Ha. Rituals.

I listened to "When We" by Tank blastin' through my headphones and that got me right where I needed to be to start the night off right. I took extra time to do my make-up just to make sure everything sat right. About 30 minutes later, I sprayed my face with rose water made with roses from Momma's garden. I finished gettin' dressed just in time to hear Danny start introducin' me to come out to the stage. Mila ran behind me and pulled me into a hug.

"Bitch I been dancing beside you every night for the last two years, and this our last night gracin' this stage. You better fuck it up, you know I feed off of your energy. We need to leave with bands to put in the bank tonight." She smiled as she dapped me up. It was my turn.

Mila slapped my ass as I ran out. "FUCK IT UP BIHHHH!" she screamed.

Tonight, I was a little bit nervous because there was a special guest in the audience. I walked on stage and wiped down the pole. I couldn't see into the crowd yet, the only thing lightin' my way was the lights on stage. "Nobody" by Keith Sweat and Adina Howard started to play as the lights hit the stage. I walked around the pole seductively, and already all eyes were on me. I pulled my body half way up the pole and started swinging sideways, using only my thighs to keep me balanced. I hit a split and flip at the same time while I felt money hittin' almost every part of my body.

That's right. Pay them bills.

I snaked my way back to the top and twisted and turned my body in every direction I possibly could. While hanging upside down, I spotted my guest with a grin stretched across his face. In just those couple of seconds my body started sweating and I was tryin' like hell not to lose balance. Legend sat FRONT ROW in the crowd with his drink in his hand, chillin'. His eyes were glued to me as I made my body a human pretzel.

As "Lovers and Friends" by Lil Jon started playin', Mila joined me on stage. Usually, we danced on separate polls but to tonight was special. It was the last time both of us would touch a pole for a while, if ever again. Already bein' amped by her energy, I climbed the pole and once I was up far enough, I waited for her to do the same. She met half way and we interlocked legs and begin to swing. There were so many bills being thrown on stage I could barely see the floor anymore. Mila flipped upside down and positioned my body to flip over her. After pullin' it off successfully, we did what we always do and had people drooling by the time our set was done.

People threw flowers and other shit on the stage, to say goodbye to us. Henny's had given us a good run. People like to look at strippers like it was some hoe–ish profession and I never understood that, especially after workin' here. I was always treated with the utmost respect and expected nothin' less. I had tons of regulars and the cash flow was more money than I had ever seen in my life. I had made more money in two years then people work their whole lives for. I always tell people, fuck what other people have to say. If you can live with your choices, do you. We're all gonna die someday (well in my case that's up for discussion), so why not spend it doin' what the fuck makes you happy? People don't understand that all sexual energy boils down to is creativity. I chose to use my creativity to make me hella money, and I wasn't gonna apologize for it.

I made my way back to the dressin' room with Mila, and we chatted with the other girls while we got dressed. I packed up all of my stuff and left it on my booth, because now it was time to party. Hell, it was my party. Jr, Hussein and Marcus were set to meet us at the club after our set. Jr. was all down for the strip club, but he wasn't tryna see me out there like that. That's weird as fuck. I walked over to the hostess and asked for a booth for seven. She sat us up and got our drinks while I snaked through the club to find Legend. After lookin' for a few minutes and not bein' able to find him, I shot him a text.

"Hey, got a table. Where you at?"

*"Why don't you come find me and show me those tricks you did a few minutes ago. I won't tell nobody, I promise *wink*"*

"Um sir I'm a freak in private, not in nobody's public nothin'. Where are you stupid?"

"I'm dead ass, come find me. We could make it one for the books."

"Legend, if you don't tell me where you at you're not gonna get what I have planned for you tonight, don't play with me."

"Aw shit! If that's the case, I'm at the bar. Head over to the table, I see Mila sittin' there. I'll be there in a second."

I started to tell him there was no need to buy drinks because we had endless bottles from all my goin' away gifts, but fuck it. I came and sat down beside Mila and Devon as they took shots from our bottles and danced in their seats. Eventually, we were joined by the fellas. We all had a ball, and it was really a night for the books. The night cap I was broke off with wasn't bad either. I wish life could be like this every night, but I had a grandmother to find and spiteful bitch to kill.

I laid in bed beside Legend, who was snorin' loud enough to wake the dead. I couldn't fall asleep, but it wasn't on account of him snorin'. We were all set to leave in the morning for New Orleans, and up to this point I thought I was ready, but fear was starting to creep in. Not fear like I was scared I was gonna be put in danger, which I expected. That's why I got trained. I was more scared of what more I was gonna find out. One thing that Nairobi and O'Mere stressed to me durin' trainin' was believe only half of what you see and none of what you heard, especially in other timelines. That, and the fact that while I knew a lot and learned a lot, there were still things that were hidden from me. Nairobi didn't think it was up to her to tell me. "It's all part of your journey," she justified not telling me.

I continued to toss and turn for another thirty minutes. I remembered that Jr. had made me some sleepin' oil to help with my insomnia. I grabbed it off of my night stand and rubbed it all over my neck, behind my ears and under my nose. I laid back down to try it again. I laid there playin' with Legend's locs as I felt myself start to nod out.

I sat still, legs in a crisscrossed position waiting for the transport back. Flashes of light surrounded me in a golden hue, letting me know it was soon to come. I had never felt this uncomfortable. I had also never been this deep in. Feeling the anxiety rising in me, I attempted to force myself back awake hoping maybe it would speed this shit up. Deep down inside I knew better. I knew these things didn't happen on my time. Lifting my head, my eyes dilated from pure shock. There was a different feelin' this time. A knowing. I had never experienced these emotions before.

Surrounding me were rows and rows of books, golden glowing books. Shelf upon shelf that stretched on for what seemed like miles. I had never been here before, but my gut told me this was no mistake. Nothing that ever happens during these crazy ass trips is a mistake. Everything is always carefully and strategically placed. Shaken, I got up from my safe position and began to search the shelves, when I felt all the air leave my lungs. Every book I looked at had my name written on the binding. Every book. Visibly shaken and hella disturbed, I reached for the book entitled "The Fool." I had been here before. Every time I got ready to open this book, I would travel back to my body. I braced myself for what I knew was about to happen, but it never came.

Shocked, I sat crossed legged in between the two large bookshelves that stretched on for what seemed like forever. I was here. I was finally gon' do it. Shakin' like booty meat, I opened the thick, golden cover of the book. The first page was blank, and so was every page after it. I flipped back and forth through the book to make sure I wasn't missing anything. Right before I went to close it, I noticed some writing on the inside of the back cover.

Solelil,

This is your book, I guess you can say it's almost like a clean slate. As you go on your journey, you will notice the pages of this book will fill up on their own. Beats the hell outta writin' it by hand, huh? Once you have completed this particular phase on your journey, this book will leave you. Don't bother lookin' for it, because you'll never find it. At that time, it will be time for you to start another. This journey that you're about to go on starts you back at zero, like a baby thrust into the world. Innocent. No remembrance of past lives lived before, ready to build a new one. Learning all over again. This is you right now. Travelin' out into the unknown. On this journey, you haven't endured all the lessons that come with it, I call that blissful ignorance. You may think you know how this will end, but does it ever? That's up to you. You have planted the seed, now it's time to nurture it and watch it grow. You have endless possibilities. Training with O'Mere I'm sure your mind is sharp as a tack. I'm waiting for you. I've always waited for you. Safe travels.

FOOLISH

Love you dearly,
Grandma Odessa

I closed the book and sat there smilin'. Knowin' that my grandmother was waiting for me brought me comfort. I got up, and prepared myself because I knew my ass was about to get sent back. As I tried to quiet my mind, I heard the clickin' of heels comin' from behind me. I wanted to turn around, but in my gut I already knew who it was. I smiled as she placed her hand on my shoulder. Somethin' urged me not speak, and let her do all the talkin'.

"I see you finally saw me the other night. I told you I wouldn't be far. Sorry if I pissed you off that night at the club...I had to make myself seen to you. I just wanted to tell you that we got this. I'll be here, anytime you need me. That little whisper? That gut feelin'? Don't try and rationalize it. It's just me tryna make you great," she giggled. I turned around to face myself. Damn my higher self was beautiful.

"I'm only a reflection of you, boo" she winked. "It's time to get you back, you have a long road ahead of you girl." She grabbed my hand as I felt my body project forward. The next thing I knew, I was standing beside my bed. Lookin' at my body lying next to Legend, I smiled. We looked damn good together. I did something I didn't normally do, and just looked at myself for a second. I was proud. I had been through so much in life, and it all came down to this. All the times I thought I was crazy, all the times I was made fun of...it was all worth it now. I don't know what lies ahead in this journey, but I know I'm well equipped. I slowly lowered myself back into my body, wrapped my arms around Legend and fell back asleep.

I woke up and found myself staring into the picture of my

parents I had on my nightstand. I still couldn't believe they were gone, but we were about to fix that. Feelin' myself get sad all over again, I got up and went to the bathroom to wash my face. I had no time for emotions like that his morning. I checked the time on my phone and it read 4:30am. I walked into the living room, prepared to have some me time but surprisingly Mila was up reading and Devon was scrollin through his phone.

"Bitch have y'all even been to sleep yet?" I asked them with an ashy, groggy voice.

"Nope. Do you hear your brother in that room snoring? Sleep where?", she laughed.

"Hell, you know I'ma night owl anyway," Devon answered.

"Bitch I feel your pain, Legend in there cuttin' down the whole fuckin' forest." I joked back. She closed the book she was reading and looked at me.

"So you ready? I mean, I don't know how ready somebody could be for some shit like this but, you know what I mean." She laughed.

"I guess man. I mean, can you ever be ready for some shit like this? A couple months ago I was just a regular ass girl workin' at a strip club. Now I'm captain save everybody. Guess that's what was in the cards, huh?" I rolled my eyes.

I sat there, wondering how I should bring up this next topic. I don't know if I was the only one who noticed, but Jackie had been keepin' a closer eye on us than I realized. I was shocked when she showed up at the memorial. At first, I didn't understand why she was there. By the time she called me out, it dawned on me. Detective Moreau. I didn't even make the connection at first. Jackie was in on it all along, from the house fire, to tellin' us our parents bodies were missing. She had to throw us off.

"I know, I was waiting for you to tell me," Mila replied. Damn, she can hear my thoughts too?

"Sorta," she responded laughin'. "Not all the time, just about half."

"Why didn't you say anything?" I asked.

"Honestly, I knew the day you and Ky went and talked to her. When you were tellin' me everything, I just connected the dots. I wanted to tell you, but I wanted you to build your strength up at the same time. I can't point out everything to you, you get lazy that way. It teaches you to look at everything with a fine-tooth comb. I'm not gon' lie, I was worried you weren't gone catch it. Your brother told me to give you some time and I'll be damned if he wasn't right." She smiled.

I couldn't even be mad at her. I was so happy I had a best friend who was on the same page as me. I would be lonely as fuck without her. She's taught me so much, without even realizing it, and I was happy she was chosen to go on this journey with me. I heard motion in the hallway, and turned my head to see my brother walkin' into the livin' room.

"Well look at this. At least I didn't have to wake yall up. It's these other two niggas I gotta worry about." He chuckled.

Legend walked in behind him. "Nigga you worry about yourself, how bout that?" he joked as he pushed him.

"I agree, nigga I'm not your son. I know how to set an alarm clock." Hussein said as he came out the bathroom. I laughed at these clowns. I love my tribe. We all slowly got dressed and when we were done, walked the three blocks to the Warehouse where we were meeting up. Marcus was already there, goin' over stuff with O'Mere and Nairobi. They smiled as we walked in the building.

"See y'all early, that's what I'm talkin' bout! Even if y'all do look like the walkin' dead," O'Mere joked. "Don't worry about it, your first day there's nothin' excitin' happenin'. I do however suggest y'all get some rest when you get to New Orleans. They'll be other times to check out the party scene. Y'all need focus right now, and sleep will be your best friend when you can get it," he mentioned.

We all took a seat around the table, while O'Mere went over some things with us. "Nothin' has changed, Sol needs to be with somebody from security at all times. She is not to be left unattended." He urged. I know they were tired of hearin' that, but I understand why it was stressed so much.

"Your mission right now, is to find Odessa. That other shit, we will cross that bridge when we get it to it. That means Andre, Kyleena...Jackie. Y'all can't do take down shit without Odessa, so put that out your mind. Sol, like she told you in that letter, she hid things for you in different timelines in New Orleans. Each of the seventeen Wards in New Orleans is a different timeline. That is your focus. Find them. The first one is a Golden Chalice. This Chalice won't be in an obvious place. Use your heads, think outside of the box. One you collect all of the items, you will report back to me and I'll tell you where to take them. I have bags here, filled with anything you need. Herbs, tonics, tinctures, tools...you name it, it's there. Thank Nairobi for that." He stopped and looked around at us before he continued.

"You wanna tell 'em this next part Nairobi?" he asked.

She smiled and got up from her seat. "In each Ward, I have set up houses for you all to stay in durin' your time in that Ward. All the Wards won't have the items that you're lookin' for obviously, but you will run into someone who will help you along your journey. It is your job to find these people, they will not make themselves obvious to you. Once you find either the item or the person, you will leave the house and not return. We need to keep the ones who are watchin' guessin'. We can't get too familiar."

She turned and looked at me. "Solelil, you are the entry into each house, your fingerprint. Nobody can enter these houses without it. Watch yourself. Stay alert. All of the homes are furnished and stocked with food and other necessities, so that's one less thing to worry about. Should something happen and you need to escape, directions for each house are in the manual included in your bags. I suggest you all get real familiar with it and read."

Once she finished talkin', she looked at O'Mere. "Once you have gathered all the items and reported back to me, it is then you will be lead to Odessa. This is the only way to her. Don't fall for anybody sayin' they can take you to her. Does anyone have any questions?"

We all looked around the room at each other. It was finally time. As nervous as I was, I knew I had my team with me. While O'Mere spoke with Security, I stepped outside to smoke a cigarette and have a moment to myself. I had come so far, and this would put me one step closer to finding my mother. I still worried about Kyleena, but like O'Mere said, one thing at a time. Just to think, my gifts use to scare me to now realize they were only my ancestors trying to speak to me and guide me. So far, while I took some L's, having my brother back was the most beautiful thing I've ever experienced. Speakin' of the devil, he joined me outside.

"So this is it, huh? You ready?", he asked smirkin'.

"I guess so," I answered him.

He came and stood in front of me. "Yo, I don't want you worryin' about shit. We got this. O'Mere wouldn't let us do it if he didn't have faith in us. We're gonna find Grandma so we can handle our business. I gotchu. I always have."

I nodded at him. I knew he did. O'Mere called us all back in. "If there aren't any questions, I need everybody to gear up and meet me in the middle of the room." We all grabbed our bags and our crystals that Nairobi provided us with and walked toward the middle of the large concourse area.

"Jr, come here man." O'Mere called him over into the middle of the circle.

"You the strongest, so I trust your jumpin' skills. Think you can handle it?" he tested him.

"Hell yea man, I got this. Aye y'all, tight circle. Bring it in," he motioned.

Mila, Devon, Legend, Huessien, Marcus and myself all surrounded Jr. We all held on to each other as O'Mere walked around us, makin' sure everybody was secure. "Remember, if you need us, we'll be there. Good luck to you all." O'Mere stepped back away from the circle.

Jr. told all of us to close our eyes and not to open them until he gives us the ok. He started chanting quietly, and as he got louder, I felt my body project. It felt like someone had took some type of electricity and sent shock waves through my body. That lasted for all of a minute. Before I knew it, my feet were on solid ground again.

"Aight, open up," Jr yelled. We all opened our eyes and were standing in the most beautiful house in the middle of a bayou that I had ever seen.

FOOLISH

It kinda reminded me of the house and yard from "Eve's Bayou", one my favorite movies. There were lush green weeping willow trees, and an even greener yard. There was exercise equipment for DAYS planted around the huge backyard. We all looked at each other and ran toward the house in excitement. I put my finger into the device and unlocked the door. We all went runnin' in, just to get stopped dead in our tracks. To our surprise and utter disgust, Andre and Amir stood in front of us. Behind them was a painting of Jackie, what had to be hundreds of years ago. We all looked around at each other, not sure of what to make of this. I felt all the anger that ever existed in my body rise to the surface.

Andre stood smirkin' with Jr.'s gun pointed right at the center of his face. "Well hello to y'all, too. I'm glad to see you all made it safely. Welcome to the Moreau Plantation."

Acknowledgements

I just wanted to thank everybody who have been with me from the beginning, and those who joined me along the ride. I never thought that I would be able to write a book, much less self-publish it. It has been a long, rocky road but much like Sol, my journey is just beginning. A lot of people ask me is my story similar to Sol's, and at first the answer was no. As I continued to write her character, I saw pieces of me in her. The fear. The not wanting to accept who I was: a witch, oracle, lightworker...whatever label you want to stick on it. In writing this book, I've come to learn myself all over again, through Sol.

I just want to thank a couple key people who have had a major impact on the creation of this book:

Trey, Jon Jon, Jhneanelle & Brittany: I literally could not have written this book without yall. From the idea provoking conversations in the middle of the night/early morning, to yall talking me down off the ledge when I'm losing my shit, I thank yall. I thank yall for being the dopest people in the world. Yall are my real life tribe, and I thank God every day for yall.

Natasha: Thank you for not only giving me the space and allowing me to pick of the pieces of my life, but for pushing me to write this book. You have cheered me on from the moment I started writing. You are such an awesome, giving person and I'm proud to call you my cousin! Love you much!

Antoine: I don't even know what to say to you dude lol! You have been one of my biggest supporters, even before this book came about. You always said you saw greatness in me, even when I couldn't see it myself. Meeting you was no mistake, you're one of my best friends and I don't call you my fave for no reason. No matter what, you never have to question my loyalty and support. I love you.

My Knowledge: I love you. Knowledge and wisdom bring forth understanding. Understanding is the highest form of love.

Me: Last but not least girl, you did it! Just like Solelil, everything that has happened to you has brought you to this moment. Bask in it, and realize that there is more to come. You've turned into such a beautiful person, who finally learned to love herself above ALL. Don't let anybody tell you how to do you, here's to many more!

About the Author

Who is SAI MECCA?

In 2013, **Sai Mecca** ran across her first set of tarot cards and never looked back. Lover of all things voodoo, metaphysical and spiritual, her goal is to use her creativity and passion to unlock the doors of every hood witch's broom closet one by one.

You can find her curled up with a good book, shufflin' up her tarot cards or developing more story plots to snatch your wigs. She resides in Fayetteville, North Carolina.

Email: submit.ether@gmail.com (business inquiries only)
Instagram: JessaIreen
Twitter: JessaIreene
Snapchat: JessaIreene

Made in the USA
Middletown, DE
16 September 2021